Enterprising Widows

*Three ladies taking the business world—
and the men who run it—by storm!*

The Champagne Magnate

When Emma finds herself at the head of the family's
struggling wine business, she must partner with
neighboring vineyard owner Julien Archambeau,
the brooding, reclusive Comte de Rocroi.

The Retailer

To honor her late husband's legacy, Antonia is
on a mission to turn the ramshackle London property
she inherited into the ultimate shopping experience!
But she must rely on the guidance of her
handsome rival, Lord Cullen Allardyce!

The Publisher

Saddled with extreme debt and an ailing publishing
house, Fleur needs an investor to revitalize the
business. But sparks soon fly when that investor
comes in the form of Jasper Bexley...

Find out what happens to the
Enterprising Widows in

*Liaison with the Champagne Count
Alliance with the Notorious Lord
A Deal with the Rebellious Marquess*

Available now!

Author Note

This series has centered on the Holmfirth flood of 1852, and I've tried to be faithful to the history of the event. The names of the people involved, like coroner Dyson, are historical figures. Captain R.C. Moody, whom Fleur meets with in chapter one, is real, as is his role in investigating the flood. The butcher store market that Fleur visits is real, as is the reference to the Water Street houses not being rebuilt. Those Easter eggs make for interesting reading. Also true, no legislation was ever passed regarding an improvement to dam oversight. In 1864, another dam accident took place at the Dale Dyke Reservoir that was even more deadly.

The collapse of the dam could not be pinned on any one person because it was indeed a case of collective error. Many things went wrong at many parts of the process. The Holmfirth Reservoir Committee was financially mismanaged among other things and the Huddersfield Bank did loan them money (as noted later in the story). (The banker who helps Jasper and Fleur was a real historical figure and truly did write the essay referenced.) So, Orion's disaster is not too far-fetched, although Orion is fictional, as is his involvement in the dam.

For more about the details of the Holmfirth flood, I highly recommend Ian Harlow's book *The Holmfirth Floods: The Story of the Floods in Holmfirth*, which I heavily relied on for details.

A DEAL WITH THE REBELLIOUS MARQUESS

BRONWYN SCOTT

HISTORICAL

Harlequin®
HISTORICAL

ISBN-13: 978-1-335-59625-3

A Deal with the Rebellious Marquess

Copyright © 2024 by Nikki Poppen

Harlequin Enterprises ULC
22 Adelaide St. West, 41st Floor
Toronto, Ontario M5H 4E3, Canada
www.Harlequin.com

Printed in U.S.A.

Bronwyn Scott is a communications instructor at Pierce College and the proud mother of three wonderful children—one boy and two girls. When she's not teaching or writing, she enjoys playing the piano, traveling—especially to Florence, Italy—and studying history and foreign languages. Readers can stay in touch via Facebook at Facebook.com/Bronwyn.scott.399 or on her blog, bronwynswriting.blogspot.com. She loves to hear from readers.

Books by Bronwyn Scott

Harlequin Historical

"Dancing with the Duke's Heir"
in *Scandal at the Christmas Ball*
The Art of Catching a Duke
The Captain Who Saved Christmas

Enterprising Widows

Liaison with the Champagne Count
Alliance with the Notorious Lord

Daring Rogues

Miss Claiborne's Illicit Attraction
His Inherited Duchess

The Peveretts of Haberstock Hall

Lord Tresham's Tempting Rival
Saving Her Mysterious Soldier
Miss Peverett's Secret Scandal
The Bluestocking's Whirlwind Liaison
"Dr. Peverett's Christmas Miracle"
in *Under the Mistletoe*

Visit the Author Profile page
at Harlequin.com for more titles.

For the puppies: The first book without Huckleberry sitting beneath my desk, but also the first book with Stevie beside me, because for every ending there are new beginnings. And always for Bennie, who is celebrating his twentieth book with me.

Prologue

Holmfirth—
February 5th, 1852

Fleur Griffiths loved her friends more than she hated whist, which explained why she was up an hour past midnight, playing poorly at cards in Mrs Parnaby's lace-curtained parlour and being positively trounced by Emma Luce, who was on her way to navigating a grand slam. Normally, by one in the morning, she would be asleep beside her husband. They all would. Except *this* evening they'd sent their men home without them. Fleur sighed and tossed out a useless card—Emma was unstoppable tonight—and reassessed her reasoning for the late night. It wasn't all due to her affections for her friends. It was about the quarrel, too. She was here because she didn't want to be *there*, in their temporary lodgings with Adam, not yet. Her temper was still too hot.

She and Adam had fought—hard—tonight right before all three couples had left their lodgings on Water Street in the nearby village of Hinchliffe Mill for supper at Mrs Parnaby's in Holmfirth proper. Beneath the table she pressed a hand to the flat of her stomach. They'd fought about the baby, or rather the potential of a baby. Nothing was certain yet. She wanted children, Adam did not.

Neither had made a secret of their preferences when they'd married eight years ago. She'd always assumed the issue would work itself out, that Adam would come around in time. But he remained adamant in his stance that a man should not start a family in his late fifties. Now, though, it seemed possible that nature disagreed with him. Her courses were late and with each passing day, her hopes rose that there would be a son who would grow up and take over Adam's news syndicate, a collection of newspapers that stretched from London to York in the north and all the way to Bristol in the west.

Surely, with such a legacy on the line, Adam would see the merit of having a son, someone to carry it all on. What was the point of all this work and sacrifice to build the newspaper empire if there was no one to leave it to when she and Adam were gone? But Adam had been grim tonight when she'd floated the idea. 'Let's hope it's just stress causing the lateness,' he'd said. She should have left it alone. After all, nothing was decided. But she'd pushed the issue. She'd gone to him, helping him with his neckcloth, pressing up against him, flirting as she fussed with his clothes. 'Would it really be so bad?' she'd cajoled, hoping for a smile. She did not get one.

'Yes, yes, it would,' was the terse response she'd got instead and, because there was a real possibility the child was no longer the hypothetical subject of an old argument, she'd not let the discussion go. Hot words had been exchanged along with blunt opinions that had sustained hurt on both sides.

She tossed another card. Would this hand ever end? It wasn't she and Adam's first fight. They were a rather volatile couple in private, something that would surprise Emma and Antonia with their perfect marriages and doting husbands. *They* didn't have disagreements. They had discussions. Not so with her and Adam. Fleur prided herself on having a 'real' marriage where there were quarrels and hard truths and imperfections but where there were also apologies, commitment from them both to do better and sex—the glorious, heated sex that reminded her that, beneath it all, Adam loved her and she loved him, desperately, completely. Together they could conquer anything.

Tonight had felt different, as if here at last was something they'd not get past. When Emma had suggested an impromptu round robin of whist after supper, Fleur had let Adam go without a kiss or whispered, 'I love you.' She'd stood apart from him in the hall while the others had said goodnight to their husbands and the three men had headed back to the Water Street lodgings. No doubt, the men would stay up a while, have a drink together and discuss the business of the mill that had brought them all to Holmfirth. Then they'd retire.

She knew Adam would retire first. He didn't like late nights. In London, he preferred to rise early and get into the office while it was still quiet. She knew his routine, his preferences, intimately. She'd spent eight years adapting her schedule to fit his. If not, she might never have seen him. Adam loved his work as much as he loved his wife. On nights like tonight, nights where they fought, she wondered if he didn't love it more. Or perhaps she was just selfish in wanting all of his attention.

Emma was just about to claim the last trick when Fleur heard it—a sound in the street: running feet, a shout. She froze and looked up from her hand. She could not hear the words, but she knew what panic sounded like. The shout came again, closer now. 'The embankment's breached, the river's in Water Street!'

Oh, God, the men! Adam, asleep in his bed. Would he even have a chance? Similar thoughts were mirrored on the faces of Emma and Antonia. Fear galvanised them. The four women raced to the lace curtains to peer out into the night. They could see nothing but darkness, but they could *hear*. Even at their safe distance, they could hear the river ravaging, hear its heavy churning as it rushed through Holmfirth, hungry to devour the next village in its path.

'We'll be safe here,' Mrs Parnaby tried to assure them, but Emma was inconsolable in her panic. She raced for the door.

Fleur grabbed for her. 'Help me, Antonia! Help me hold her!' The silly fool meant to go out after them. With Antonia's help, she wrestled Emma from the door. 'What do you think it will accomplish, you running out there? You can't see a thing,' Fleur scolded her friend too harshly in her own panic. 'It's too late to warn them.' She forced Emma to sit.

Antonia took Emma's hand and knelt beside her. 'They're strong men, they can take care of themselves.' That was Antonia, always the optimist. Fleur could do with a little of that optimism herself right now.

Mrs Parnaby was all bustling practicality, ordering a

tea tray. 'We'll go help when the water has settled and there's less chance of us being another set of people in need of rescue ourselves.' Fleur knew what that meant. It meant there was nothing to be done until daylight. Fleur noted the grimness around the woman's mouth. Despite her hopeful words, Mrs Parnaby already feared the worst and, in truth, Fleur did, too.

It was the longest night Fleur could remember, especially given that their vigil hadn't started until half-past one, the night already well advanced. But the five hours until there was enough light to be abroad dragged at a snail's pace, the hall clock seemingly frozen in time. None of them could sleep. They spent the night wide awake in the parlour, ears craning for the sound of footsteps, for a knock on the door. None came.

The moment it was light, they donned cloaks and followed Mrs Parnaby to the Rose and Crown Inn, but morning did not bring relief, only reality, and what a grim reality it was to see the result of what they'd heard last night. Fleur noted it all with a reporter's eye as they picked their way through mud and debris: the dead cow mired in the muck, the various parts of metal machinery deposited willy-nilly wherever the river tired of carrying them, the heavy oak furniture reduced to sharp, dangerous splinters, the timbers and stones that had once been houses, torn asunder, the sheer amount of ruined home goods, and the oddness of the things that had survived intact.

They passed a credenza still whole and a set of un-cracked blue dishes. Fleur wondered if their owner would find them. How many miles had that credenza travelled down the river? There was hope in that. Some things in the river's wake had survived the night. Perhaps that meant their husbands had, too.

Others were at the Rose and Crown. It was fast becoming a gathering point, a place where families could find each other, where people could exchange news and where those in need could get help, medical care, a blanket and a hot meal.

Fleur tied on an apron and went to work immediately. There were children who'd come in alone, bedraggled and looking for parents, armed with horrifying stories of having spent the night clinging to the roof timbers of their homes and praying the water wouldn't reach them. Those were the *least* horrifying tales. Others told terrible stories of watching their families being swept away in the raging current.

She spent the morning washing faces, spooning broth, the journalist in her avidly listening to stories and asking questions. She offered reassurance where she could. Across the room, she saw Antonia do the same, quite often with a small child on her hip. Antonia had always been good with children. Fleur tried to keep her eyes from the door, to keep her attentions on those she could help. She tried not to think of Adam. He would come. If he was with Antonia's husband, Keir, he'd be out there helping those in need first before helping himself. He would come when he could.

There *was* good news. James Mettrick, one of the men they'd come to do business with who also lived on Water Street and had been in his residence at the time of the flood, straggled in mid-morning, bruised but alive.

This was tempered with the reality that his family had not survived. Fleur clung to the knowledge that survival was possible. If James Mettrick had survived, perhaps Adam had, too. Perhaps Adam was still out helping others. Perhaps he'd been pushed downstream and needed transport back, or perhaps, heaven forbid, he was hurt and even now some kind stranger was caring for him as she was caring for others. It gave her own hope a much-needed second wind.

That second wind was short-lived. At ten o'clock, George Dyson, the town coroner, arrived. Fleur tracked him with her eyes as he sought out Emma. Fleur watched Emma nod before Emma turned her direction with a gesture that indicated the three of them should adjourn to the Rose and Crown's private parlour.

In the parlour, Antonia stood between her and Emma, gripping their hands as Mr Dyson cleared his throat and addressed them, using Emma's title, Lady Luce. The formality lent an ominous quality to his tone and Fleur braced herself against words that never prefaced the positive. 'I wish I had better news.' Oh, God. Fleur felt her stomach sink. 'I will be blunt; Water Street didn't stand a chance. The river hit it from the front and the side, absolutely obliterating the buildings.' He paused and swallowed hard.

How many times today had he needed to deliver bad news? Fleur wondered. But the wondering didn't make his next words any easier to hear. 'James Mettrick's family and the Earnshaws, with whom you had business dealings, are all gone. Their homes are entirely destroyed.' Homes that had been next to the ones Fleur and her friends had rented.

The world became muffled to Fleur. She was vaguely aware of Emma arguing something about James Mettrick, the son, surviving. Dyson was shaking his head, delivering the death blow as gently as possible. 'Lady Luce, the bodies of your husband and his friends have been recovered.' There was more. Fleur didn't care. She'd get the details later. For now, all that mattered was knowing they were gone. Garret was dead. Keir was dead. *Adam* was dead.

No, it had to be a mistake. Adam couldn't be dead. Not when there was unresolved anger between them. Not when there might be a child to raise. Her world reeled. She staggered forward, catching herself on the fireplace mantel lined with blue ware pieces like the set they'd seen in the mud, unbroken and whole. Rage surged. Damn it all! Why should the universe choose to save dishes over the life of one good man, *her* man? It wasn't right. But she could make it right. She picked up the blue ware piece nearest her and threw it hard against the wall, watching it shatter into a thousand pieces. Like her heart. Her life. Her very soul.

Anger began to burn, a source of fuel against her grief. This was what Adam had feared—that the dam was insufficient to its task. It was the reason Garrett had asked him to come, to bring his investigative journalistic talents to bear on determining the quality of not only the mill, but the river that mill depended on. Now the very worst had happened. Naturally? Or as the result of human error? If it were the latter, she could make sure someone paid for all they'd taken from her.

* * *

Apparently, one could live on anger, at least for four days. While Emma and Antonia had stayed in with their grief at Mrs Parnaby's, Fleur had gone out, channelling her rage into walking the muddy, ruined streets of Holmfirth. She helped with the recovery effort from daybreak to sunset. She helped rehome those who'd lost everything. She sat on the committee charged with collecting funds to distribute to those in need—of which there were many when the realisation set in that the river had destroyed homes *and* jobs. There was no work to go back to, no income to earn. In the evenings, she wrote copious articles to the newspapers Adam owned, sharing first-hand testimonies of survivors and reports of the developing situation. She instructed the editors to send artists to draw pictures. She wanted lithographs printed, she wanted word spread far and wide about the depth of tragedy in Holmfirth.

Anger could only go so far, though. It kept her fuelled and busy. But it could not change the fact that Adam was gone. 'We're widows now. Widows before the age of thirty,' Fleur ground out, pacing before Mrs Parnaby's fireplace. The woman had been a generous hostess, taking in three women who were only supposed to have been dinner guests.

Emma spoke up as if reading her thoughts from across the room. 'I think it's time to go. There's nothing more we can do here.'

Fleur raised an eyebrow in challenge. Nothing more to do here? There was plenty to do here. She couldn't possibly leave now. But of course, Emma would be thinking about concerns with Garrett's estate and his investments. She would need to be in London. Antonia nodded agreement, citing the need to take over the reins of Keir's department store project. That was a bold move on Antonia's part. Fleur was aware of Antonia's gaze on her as her friend asked, 'Shall we all travel together as far as London?'

Fleur shook her head, not daring to look at her two closest friends. They would argue with her. They'd not been out in the streets and seen what she had seen. 'No. I think I'll stay and finish Adam's investigation. There are people to help and justice to serve.' She would take rooms at an inn if Mrs Parnaby needed her privacy back.

Emma's face showed disagreement. 'Do you think that's wise, Fleur? If this disaster was man-made, there will be people who won't appreciate the prying, particularly if there's a woman doing it. You should think twice about putting yourself in danger.'

'I don't care,' Fleur snapped. She loved Emma, but they often butted heads, both of them stubborn. 'If Adam died because of carelessness or greed, someone will pay for that. I will see to it and I will see to it that such recklessness doesn't happen again.'

Emma's gaze dropped to her waist and Fleur snatched her hand away from her stomach. She'd been unaware she'd put it there. But it was too late for Emma's sharp eyes. 'And Adam's babe? Would you be reckless with his child?'

Fleur reined in her anger, softening her voice. 'I do not know if there is a child. It is too soon.'

Emma relented with a nod. 'Just be careful, dear friend. I do not want anything to happen to you.' Emma rose and came to her, Antonia joining them. They encircled each other with their arms, their heads bent together. This would be their private farewell. 'We're widows now,' Emma echoed her words.

'We have lost much,' Fleur murmured, 'but we are still friends. Whatever else changes, that will not, no matter where we go, no matter what happens.' She looked at the pale faces of her friends, her resolve doubling. For Garrett, for Keir, for Adam, for Antonia, for Emma, and for herself, there would be justice for them all.

Chapter One

There'd been no justice, just a vituperative, albeit sincere, outpouring of extreme dismay from the Government Inspector over the negligence surrounding the construction, maintenance, and oversight of the doomed Bilberry Dam. If one thing had been made clear in the investigation, it was that the dam had been plagued with misadventures from the start on all levels.

Sympathy and outrage were not enough for Fleur. It had not been enough last February when the inquiry concluded with a call for increased legislative oversight to prevent future disasters and it was not enough now, fifteen months later, which was why Fleur had scheduled a morning meeting with Government Inspector Captain R.C. Moody at the *Newcastle Forge*, one of the Northumberland papers owned by the Griffiths news syndicate. Owned by *her*.

It was one of the myriad changes that had occurred in the past year. Adam's empire was hers now, hers to look after in his place, although it was not a role she would have chosen for herself. Being a newspaper magnate had been Adam's dream, not hers. She'd wanted to be a storyteller, nothing more. Running the syndicate was a daunting task, but one that offered her the leverage to continue to pursue justice for the dam accident.

If the truth wouldn't come to her, she would go to the truth. So, here she was, in Newcastle upon Tyne, sitting in Adam's regional office, surrounded by Adam's things, sitting behind the desk in the chair Adam used to occupy when he was in town. The company might be hers, but the office was still very definitely his. She took strength from that, from feeling his presence. Before her on the desk were the documents regarding the dam accident. How many times had she read them in the hopes that she might uncover something new? She tapped her fingers, impatient for Captain Moody to arrive. A glance at the small desktop clock encased in masculine walnut indicated her impatience was not warranted. Moody wasn't even late yet. There was no basis for it except her own eagerness.

She'd met Moody before during the inquest. He'd been a perfect gentleman, considerate and well spoken, aware that his task as the Government Inspector was not only to investigate the cause of failure, but also to ensure the region recovered. He'd been sensitive to the rawness and depth of loss the people had experienced. In those days, she'd been just another widow, angry and grieving. Today, she was a businesswoman at the helm of a newspaper empire. She could not be handled with platitudes and consolation. Today, she wanted accountability and truth.

A knock on her closed door was followed by the paper's receptionist announcing Captain Moody's arrival. Fleur rose and ran a smoothing hand down her bodice and her green tartan skirts before straightening her shoulders. She would be politely charming, personally enquiring and, above all, professional. The past months had taught her the merits of such decorum when dealing with Adam's testy board of directors who hadn't liked change when it came in the form of a woman. 'Send him in, Miss Grant.'

She could hear Miss Grant in the outer office. 'Mrs Griffiths will see you now, Captain.'

That was her cue to come around the desk and extend a hand in greeting as the Captain entered the room, *her domain*. This was her space; she was in charge here, despite it being marked with Adam's effects. 'Captain, it's so good of you to come. I know you're a busy man these days overseeing the Royal Engineers in Newcastle.' She smiled. 'And somewhat recently married, too, I hear. Congratulations.'

He smiled the smile of the newlywed bridegroom, part-blissful enchantment, and part-bashful humility as if he couldn't quite believe his good fortune. 'Yes, Mrs Griffiths, you've heard correctly. Mary and I were wed last July.' Quite the marriage it was, too. Fleur had done her research. The Captain's wife was the daughter of an extremely wealthy industrialist and, rumour had it, already expecting their first child—not that she would bring that up.

'Please, have a seat.' She gestured to the leather club chair set on the guest side of the big, polished desk. She crossed to the matching console where Adam's Baccarat decanters and a silver coffee urn were displayed. 'It is probably too early to offer you a drink, Captain, but I have hot coffee and fresh rolls.'

'Coffee, thank you, Mrs Griffiths.' He took the seat, sitting with evident military bearing. 'How have you been?' he asked as she passed him a warm mug of coffee and a pastry plate, his question a reminder of how differently the year had treated them. Her marriage, her hopes for a family, had ended while his had begun.

She took her own seat behind the desk, a hand slipping surreptitiously to the flat of her stomach. There'd been no child. Perhaps there never had been. Perhaps all that had ever been in her belly was hope: hope for a child, for the type of family she'd been denied growing up, hope to redirect a marriage she'd sensed was coming to a volatile head between two strong-willed people who wanted different things. Instead of new life, she'd got death.

'I've been well, thank you.' It wasn't quite a lie. She'd been busy and she supposed that was as close to well as she'd get these days. Busy enough to not miss Adam every waking minute. Busy enough to not be entirely eaten up with the regret and the guilt that surrounded that fateful night in Holmfirth. Busy enough to convince herself she was indeed moving on, that she was making progress in a man's world with a board of directors who'd sooner oust her than support her. Some days she actually believed in that progress.

She took a sip of her own coffee and got straight to business. 'I've asked for this meeting because it's been over a year since the inquest delivered its verdict on the dam and nothing has been done. There has been no preventative legislation introduced and now I fear that momentum has been lost. The public has forgotten the urgency behind the issue.' But she had not. She would never forget the horror of Holmfirth and the terrible days that followed when she'd roamed the streets helping survivors, grappling with the loss of Adam and all it meant.

Captain Moody gave a slight nod, but it was a nod of empathy, not agreement. She hoped he would not condescend to her with pity, which seemed to be a man's default when dealing with a widow. 'Mrs Griffiths, you were there when the verdict was read, and prior to that, when my own conclusions were presented. Even now, I will still stand by every word of my statement. While there was proof of gross negligence and ineptitude of such capacity that it turns my stomach to think of it, there was no one person or firm who could be charged with the irresponsibility that led to the dam's demise. This made it impossible to render the charge of manslaughter,' he explained patiently. 'Truly, I understand how disappointing such a finding must be for you.'

Disappointment did not encapsulate the entirety of her feelings in that regard. She knew the words of those findings by heart. She'd heard them spoken out loud at the original presentation of the jury's verdict. She'd read them over and over when the report had been published.

We regret that the reservoir being under the management of a corporation prevents us bringing in a verdict of manslaughter, as we are convinced that the gross and culpable negligence of the commissioners would have subjected them to such a

*verdict had they been in the position of an indi-
vidual or firm.*

Regret was a mild word compared to the *devastating*
guilt she felt. Regret was what one felt when one had
to decline an invitation to afternoon tea. It was a polite
word. Politeness had no place when discussing the loss
of eighty-one lives, or the deaths of people swept from
their homes in their sleep. Mildness was an inappro-
priate response when listening to the tales, as she had
in the early days of the flood's aftermath, of those who
watched, helpless, as loved ones were carried away by
the angry torrent. There was no room for complacency
when people realised the river had stolen lives and live-
lihoods, that the flood had devastated their economic
well-being.

She wanted to give in to the rage the issue deserved,
but she remembered in time the promise she'd made herself earlier. She would be professional. No one respected
hysterics. A man was entitled to an angry outburst, but
a woman, never. 'You are right, Captain Moody. It is
extraordinarily disappointing.' Fleur cultivated careful
neutrality, letting him see only the steady steel in her
gaze instead of the rage in her heart. 'Especially when
you acquired an impressive record of names. Your enquiry clearly stated that if there was an individual or
firm on which blame could be fixed, prosecution would
be possible.' Justice would be possible.

His gaze narrowed. 'What are you suggesting,
ma'am?'

'That your enquiry, while timely and thorough,
should be viewed only as the beginning, not the end of

the interrogation on the dam.' The government *had* acted
with surprising alacrity. The inquest had opened immediately on the sixth, the day after the flood. By the eigh-
teenth of February, Moody had given his report to the
jury and by the twenty-seventh, the jury had come back
with their final conclusions. The amount of paperwork
he'd amassed in those two weeks had been impressive
and detailed, as was the list of names, both of individuals and companies who'd been involved with the dam
at any point in its construction and maintenance. 'The
inquest should be reopened and individuals investigated
more thoroughly.'

To his credit, Moody took the suggestion seriously.
'On what grounds? It is not the custom to try a man or
a firm twice for the same crime unless there is new evidence come to light that reshapes our understanding.'

Fleur reached for a folder lying beneath the papers
on her desk. 'There is this.' She slid it across the desk
to him and gave him a moment to peruse the single
sheet inside. She steadied her own breathing. Everything hinged on this. Some might say her case hung by
a thread, but she thought it wasn't so much a thread but
a rope—a strong rope made of hardy hemp, the kind
that didn't unravel at a first picking.

She'd spent the last fifteen months reviewing every
detail, retracing every step that had led up to the dam
disaster, starting seven years prior. She'd had the time
to dig deeply that Captain Moody had not. And she'd
found something. *Someone.* A singular person whose
actions had caused the disaster. The singular person
needed who could be prosecuted and held accountable.

'Lord Orion Bexley?' Moody quirked a brow and

set the folder down. 'You want to go after *him*?' It was not a challenge, but an opportunity to make her case.

She gave a sharp nod. 'He's the only one who was a consistent presence at the dam. The others—Mr Sharpe, Mr Leather, Mr Littlewood—they're contractors, inspectors, and masons. All of them are people who temporarily intersected with the dam at various points in its development. None of them was singularly responsible for the accident, although,' she added a stern pause, 'all of them do *share* in the blame, all are responsible in part.'

'But you feel Lord Orion is somehow more responsible?' Moody asked.

'Yes, he was on the board of commissioners and didn't sign off on certain reports. It's all there. Much of the mismanagement can be traced directly to him. Particularly this order, which was initiated by him, but, even after funds were delivered, the repairs were never executed.' Follow the money. Adam had been fond of claiming that as one of the top rules of good investigative reporting. Money and blood always told.

Captain Moody was silent for a long while. 'I admire your tenacity and your zeal to see justice done, Mrs Griffiths,' he said at last in quiet tones. 'However, I do not think you are aware of what or who you're up against. It will be legally difficult to get to Lord Orion Bexley even if you had an ironclad case against him, which you do not. You have some interesting leads and conclusions, but be honest—they are not airtight.' He was right. She had strong leads, but it was entirely possible they might go nowhere. Still, she wouldn't know until she tried and she simply couldn't give up.

'What do you mean that I cannot get to him legally?'

That had grabbed her attention. 'No man is above the law. Just because he has a title does not mean he is automatically blameless.'

Moody chuckled. 'Unless that man is the brother of a marquess. Then it's a bit trickier. You know that, Mrs Griffiths. No *common* man is above the law. Lord Orion Bexley is far from the common man.'

She sighed. She knew first-hand that the peerage played by its own rules when it suited them. She'd learned that lesson the hard way through her uncle. She hadn't realised Bexley ran quite that high in the instep, though. 'A marquess?'

'Yes, the Marquess of Meltham, an old and venerable title. The family seat is near Holmfirth,' Moody supplied, discreetly filling in her gaps. She'd not looked up Bexley's title specifically because she preferred to let a man's actions speak for him rather than a title he had not earned beyond the accident of his birth.

She refused to be daunted. 'Well, if I can't get to him legally, perhaps I can get to Lord Orion Bexley socially.' An idea was already taking shape in her mind—a publicity blitz. 'I would think some articles suggesting Lord Orion's culpability would bring him under social censure.'

The Griffiths news syndicate owned seven papers in the north that spanned the distance between Newcastle-upon-Tyne and Sheffield. Those papers could expose the role played by Lord Orion Bexley and apply pressure by making regular appearances. The more often the public saw an issue in print, the more likely they were to view that issue as important and give it their attention.

'The peerage may not have to answer to the law, but

it does answer to society and popular opinion. No one cares to be disliked. Society has its own unwritten rules. Blacken a person's name enough, throw enough aspersion in one's direction and there will be socially unpleasant consequences.'

'Unpleasant consequences for both parties, ma'am, if you don't mind me saying so. If you were wrong, for instance, it would go poorly for the papers and for you. I do not know the Marquess personally, but I would guess he'd not take kindly to his brother, his family, being slandered.' It was only slander if she was wrong. And she knew in her gut she wasn't.

'Truth is indeed a double-edged sword, Captain.' She gave a polite smile. 'I have lost my husband, sir, due to carelessness and cavalier neglect. His death and the death of others were senseless, purposeless. That loss will not go unavenged while I have the ability to see justice done.' She rose to signal the meeting was concluded. 'Thank you for your time, Captain.'

Moody stood. 'I wish you luck and I urge you to take care. Tweaking noses can be dangerous work, Mrs Griffiths.' Especially when those noses belonged to powerful marquesses, but such was the price of justice, and she would pay it if need be. She might not be able to get to Lord Orion Bexley legally, but often, what the law couldn't do, the press could, and it would start today.

Meltham House, London—
Three weeks later

Jasper Bexley, Marquess of Meltham, liked to start his day with quiet and coffee in the morning room, a bun drizzled with icing for his sweet tooth at his elbow, a plate of fluffy scrambled eggs before him and the latest newspapers at the ready. But if he had to choose between the food or the quiet, he'd choose the quiet. He preferred quiet above all else.

Quiet was a sign of order, of steadiness, of readiness. Most of all it was a sign that all was right in his world and Jasper Bexley was a man who valued that rightness in all its forms. It allowed a man to think rationally, plan methodically, engage with his world logically. For him, silence was indeed the golden currency of quietude, especially during the Season when the demands on a marquess's time were extreme.

So, when his brother's strident tones, accompanied by the loud *thwack!* of a newspaper on the polished surface of the breakfast table set Jasper's cup to jangling and his coffee to sloshing in its saucer, much more than the pristine silence of the room was broken. His train of thought was broken, the peace of his morning was broken, and such things were not easily mended or restored.

Jasper sighed and dragged his gaze from *The Times*. The morning was giving every sign of going downhill from here. He took off his wire-rimmed spectacles and set them aside. He suspected it would be a while before he got back to his reading. With Orion it was never just a single interruption, but the beginning of a long line of other disturbances.

'Don't you have rooms at the Albany?' he queried coolly, fixing his younger brother with a freezing stare, both of which were meant to remind him that this was to be the Season of his living independently and embracing his adulthood. It was beyond time. Orion was thirty, eight years older than Jasper had been when he'd become the Marquess.

'They can't keep saying these things about me! There's been articles up north and now there's one in the *London Tribune*.' Orion abused the table with another swat of the newspaper, slouched into the chair and conveniently ignored the question.

'Conveniently ignoring' was a coping strategy his brother had cultivated as a boy and honed to perfection as an adult. The only other thing Orion cultivated with such care was his appearance—always immaculately groomed and expensively turned out, even, Jasper noted wryly, in the midst of his latest crisis. This morning, Orion wore a grass-green silk waistcoat, a sky-blue silk cravat and a bottle-green jacket of superfine, his jaw clean shaven, his champagne-blond hair—Orion's term for a hue that was not quite gold or brown—neatly trimmed.

Jasper always felt a bit rough around the edges compared to his brother. His own hair was decidedly longer, a collection of unruly nut-brown waves that tangled easily no matter the amount of pomade his valet applied. He was too busy to think about clothes. He left that to his tailor and valet. Between them, they hadn't failed him yet.

Jasper breathed in through his nose and gave a long exhale, preparing to jump into the impending fray. 'What is it this time? Did the society column not care for your latest waistcoat? Or is it money trouble again?' Perhaps a gaming debt that had lingered too long for repayment. It wouldn't be the first time. He hoped that was all it was. He hoped it wasn't worse—a wronged earl's daughter caught kissing Orion in a garden at a ball, perhaps—because Orion would make a terrible husband. He loved his brother, but that didn't mean he wished Orion on an unsuspecting wife.

'Brother, you have to make them stop. It's gone too far. It never should have been allowed to start.'

Jasper did not care for the accusatory tone with which the last part was said. Nor did he like the feeling that he'd entered in the middle of a play and didn't understand the plot. He rubbed the bridge of his nose. 'I am going to need more detail than that, starting with who "they" are in this little drama and what *is* the drama?' Because it was always drama with Orion. Mountains from mole hills were his speciality, usually because they'd been ignored too long before they reached Jasper's attention.

Orion shoved the paper the length of the table. '"They" are the *London Tribune*, the *Leeds Messenger*, the *Sheffield Tribune*, the *Bristol Intelligencer* and a host of smaller papers from here to York.' Orion's chagrin seemed genuine for once and, for a moment, Jasper sensed something else beneath it—authentic concern? Perhaps a sincere sense of worry? But it was gone as quickly as it came. Still, he thought, the observation was worth filing away.

Jasper reached for his glasses and picked up the paper, his brow furrowing as he read the half-page article, which was quite a bit of space devoted to an issue that was over a year old and one that had been settled. 'This is about the dam accident in Holmfirth last February.' More specifically, it was about the enquiry that had occurred afterwards. Orion had been on the Board of Commissioners for the Holmfirth Dam project, a position Jasper had arranged in the hopes of giving Orion a sense of purpose and direction when Orion had finished a brief, disappointing stint in the military with the engineering corps.

He looked up at Orion. 'What does this have to do with you? The verdict was clear: there was no one person or organisation that was accountable for the accident.' The dam had been a tragedy of collective errors, to be sure, and a travesty of bureaucratic nonsense.

'Someone is attempting to reopen the investigation,' Orion groused, reaching for the silver coffee pot and pouring a cup before pulling out a flask to enliven the brew. Jasper frowned. It was barely half past eight. A bit early, in his opinion, to be 'enlivening' beverages.

'Let them search. They are not bound to get far. The law won't retry a case without new evidence and there was no conviction last time due to there being no one or no group *to* bring to trial.' Jasper failed to see what the worry was.

'But that's the point. Someone *is* looking for a person to pin it all on and that person is *me*!' Orion blurted out with dramatic angst. 'The newspaper articles have named *me* in a manner that suggests I am the someone who should be held accountable and whoever is doing it is using the papers to whip up support. You must put a stop to it,' he insisted.

'You want me to use my title to suppress the press?' Jasper surmised bluntly. And when *or* if that failed, Orion would want him to use his title to suppress the individual citizen behind it. Did Orion even see the irony in that, given his voting record in Parliament regarding lowering the stamp tax on newspapers and abolishing the excise tax on printing paper? He championed free press. He didn't censor it.

Orion leaned forward in earnest. 'I want you to use your title to suppress slander, Brother. Someone is trying to ruin me.' It was said with all the aplomb of a Drury Lane thespian—he was giving *quite* the performance.

Jasper nodded. Orion *was* named specifically. That alone required his attention. The family name must be protected from unrighteous scandal. But he also knew that with Orion there was always a nugget of truth involved and many other types of nuggets, too. There was likely more to this than what Orion was letting on. He just had to figure out what that more was. Regardless, the situation would have to be handled delicately.

If the press was indeed slandering Orion, it would indirectly be akin to slandering the marquessate, which Jasper would not tolerate. His father had taught that lesson well and often. The Marquess must protect the family. Of course, that assumed that was indeed happening. Cases were *never* black and white with Orion. He would not let his brother be wronged, but neither would Jasper risk the marquessate's good name by using it to undermine a free press, one of the life bloods of an evolving society, a view that often made him unpopular in the House of Lords. It was a view he'd fought for on more than one occasion because ideas—scientific, philosophical, or otherwise—were critical if a society were to modernise and advance, something the reclusive and often eccentric Marquessate of Meltham had long believed in. It was a legacy he was more than happy to keep alive.

He sighed. This was going to be tricky indeed. 'I'll

look into it right away. Get me a list of all the papers that ran articles about you.' He was already mentally reorganising his morning to move this to the top of his task list as a thousand questions clamoured for his attention, mercilessly drowning out the quiet.

Chapter Two

If the British system of primogeniture had not so mercilessly designated that Jasper Bexley be a marquess's heir simply on the merit of his birth and sex, he would have, by his own choice, been a scientist, a participant in a field of discovery that was rooted in logic and careful, reliable methodology that sought predictability. The scientist's life was a quiet, orderly life of logical experimentation that led to logical outcomes, where everything had explanations and reasons.

Since his first encounter with Francis Bacon's treatise, *Novum Organum*, which he'd ponderously and determinedly waded through in its original Latin at eighteen, the year his father had inexplicably taken ill, the Baconian Method had become the lens through which Jasper processed and understood the world— logical reasoning through classifications instead of syllogisms, and most of all the discovery of truth, of knowledge through an organised process that began with questioning and observation.

Bacon had appealed to him at a time in his life when he'd been desperate for answers. His father, a generally hardy and robust man, had taken ill with pneumonia and had never recovered despite four years of trying. Both the illness and the lack of recovery had seemed random and inexplicable occurrences to Jasper.

How was it that a healthy man like his father could be cut down still in his prime? He'd sought answers and reasons in his craving to rationalise the tragedy playing out before him. His father dead at the age of fifty-four. The title and the responsibility of leading the family his at the young age of twenty-two. Since then, Bacon had become a tool to guide him through managing the title and a tool for managing his life so that he might use the order of logic as a shield against the chaos and pain of emotion.

That tool was serving him well today. Questions were a scientist's stock in trade and there were plenty to ask at present. Jasper dedicated his morning to doing that asking: why was someone seeking to reopen a decisive, thorough investigation? Who might that someone be? Why was his brother the target? Why was his brother worried about being the target if the previous investigation had turned up nothing directed at him? What was different this time?

Questions led to research. To create answers, one had to gather information—*objective* information. He could not resolve the situation if he didn't understand the *whole* situation. Too many people, Orion included, saw the world as *they* were, not as it factually was. Truth, by its very definition, could *not* be subjective. It must remain inviolable.

As long as one asked the right questions, that truth was not so hard to come by and, by the late afternoon,

Jasper had discovered two interesting pieces of information. First, all the papers were owned by the Griffiths News Syndicate. Second—and this was where it got interesting—the *woman* in charge of the syndicate was Fleur Griffiths, who'd lost her husband in the flood. A woman. A widow. Certain conclusions could be drawn.

Jasper drummed his fingers on the surface of his desk as he imagined the scenario the information provided: a grieving widow with a news organisation at her disposal and a proverbial axe to grind. Motive didn't get more obvious than that. She'd lost her husband. She would have been disappointed with a verdict that didn't assign clear blame. Clear blame would have given her closure and the explanation she was no doubt looking for: why had this random, freak accident claimed her husband's life? Without that explanation, her grief remained unassuaged, unable to rest.

He knew those feelings. They were the feelings he'd had when his father had died. He'd taken comfort in his Francis Bacon, searching for that understanding. She was out looking for vengeance and wielding her presses to do it. Perhaps she hoped if she could find a culprit, it would appease her grief, close her wounds. No. Strike that last part. He was extrapolating now about a woman he had never even seen. He would need to rectify that.

One had to be careful not to infer too much. After all, he didn't know anything *factual* about Mrs Griffiths's character, another reason why it was necessary to encounter her. His scenario upon which the 'obvious motive' was based assumed she grieved, which was based on another assumption—that all women grieved. Mrs Griffiths was a woman, therefore she grieved. Wasn't this the very concern of syllogistic reasoning that Bacon had railed against? One must test each step in that dangerous ladder.

He strode to the sideboard against the wall and poured an afternoon brandy, testing those logical rungs in his mind. Perhaps she did not miss her husband? Perhaps she was glad to be free of him, free of matrimony? Especially when she now had a fortune and empire at her disposal. He knew there were such women in the world who aspired to be more than wives and mothers. Perhaps she was one of them? But that brought another set of assumptions to test. *Did* she have a fortune? An empire? Perhaps there were others controlling it? Perhaps she was nothing more than a figurehead? Perhaps someone was controlling her?

By the time his secretary, a tall, slim, serious, dark-haired fellow, appeared for further instruction, two items had become clear. First, Mrs Griffiths was a person of interest to him and he needed to confirm she was the person responsible for these articles both up north and in London. Second, to move along his understanding of the situation he needed to know *her*. A good critical thinker tested not only the content of the argument being made, but the source who made the argument. He could not answer his remaining questions or form a viable hypothesis without that. To know her required meeting her, but not as the Marquess of Meltham. She would never receive Meltham and even if by some miracle she did, she'd be on her guard, wanting to protect herself.

'I need you to ascertain if Mrs Griffiths is in town,'

he told his secretary. He was fairly sure she was. It was the Season, Parliament was in session and all the news was here, after all, as well as the syndicate's headquarters. 'If she is in town, I want to know where she'll be tonight.' And he would miraculously be there, too. Not as the Marquess, of course, but in the guise of one of his lesser titles. Perhaps the Baron, Lord Umberton, would make an appearance this evening. The irony did not elude him that sometimes acquiring the objective truth often required a bit of subterfuge and, according to his secretary when he returned a couple hours later, a ticket to the theatre.

The Adelphi on the Strand was not the type of theatre Jasper was used to. It was not Covent Garden or Drury Lane—the theatres where *he* had boxes—but its façade was imposing despite its less than aristocratic population. Jasper tugged at his white waistcoat, feeling a bit overdressed. To be fair, there were a few aristocratic swells in the crowd—young bucks out for adventure beyond the confines of Mayfair—but most of the attendees were salaried clerks who worked at Gray's Inn or at firms throughout the City writing briefs, tallying ledgers and hoping for eventual promotion. Certainly, it was an educated if bourgeois crowd. Still, these were not *his* people. However, they *were* Mrs Griffith's people and that was interesting, informing.

Jasper purchased a playbill from a young usher and tried to draw a picture in his mind of Mrs Griffiths; perhaps she was a stout, determined older woman. He could imagine the sort: iron grey hair, a double chin from good living, a bosom worthy of a ship's prow and a waistline that corseting had long since failed to define. Perhaps, despite her age, she enjoyed an evening out among the younger set and embraced the novelties of the new modern era, which seemed likely if she had indeed taken over her husband's news syndicate after years of perhaps assisting him from the sidelines.

His own mother would be the first to tell him behind every great man there was usually a strong, tenacious woman and Adam Griffiths had been at least a great businessman to have acquired such a news network. Aristocrats didn't hold the monopoly on greatness as they once did. His father had predicted it, prepared him for it, prepared him to embrace change even as those in his set resisted it with every fibre of their being.

Jasper scanned the crowd as he took a seat on the floor. He'd not sat on the floor amid the masses before. But he didn't plan on being here long. He took out a pair of opera glasses and scanned the boxes. *She'd* be in a box. Griffiths would have been on top of the food chain here, the very sort of man these clerks aspired to be.

Jasper began dismissing boxes as his opera glasses roamed. No, not that box, not that one, not this one…all of them were full of grey-haired businessmen with their wives or perhaps, in some cases, their mistresses. Whoa! His opera glasses came to a full stop on the woman in the second box from the end. A lone woman dressed in a gown of burnished gold silk, cut fashionably low to show off a lovely bosom, auburn hair smooth and well coiffed, her bearing straight-backed and regal amid the heavy red velvet draperies framing the box. *Maybe her?*

Or was that just wishful thinking because she was positively stunning and bore no resemblance to the picture he'd drawn in his mind? His opera glasses would have lingered on her regardless of his errand. But it was her posture that made him consider her as a candidate for being the woman he sought, because goodness knew nothing else about her fit the anticipated mould of what he'd expected Adam Griffiths's widow to look like—a woman who was commensurate in age to Griffiths and well past the first blush of beauty.

This woman was thirty at most and she sat like a queen, her spine straight with authority, her shoulders squared with confidence, her chin tilted up a fraction of an inch as if to say, 'I dare anyone to come to my throne.' And like a queen, she was alone, unapproachable, untouchable. Thoughts of Queen Elizabeth teased the edges of his mind. Perhaps it was the red hair that sparked the comparison.

He checked the remaining box to be sure he wasn't overlooking anyone. No contenders there, just an older man and a woman with white hair—too old for what he was looking for. Jasper returned his opera glasses to the prior box, to his queen. Despite her surprising youth, it had to be her—the expensive gown and the confident bearing of one who was used to being in control. And she was alone, which spoke volumes to him as the house lights flickered, prompting the audience to take their seats. Before the house went dim, he summoned a fruit seller and pressed a coin in the girl's hand. 'At the intermission, tell me which box belongs to Mrs Griffiths.' He needed to be one hundred per cent right on this. He didn't want to make a fool of himself and approach the wrong woman.

The play was a performance of John Morton's *A Des-*

perate Game, a one-act farce which would be followed
by other performances after the intermission, but sitting
in the dark as those around him were excitedly impatient for the curtain to rise on the stage, Jasper's attentions were engaged inwardly instead, mulling over the
woman in the box above him and her defiant aloneness.
If he set aside his adherence to Baconian Law and engaged in the luxury of the loose logic of assumptions,
things began to make sense now that he was sure he'd
sighted her.

Bereft too young of a husband, she wanted justice.
No, she wanted more than justice. She wanted rectifi-
cation. She wanted someone to pay for her husband's
death and she thought that someone should be Orion.
It was there in the tilt of her chin. She would *hunger*
for it perhaps with a vengeance, a passion, that had become misguided despite the purity of its initial intent
to see right done.

He knew a bit about good intentions gone wrong.
Much of what he tried to do for his brother seemed to
end up in that category. He could certainly empathise
with the wanting to do good. But he could not sym-
pathise with it when it meant allowing the marquessate
to become the whetstone for the brutal knife of her grief.

When the house lights went up, the fruit seller was
waiting to confirm his hopes. The woman alone was indeed her. He made his way to the stairs leading to the
boxes and fought his way upstream. The Adelphi did
brisk business among the middle classes and the house
was full tonight. At last, he reached the box tier. It was
quieter up here and far less crowded. Ushers were po-

sitioned outside the boxes to see to the needs of the patrons within them and at the entrance to the saloon in order to prevent interlopers from intruding.

Jasper counted the boxes and approached the one containing his quarry, another coin at the ready, just in case he needed it, a hum akin to the thrill of the hunt thrumming in his veins. 'I'm here to see Mrs Griffiths.' He watched the usher's gaze move over his dark evening clothes and white waistcoat and conclude he was someone of import. But it wasn't enough.

The usher consulted his list. 'Mrs Griffiths is not expecting anyone in her box tonight.'

'Of course,' Jasper demurred in agreement, ingratiating himself to the usher. 'I did not know if I'd be able to attend tonight. It was all rather last minute.' Not a lie. He'd not had a ticket until two hours ago. 'If you could tell her Lord Umberton is here, it would be appreciated.' He offered the coin. He'd let the usher do his job and announce him. He had no desire to get the young man into trouble, but he would follow him in. He wasn't going to stand outside the box waiting to be refused. It was much harder to evict a man once he was inside. He did do the usher the courtesy, however, of a two-step head start.

In the dimness of the box, the usher cleared his throat. 'Mrs Griffiths, Lord Umberton to see you,'

Jasper stepped around the usher as she turned her head, meaning to take advantage of the moment of surprise only to find the tables entirely turned on him. Viewing her from a distance had not done her full credit. Stunning was an inadequate word to describe this woman. Proximity provided details. Up close, her eyes were green. Her skin was pearly luminescence and porcelain smoothness from the sweep of her check to the expanse of decolletage. She rose and the susurration of gold silk called attention to the exquisite simplicity of her gown and how it made love to every curve and angle of her, the body within the gown's only ornamentation. She was elegant beauty personified and his body answered to it, roused to it, most dangerously, because this was not logic.

In the heat of the moment with his usually organised thoughts in a riot, he could not recall the last time he'd responded so immediately, so thoroughly to a woman and so inconveniently. Very well, he rationalised. Being aware of the nature of his attraction meant he was forewarned against it. He was here to take her measure—objectively. Her green eyes were on him in cool perusal, his moment of surprise slipping away. He found the words to intercept the refusal before she could evict him. 'Pardon the intrusion. When I saw you were in attendance tonight, I wanted to take the opportunity to share my interest in the articles your paper has been publishing about the Bilberry Dam.' Also not a lie. He was interested but in a way that differed from the interest of her news syndicate.

A slim auburn brow arched. 'I do not come to the theatre, Lord Umberton, to discuss business.' It was meant as a rebuke, a cool scold, but it did not entirely hide the spark of another type of interest. Neither did he miss the subtle sweep of her gaze. She might not approve of the interruption, but something in her gaze said she approved of him.

He pressed his advantage. 'Perhaps I might persuade

you to join me for supper afterwards. I have a private table at Rules. What do you say to oysters and champagne?' He could see the idea tempted her even as they both understood how daring the offer was. In the circles he usually ran in, such an offer would not be made. They'd not been formally introduced. But this was not a pink-wool-wrapped debutante. This was a woman of the world, a woman of a man's world, to put a finer point on it. She ran a newspaper syndicate. One could not do that without getting a little dirty.

Her hand fingered the gold and pearl pendant at her neck, her auburn head tilting in consideration. 'Since I do not know you, Lord Umberton, nor you me, I will take mercy on you and offer you a lesson instead of a set down. I do not come to the theatre to discuss business, or to spend the evening in the company of gentlemen with whom I am not familiar.'

He chuckled. He probably deserved that. He'd behaved audaciously and he couldn't remember the last time he'd done that either. Still, he was no quitter. He might not know her, but neither did she know him. It was his habit to never leave a room until he got what he came for. Her refusal only meant she was careful, not that she wasn't interested. He gave a nod, allowing himself the luxury of a little flirting. 'What *do* you come to the theatre for?'

She snapped open the fan that hung at her wrist, an expensive black and gold creation. 'I come to forget, Lord Umberton, to set aside the world for a bit.' It didn't take much to read between those widely spaced lines as she no doubt intended. The house lights flickered. It was time for him to close the deal.

'I do apologise for my poor timing.' He gave a gracious bow. 'Perhaps tomorrow at your London offices would be more appropriate. I shall call on you at ten o'clock.'

'Will you be up by then?' she queried. He was up right now, to be truthful, but that wasn't the kind of up she was referring to. 'I was unaware lords rose before noon.' There were all sorts of wicked responses he could make to that given the rising action he was experiencing at the moment—nothing outrageous or obvious, he had more self-control than that—but certainly his interest flickered like the house lights, prompting, prodding.

'Rising by ten will be no problem for me, I assure you.' He offered a cool half-smile. 'I'm a different sort of lord, Mrs Griffiths. You'll see.' He exited then, before she could refuse. He'd got what he'd come for and quite a bit more, but it appeared he was up for it in all ways.

Chapter Three

Fleur had been up most of the night. The unexpected visitor to her box had been the perfect—as in perfectly upsetting—ending to an already difficult day: Adam's birthday. He would have been fifty-nine. She'd not been in the mood for people. But the man himself had been upsetting in an entirely different way that transcended the intrusion.

Even now, as she paced her office at the *London Tribune* waiting for the clock to chime ten, her sleepless body was full of restless energy, her mind insisting on recalling every detail of Lord Umberton in vivid colour and imagined tactile texture: the tousled tangle of rich nut-brown waves that tempted a woman to run her fingers through them, to tame them as a woman might wish to tame the man; the topaz depths of his gaze that managed to be both gem-sharp and warmly inviting; an intriguing combination which explained why she'd almost accepted his offer of oysters and champagne at Rules. That, and the fact that she'd been vulnerable last night, missing her friends. Missing Adam.

The box was too lonely without Antonia and Emma to join her. Their husbands had purchased the box to-

gether years ago and the six of them had spent count-
less evenings there. Now, Antonia was sailing for Tahiti
with Lord Cullen Allardyce. Last month, Antonia had
literally walked away from her life, her business, her department store in London, with nothing but the clothes
on her back to be with him. Emma was in Cumières,
France, running champagne vineyards with her husband, Julien Archambeau, Comte du Rocroi. Both of
her friends had gone on to new lives, new loves, and
she'd been left behind with an empty theatre box and
an empty bed.

But more than she missed her friends, she missed
Adam. She missed the bed and the sex the most. She
and Adam had fought hard and fornicated harder… And,
oh, how she missed it. Sex had been on her mind all day
yesterday, making her ache, making her want as she'd
gone through the ritual and the pain of privately mark-
ing Adam's birthday. Last year, Antonia had been with
her. This year, she'd had to face the day alone.

It wasn't just the physicality of the sex she missed, it
was the emotional connection, too. The knowing look
they could cast one another across a room that said *I
want you. Only you in this whole wide world.* The precious moments afterwards when the world narrowed
to only Adam's arms, when there was peace, when the
newspaper didn't intrude and it was truly just the two
of them. Bed was their safe space. Perhaps that's why
she liked it so much. In bed, they could talk about anything, say anything. She'd never felt more connected to
Adam than when they were in bed together. In bed, she
could forget all she'd given up for him and remember
the glory of what they had together.

That was what she missed, what she craved, what she envied Emma and Antonia for. They had that again, for a second time. Of course they did. They were both generous and kind. They'd loved their first husbands. They'd been good stewards of the love they'd been given. They'd proven to the fates that they were worthy of having that love again. She wasn't like them. She'd fought with Adam, she'd resented that Adam wouldn't allow them a child, that she'd given up her family, such as it was, and the life she'd thought she have for him. In return, she'd expected some sacrifice on his part. But there'd been none. Adam was uncompromising, unyielding in all aspects of his life and his principles, even when it came to his wife.

She'd not honoured those principles as she should have. She'd lost a good man and that loss posed a dark question that loomed large in the deep hours of the night when ghosts walked hand in hand with regrets: was she worthy of love a second time? She had to prove herself worthy of love, of Adam. Justice for the dam would do that, would prove that she'd been a good and loyal wife who had loved her husband.

Then, *he'd* appeared in her box, Lord Umberton, and made it clear she needn't be alone, at least not physically. Oysters and champagne could easily lead to other things—things she might have taken him up on last night if her common sense hadn't intervened. He could only give her sex. He was a stranger. He couldn't give her the rest.

In the moment, his invitation had made her wonder if the interest in the Bilberry Dam had simply been an excuse, a conversational opener, a reason to meet her. The thought had lasted until he'd manoeuvered the morning appointment out of their interaction. Either he didn't take no for an answer, or he truly did want to discuss the dam. The businesswoman in her hoped for the latter. Perhaps her articles were beginning to bear fruit, perhaps this man might become an ally. The businesswoman also hoped that by morning light with her vulnerability caged, he would not be so handsome and that he'd be late—something that would make him unlikeable. She desperately needed him to be unlikeable, desperately needed to have something with which to temper her reaction to him.

But he wasn't late. Nor was he early, not even by a blameable minute. He had the audacity to be punctual *and* he was still handsome, perhaps even more so than he'd been last night. In the daylight she could make a study of the interesting juxtapositions he presented: the tousled waves contrasting with the immaculate clothes; the razor-sharp nose abutted by the soft gaze of his eyes from behind the round rims of wire frames.

Had spectacles ever looked that sexy on a man before? They were a definite lure, baiting a woman to draw near, to sit on his lap—no, not merely *sit*—to hike her skirts to her knees, straddle him and face him eye to eye as she removed those wire frames so that nothing stood between their mutual gaze while she went on to remove other items: his cravat, the ruby tie pin within its folds…

She refocused her thoughts on the study she was making of him. If it weren't for the obviously advertised expense of his clothing and its excellent cut, one might take him for a new Bohemian—who lived outside of society's restraints. But he was quite the opposite by dint of his title. Anyone bearing the title 'Lord' was *not* outside society's constraints. Her uncle had been keen on reminding her of that. A lord's niece, like herself, had obligations, too. Obligations she'd not upheld. She'd been cast out for those transgressions.

It was a reminder, also, that for all the lap-straddling fantasies running through her head—fantasies in which she was the initiator—that he was not powerless. She had only to look at the body beneath his high-end clothes to know that. The breadth of his shoulders, the leanness of his waist, the long length of his trousered leg all reinforced the message that beyond the inviting depths of his curls and the warmth of his eyes, he was a man confident in his own power, his own appeal.

'I trust I don't disappoint?' Umberton said casually, taking a seat as the door shut behind him. *There* was that confidence she'd noted in him, the confidence to nonchalantly toss off a nuanced phrase with its double meaning and the confidence to correctly attribute her gaze to the interest he raised in her. It was not arrogance that drove him to it. Experience, perhaps? How many women had looked on him and not found him wanting? Perhaps it was the same experience that led her to understand his interest in the box last night had extended beyond their mutual fascination with the Bilberry Dam. This was like recognising like.

'Not in the least, Lord Umberton.' She took her seat behind the desk, noting that his gaze had followed the swish of her skirts. 'Did you enjoy the rest of the performances last night?' She would test him and his authenticity before they went any further. Was he really interested in the dam? How truthful would he be about his motives?

'I did not stay, Mrs Griffiths.' He favoured her with a smile and his topaz eyes teased. 'There didn't seem to be a reason to after you turned down my table at Rules.' Score another point for him. Lord Umberton was punctual *and* truthful. He had indeed departed the theatre straight away when he'd left her box. She knew because she'd spent the rest of the evening scanning the crowd for him and not caught sight of him. Not that she'd admit it, especially not to him. There was a thin line between confidence and conceit, and she would not unnecessarily feed his ego.

He asked the reciprocal question demanded by politeness. 'Did you enjoy the performances, Mrs Griffiths?'

'They did what they were supposed to do.' She offered a polite smile and smoothly moved the conversation to the business at hand. 'What can I help you with regarding the Bilberry Dam?'

He leaned forward, his gaze friendly but intent. 'I am looking to have my curiosity satisfied. The *London Tribune* has run an article this week regarding responsibility for the accident, and other articles about the same have been run earlier in regional papers owned by your corporation. I am curious as to the purpose.'

The response made her prickly. She had real work to do. She did not have time for the mere satisfying of a man's personal curiosity or answering to a private citizen. 'So, like the entitled lord you are, you thought to invade my privacy by approaching my theatre box during non-business hours at a non-business venue and simply ask me why my newspaper publishes what it does? You do see the audacity in that, don't you?'

She certainly saw the fault in it and the fault was all hers. She'd encouraged this when she should have evicted him from her box. In a moment of weakness, a moment of missing Adam on a difficult day, she'd had her head turned by a handsome man. She should have challenged him the moment he'd suggested the appointment. Instead, she'd opted for petty raillery over rising early that contained a hint of bawdry innuendo. 'Do you have appointments at *The Times* today as well? Perhaps you'd like to discuss with them why they didn't run a follow-up story to the newly signed Perpetual Maritime Truce in the Lower Gulf?'

He chuckled at her attempt to shame him with hyperbole. 'The Bilberry Dam is much closer to home and it is an issue which has already been settled. News by its very definition is *new*, something that is as yet unexplored or shared with the masses. What is there new when it comes to the dam?' He paused, a question on his handsome face. 'You *are* aware that a case cannot be reopened and retried without new facts, are you not?'

'I am aware of how the law operates, Lord Umberton.' Her temper rose. He was baiting her on all fronts. She did not care for the condescension veiled as 'politely informing' her about the function of the law.

'Then you *do* have new information?' he said eagerly. 'The articles hint at it, but one wonders what the sources might be and why they weren't brought forward earlier when all of this was considered the first time.'

The man vacillated like a weathervane. What should she pay attention to? The eagerness in his voice because he meant to be her ally and wanted to test the veracity of her claims before he aligned himself? Or should she be wary of the discreet, polite jabs his conversation took at her knowledge of the law and the lateness of presenting this recent angle? Or, a third option reared its head to make the game even more complicated, was he baiting her in the hopes of fishing for information? Did he want her to spill all she knew? If so, for what purpose?

In defence, she took a leaf from his own book. 'I'm not sure how much *you* know about quality journalism, Lord Umberton, but an honourable reporter protects their sources.'

He levelled his gaze at her, the topaz of his eyes sharpening at her tone. 'Let me ask you this, then. Are you instigating this or is the paper reporting on behalf of others?'

'I can't reveal that.' She held her ground, wishing she could dislike his line of questioning as much as she liked his gaze. Any other man would have been evicted from her office by now. 'I don't see how it makes a difference, nor do I see what business it is of yours. Why are you interested?'

'Because I sit in the House of Lords and the dam accident was the product of communal negligence. I would like to see that an accident of that magnitude does not happen again. There are other dams in England, Mrs Griffiths.' He paused before adding sharply, 'Perhaps that makes my curiosity less banal to you.'

That sounded more like an ally despite the rebuke and Fleur felt a trill of excitement race through her. It was beginning! Shortly after the dam accident last year, she'd hoped MPs would introduce legislation on their own after the call to action from the Holmfirth report which had been clear that laws were needed. But after a year, nothing had been forthcoming. Yet here was traction at last and from higher up the ladder of power than she'd dared to hope. She might get both justice *and* the long-elusive legislation passed with a man like Umberton on her side. And his friends. Where he led, surely others would follow.

'I think you and I may have almost got off on the wrong foot, Lord Umberton.' She smiled, determined to seize the opportunity.

'Almost?' He arched a dark brow, but his eyes were flirting with her. 'You've called me audaciously entitled and accused me of using that title to selfishly satisfy my curiosity.'

She answered his teasing eyes with a lift of her own brow. 'And you barged into my box, quite disrupting my night.' In ways he could not imagine. She'd had to seek self-pleasure after midnight to find any relief.

'Then we are even, the playing field levelled,' he suggested, the conversation becoming more game than negotiation.

'Perhaps we can start again, beginning with lunch. Can I interest you in an early déjeuner at Verrey's on Regent Street? If we leave now, we can get a head start on the noon crowd.'

He put on a show of considering the offer, clearly enjoying the transition to the easy by-play between them. 'You turned down my supper invitation. Why should I accept yours to lunch?'

'Because we are starting over and we are no longer strangers,' she replied, doing some flirting of her own.

'What sort of woman goes to supper with a man she's just met? I had to decline on principle no matter how tempted I *might* have been.'

He gave an infectious grin. 'You *were* tempted?'

'Maybe a little,' she answered with a smile of her own. 'I am assuming that's a yes for lunch?'

'I am not in the habit of refusing lunch invitations from beautiful women.' Good lord, how he loved an assertive woman. A debutante of the ilk his mother was always throwing his direction would never dream of inviting him to lunch. Jasper stood and held her coat. She shrugged into it and he caught a coy whiff of her scent: notes of vanilla and jasmine mixed with something he couldn't name.

It was enough to make him smile. So that was what confidence smelled like. No delicate roses or sweet lilies for this woman. Of course not. Such delicacy didn't suit a woman who sat alone at the theatre and scolded anyone who dare intrude on her sanctuary even as she flirted with her eyes and considered bold proposals—both his and hers.

It prompted him to wonder what other proposals might be made between them. But such wondering came with a warning. To make this into anything more than what it was intended to be—a fact-finding mission—came with complications. He would need to choose his response wisely. Orion and the family were counting on him, as was his good common sense. Francis Bacon would not approve of being ruled by spontaneity.

Chapter Four

Verrey's Café was an interesting choice. The main floor was long and narrow, dotted with small, square tables draped in white tablecloths that stretched back to a three-quarter wall of mirrored glass in the rear that gave the space an added sense of largeness. It was still early for lunch. Only a smattering of patrons sat at the tables.

The restaurant was quiet and of that Jasper approved as the maître d' led them to a discreet table at the back, partially hidden from common view by potted palms. Jasper approved of that, too. For all her boldness, it seemed Mrs Griffiths had a sense of discretion, as well. This was a nearly invisible table and she was dining in advance of the crowd. The woman liked her privacy.

'I can't decide, Mrs Griffiths, if you're simply circumspect in your social behaviours or if you don't want to be seen with me,' he offered wryly as they took their seats. In truth, he preferred the privacy as well. There was less chance someone would recognise him and call him Meltham.

She fixed him with her green eyes, emeralds when scolding, grass green in her softer moments. They were emeralds at the moment. 'I eat for fuel because my body demands it. I do not eat for the sake of being seen.'

He could not resist. 'And the theatre? Is it fuel or for being seen?'

'Fuel,' she answered without hesitation. 'For my mind, for my soul.'

'And yet your gown last night was made to be seen,' he prompted with a little argument. She might have sat alone, might have claimed she wanted no intrusion, but in that gold gown she had to have known she invited intrusion. She'd not passed the evening unremarked. His were not the only opera glasses that had lingered on her box.

'I like fine clothes. They are a fuel of another sort, a fuel for my eyes, for my fingers. I love the textures, the layers.' The confession carried a sensual quality to it or was his imagination running away with him at the thought of her touch on his sleeve, her fingers stroking the tight weave of his superfine coat? It was an unseemly thought about a woman who was most likely his enemy.

The waiter came and set the first course down in front of them, *oeufs à la Russe* with grey caviar for the discerning gourmet who would not appreciate black carp roe. Verrey's was one of those fine restaurants where menus were not necessary. Regulars knew already what was served or at least knew with confidence that whatever the chef chose to put on the table would be excellent. To have a menu was to mark oneself as an outsider.

'I must be seen, of course,' she added with a touch of ruefulness when the waiter left. 'It inspires confidence in those I do business with to see me out and about, expensively gowned as if I haven't a care in the world. It tells them that the syndicate is solvent, that it is business as usual even if Adam Griffiths is no longer at the helm. To become a recluse would be to inspire panic and concern.'

Her comment struck a note of empathy within him. He understood that need to be seen. If it were up to him, he'd spend his life at Rosefields, puttering with his science experiments. But the title didn't allow for that. The Marquess must be seen, the very sight of him a reassurance that all was well for those who counted on him. He spent his days in service to those people as Mrs Griffiths spent her days in service to her people.

'Did the theatre feed your soul, then, despite the need for a public display?' he asked as they ate. It seemed odd to him that one might find solace in a farce. A Shakespeare tragedy he could understand. But a comedy? They were made for laughing more than soul-searching reflection. But perhaps she'd had no choice if she wanted to be seen. What had she been looking for last night? He might examine later why it mattered so much to him to find out.

'Yes. Last night I was thinking of my friends. Remembering. My husband and I shared the box with Lord Luce and Mr Popplewell and their wives.' There was a shadow in her eyes as the waiter cleared the table and another set down plates of *sole à la Dugléré*. 'I had not been to the theatre since the accident. Last year I was in mourning, of course,' she explained, taking a flaky forkful of the fish.

Jasper felt like a cad. The evening had been of some

significance to her, a private commemoration of sorts, and he'd barged in to disrupt it. He deserved every word of her set down and more. In retrospect, he thought he'd got off rather easily. 'I must apologise again for my intrusion. It could not have been more poorly timed.'

She gave a small smile, but said nothing. What was he expecting? Absolution? Did he want her to say it was all right? She was too astute for that and he admired her for not letting him off for his intrusion. He'd behaved badly.

'Are your friends, the wives, not in town? Could they not have joined you?' Surely she hadn't needed to face the box and its memories alone last night.

She shook her head, her mood lightening slightly. 'They are both living abroad.' She slid him a sly look. 'Both of them have found new husbands.' She raised her wine glass, containing a sharp white wine. 'One of them has married the man who provides the wines to Verrey's and other fine establishments in London. The other has sailed with her true love to Tahiti. They are not married yet, but they soon will be.'

'I do recall now reading about the Popplewell department store fire and the story the *London Tribune* ran about the Popplewell's contributions to the community.' His mother had been devastated. She'd been looking forward to the new shopping experience.

'Well, Antonia has turned tragedy into triumph.'

'Yes, I hear she sold the store and her other business interests to the Duke of Cowden for a tidy sum.' Was that what Fleur Griffiths envied? Did she wish to sell and unburden herself from the enterprises her husband had chosen? After a year in the editor's seat, was it proving too much? Yet here she was, using her papers to renew interest in the Bilberry Dam. That scenario seemed unlikely.

'Do you desire to follow in Mrs Popplewell's footsteps?' He studied her, trying to read her expression. What was hidden there? Regret? Grief? Envy?

'To new lands or new husbands?' she parried, meeting him with a bold gaze. 'What makes you think I want either?'

'You said you were missing your friends. It is not unrealistic to suppose you felt their new husbands have competed for their attentions and won.' Fleur Griffiths struck him as the type of woman who enjoyed competition, but not losing. He toyed with his wine glass, shooting her a strong look at the last. 'Perhaps you miss what they now have?'

Her retort was sharp. 'And what exactly do they have?' The boldness of his question was not lost on her.

'They have love again and they both have a second chance for whatever their former lives failed to give them,' he mused out loud.

'I am happy for my friends, not because they have new husbands but because they have what they need. If that need comes in the form of a man, then so be it.' She took a swallow of her wine. The swallow was manufactured, he'd wager, to cover emotion. He'd turned over a few rocks with his comments. Why not flip another one over?

'What of your need, Mrs Griffiths? What would you do with a second chance?' he enquired.

'Perhaps I don't need a second chance. Perhaps I have all that I require. I have my work. Running a newspaper syndicate is an all-consuming job. It leaves little time for other things,' she replied hotly, outwardly offended by his assumption, but it evidently wasn't the entire truth as something shifted in her eyes, darkening them with another shadow. This woman still grieved, although not only for her husband. She'd lost something more, something beyond Adam Griffiths, something her husband had perhaps been a gateway to.

A family? Children? How ironic that her husband's job pulled him away from such things whereas Jasper's position as a marquess drew him in, binding him and his family ever more tightly together. His fate was their fate, and their fates were his. Something he'd best remember when dealing with Mrs Griffiths. His intrigue with her was slowly leading him from the intended path. The questions that filled his mind weren't about the dam or the information she had linking Orion to the disaster, but about her—what did she want from life? Did she enjoy the newspaper business?

'I have all I need, Lord Umberton.' She was cool again. 'I have my work. There is little time for anything else at present.'

He paused his questions and took a small spoonful of the *crème pistache* that had just been set in front of them—cool and green, like Mrs Griffiths's eyes. At this proximity, the comparison could not be escaped. 'Is that why you've opened the dam investigation again? Your work demands it? Or does something more demand it?' It was time to bring the conversation back to business.

'My work *is* the search for truth. That is why I am bringing the Bilberry Dam to the public's attention again. Is that not your work as well? As a member of the House of Lords?'

'And you feel the truth is that Lord Orion Bexley is at fault for the entire accident? Your articles suggest as much.' He watched her face carefully.

'His name is the one thread that runs through the paperwork documenting the building of the dam, the issues with the dam's structural integrity as well as the lax oversight of the commission. The verdict was clear that in order for a conviction to be made, there must be a singular culprit. I think one has emerged.'

She was so sure, so confident as she said the words. He saw the situation from her perspective: find a culprit, blame him, claim a verdict. And then what? Had she thought beyond that for herself, for all who would be affected? Her confidence did raise some concern for him. What did she think she knew that fuelled that confidence? What did she know that he did not? Because, not for a minute did he think Orion had told him everything. Worry in the form of sweat began to bead beneath his collar and pristine cravat.

He gathered his calm. 'Forgive me for the bluntness, Mrs Griffiths, but what have you discovered that Captain Moody's investigation and the subsequent enquiry did not see at the time? Captain Moody is known for his thoroughness. It is hard to believe something this significant went without his notice.'

'The enquiry was thorough and it was expedient,' she agreed, her tongue flicking over the tiny spoon of *crème pistache* in a manner that spoke to him of other ways that tongue might be employed. 'But while expediency has its merits, it does not allow enough time for deep truth to bubble to the surface, for patterns to be unearthed and understood. But I've had time.' The last rang like a warning in his mind.

'If I am to come alongside your new efforts, I would want to know what those patterns are. You must understand that a man's reputation is a precious commodity. I cannot squander it on conjecture.'

Her eyes flared and her shoulders straightened. 'And a woman's reputation is to be squandered on conjecture?' He'd insulted her. 'Do you think I am in the habit of running a newspaper syndicate on conjecture and rumour? I assure you, when I tell you I have real evidence by which the dots can be connected, that I have it.'

Another frisson of concern snaked down Jasper's back. *What if she did?* What if Orion was indeed involved? Orion and Trouble were fast friends. He immediately felt disloyal to his brother for the traitorous thought. The onus of proof should be on this green-eyed minx who sought to stir up that trouble.

The waiter brought coffee to signal the end of the meal, a meal that had provided Jasper with food for both body and thought. 'I would like to know your goals. What do you hope to accomplish?'

She fixed him with a long incredulous stare as if it wasn't obvious to him. 'Why, justice, Lord Umberton. It has been a year and more and there's been no legislation introduced to improve dam oversight and there's been no attempt to make a conviction.'

He was swift to correct her. 'There *has* been an attempt and it was unsuccessful because a conviction was not possible. I do agree. The lack of forthcoming legislation is immensely disappointing given that the findings at the dam strongly identified a need for it. I can give you help with legislation.' He gave a shrug. Legislation was something they could agree on, something he could help deliver.

On the strength of that common ground, she might entrust him with the information she had regarding Orion's involvement with the dam accident. If he was to test the veracity of her information, he had to have access to it. His conscience stirred a bit at that. He was walking a fine line here. But the pursuit of truth and logic demanded he set aside empathy. How else would he know what he was really up against?

He did care about dam legislation. Meltham wasn't far from Holmfirth. The dam project that serviced the rivers in that area was a constant concern for him. He'd hoped having Orion on the commission would have been a step towards better management. But the reverse had happened instead. It was imperative he know how deep in Orion was.

'Legislation is a start, but it is *not* justice for what happened,' she said in a stern tone. He could not miss the emotion beneath.

Jasper gave a slow stir to his coffee, mixing in the cream and watching it lighten as he carefully chose his words. 'And justice is not the same as vengeance. I wonder if you've confused the two.' He watched her go still and braced himself for an outburst that could very well see his coffee dumped on his lap. No matter how she tried to mask it, Mrs Griffiths had a temper. Emotion was beneath her words, beneath her choices. She wasn't afraid to boldly speak her mind. She was a woman who *felt* things, a stark contrast to his own logic.

'I think you overstep yourself on such brief acquaintance,' she said quietly. Too quietly. 'There are very few people who dare to speak to me that way.'

'Then perhaps there should be more,' Jasper countered. 'Have you thought of what happens if Lord Orion Bexley is legally prosecuted? Or even if he is just socially prosecuted by his peers, which has already begun? Let me remind you that actions have consequences, Mrs Griffiths. For better or worse, a man's life will be ruined, his family's as well simply by association. And all for what? What will that ruination achieve? What will it change?'

She gave him a long look and for a moment he thought perhaps she'd seen through him, that he'd pushed too far and given away his hand. He didn't expect his little ruse to last for ever. All she had to do was look him up in *Debrett's* if she was interested in Baron Umberton. But he did prefer it last a bit longer until he could complete his reconnaissance.

'He is the brother of a marquess. If anything, he ought to be held to a higher standard. He has all the advantages most people lack and his one responsibility is to take care of his people. He couldn't even do that.'

'Spoken like a woman who resents the peerage,' he commented wryly. 'Is that why you've picked him out? Because he's a lord, even if just an honorary one.'

'I don't hate the peerage. I'm having lunch with you, aren't I? I've picked him out because he is guilty,' she snapped. 'I can't decide, Lord Umberton, if you are friend or foe. One moment I think we could be allies in this and the next you're warning me off pursuing a legitimate culprit.'

He thought that, too. One moment he was trying to protect his brother, discover the truth of Orion's association with the dam accident, and the next his mind was running riot with a thousand curiosities about Fleur Griffiths. 'I'm not warning you off, Mrs Griffiths. I would not seek to decide for you or to know your mind.'

He certainly wasn't seeking to obstruct the pursuit of the truth. He wanted to know the truth about Orion's involvement as badly as she did, only for different reasons. 'I am, however, cautioning you to consider the long-reaching ramifications of your choices and to think about your motives for them. I am merely offering counsel since you seem to have none to rely on.'

'You mean I've been left unsupervised to run amok in the world, wreaking havoc.' Her tone was cutting. Fleur Griffiths wasn't afraid to speak her mind.

He inclined his head. 'I would hope not. I would hope you had more decorum and restraint than that. Business is not a place for hot heads. A newspaper is a powerful tool and must be wielded accordingly for the benefit of society.'

'As is a title,' she responded with the sharp heat he'd come to associate with her. He supposed some men would be turned off by her knife-edge sharpness. He was not one of them. Lord help him, but he found it deuced attractive. If it weren't for his brother being involved... Who was he kidding? If it wasn't for his brother, he wouldn't have encountered Mrs Griffiths at all.

Wealthy newspaper widows weren't exactly in his circle of association. She was of the City. He was of the *ton* and seldom did the two meet. There was only one path that would be acceptable for him to pursue with a woman like Fleur Griffiths—a private path that kept to the shadows and ended when he walked a different path to the altar with another woman. He put himself in check. Was he really considering an affair—even in the hypothetical—with the woman who wanted to use his brother as the scapegoat for her grief?

It was perhaps a testimony as to how attracted he was. If only the ladies of the *ton* were half as challenging, half as thrilling. Perhaps it was the danger, the risk that came with her that attracted him, or perhaps it was simply that Fleur Griffith made no secret of the fact that she would bite if provoked.

The bill came to the table and Jasper automatically reached for it, but Fleur Griffiths was faster, her eyes brooking no dispute. '*I* invited *you*,' she said, signing the cheque.

Well, that was an interesting change. A woman had never bought him lunch before. Jasper rose and reached for her coat, holding it for her as she slipped it on. He wasn't sure how he felt about that. It felt disturbingly as if he'd given up a modicum of control. She pulled on her gloves and stepped away from him, their eyes meeting, hers with a message: she who had her own money made her own rules.

He escorted her to the front of the restaurant, the place much fuller than it had been when they'd arrived, his hand light at her back, his body close enough to hers to breathe in the scent of her. 'I shall take a cab from here. I need to return to the office, Lord Umberton.' She made his dismissal clear. Their business was concluded. She would not allow him to drag it out with a cab ride.

He found he didn't like being dismissed any more than he'd liked having his lunch paid for.

'I'll wait until you're safely on your way,' he negotiated smoothly. His honour demanded he not leave even a self-sufficient woman alone on a street corner and his pride demanded he restore the balance of power at least a little before they parted. She needed to know that he would not allow anyone to walk over him.

He hailed her a cab. 'I'll be in touch, Mrs Griffiths, and the next time our meal will be on me,' he said, helping her inside, breathing her in one last time, memorising the scent to decode later.

'I hope our meeting was enlightening.'

'Most enlightening.' He was positively aflame with enlightenment. He could not recall the last time a woman had so tempted him while simultaneously terrifying him. She was indeed trouble. He gave away none of that turmoil. He smiled politely and shut the door, sending the cab off before his town coach pulled to the curb. His own afternoon would be busy indeed, his mind already formulating lists of things he needed to know and answers his brother needed to provide. Orion might have tangled with the wrong person this time. He'd accused her of seeking personal vengeance instead of public justice, but Jasper couldn't shake the nagging question growing in his mind. What if she was right?

Chapter Five

'You think she's right. *You* are taking her side. I cannot believe this.' Orion paused his agitated pacing before the fireplace long enough to push an equally agitated hand through his hair. Jasper wondered if he'd practised the move. Perhaps it had been a mistake to give Orion advance notice of this meeting.

Advance notice had given Orion time to think about how to posture, how to position his arguments and his emotions. Orion was nothing if not the sum of his emotions, all of which he felt entitled to display whenever he felt them. Real adults weren't ruled by their emotions, in Jasper's opinion, or at the very least real adults controlled and contained those emotions.

The thought immediately conjured images of Fleur Griffiths over lunch today. She'd been emotional, heated and then cool in turn, calm at moments, angry in others. But she'd kept those emotions under control. It was fine to feel, just not to feel too much too often, that was Jasper's credo. Too much emotion undermined Baconian law, after all, left a man feeling exposed, vulnerable. He'd had a strong taste of that after his father died. He wasn't willing to drink from that cup again.

'I am not siding with her,' Jasper corrected from the sideboard that held decanters at the ready for a pre-prandial drink. 'I had lunch with her today in order to hear her position.'

'You took her to lunch?' Orion said the words as if he'd indulged in the eighth deadly sin.

'We took lunch together, at Verrey's Café. To be honest, it had not been my intention. She invited me, if you must know.' Jasper crossed the room and handed a tumbler to his brother.

'Why?' Orion swirled the brandy and gave a sorrowful look into its depths. 'You're always asking questions. Did you think of asking that one? *Why* would she invite a man to lunch whom she doesn't know, who is, by the way, related to the man she seeks to pillory? It is not the done thing to dine with one's enemies.'

'Perhaps you should test some of the assumptions undergirding your last statement.' Jasper took a swallow of his drink and waited one beat, then two as dawning came to Orion.

'She doesn't know who you are. You've given her some trumped-up name.'

'Not trumped up, a real name. Baron Umberton. I did not lie to her. I *am* Baron Umberton.' Although he hadn't ever used that title. The Earl of Wincastle had been his honorary title growing up, one of his father's titles bestowed on him at birth.

'You made her believe you were interested in her articles,' Orion went on.

'Also not a lie. I was and continue to remain interested in her articles because they involve you, because you asked me to look into it. I did.' That took a bit of the wind out of Orion's agitated sails. It was time to be serious before Mother arrived in the drawing room. Jasper lowered his voice. 'She has convinced herself you are a person of interest, the one common thread between all the separate pieces that went wrong leading up to the accident.'

Orion merely scoffed. 'I could have told you that from the articles. That's not new. You needn't have gone to lunch to learn that.'

'But I did learn something new, though. I learned that she is the driving force behind it. She's the one who wants to reopen the investigation. She is not merely reporting what someone else has told her.' He waited for the import of that to reveal itself to Orion. When Orion remained blank, he explained, 'She is driven by emotion, by her grief. She has nothing but anger to sustain her. When she realises she has no proof she will have to let the issue drop and face the fact that she was seeking a scapegoat, not justice.'

'But in the meanwhile, I am to bear the brunt of her tirades? The aspersions on my name, on *our* name?' Orion's sense of drama returned. 'How long do you think it will take her to calm down? A week? Maybe two?'

That was a very good question. 'I don't honestly know.' After meeting her today and taking her measure, Jasper wasn't sure she'd calm down quickly or let go of her quest, not on her own at least. This certainly wouldn't be over in a mere set of weeks without some form of iron-fisted intervention. Weeks were like eons to Orion.

'It may take some time before she opens up to me and

shares what she knows. She and I are both interested in proposing legislation for better dam oversight. I hope to build on that connection in order to discover just how strong she thinks her case against you is.'

His conscience gave another kick. He did not like the not entirely honest aspects of the plan, but it was already underway and what else could he do? His father had raised him to be honest, to seek truth, but his father had also imbued him with the importance of responsibility. There was no greater responsibility than caring for the family, protecting the family. What took precedence when the two came into conflict?

'Your plan had better work,' Orion groused ungratefully, oblivious for his dilemma.

'If you don't like it, you can always try cleaning up your own messes for once,' Jasper growled. 'Just tell me this—is there anything legitimate for her to base this new case on? We cannot afford to be ambushed.' He didn't think Fleur Griffiths was someone to make idle claims. If she thought she had something, she truly might. That worried him, especially when Orion hesitated too long to answer, their conversation cut short at the sound of rustling skirts in the hallway.

'Cannot afford to be ambushed about what?' His mother, the Dowager Marchioness of Meltham swept into the room, dressed for a night out. 'I've got the Swintons' ball tonight. Colonel Taggart will call for me after we eat.' She looked between him and Orion. 'Now, what is this about an ambush?'

Orion cleared his throat, a bit of devilry glinting in his eyes. 'Jasper didn't want to be ambushed by anyone on your list of lovely debutantes for him to consider this Season.'

Jasper shot Orion a quelling look. That damnable list was a sore topic because of the subject that always followed the list: when was he going to marry and ensure the succession? 'I don't need a list. I can find my own bride.' He tried to prevent the inevitable production of the list from his mother's pocket or her reticule or wherever she'd happened to stash it at the moment. It was always on her person. But he was too late. She produced it with a flourish. He winced. It seemed longer than the last time he'd seen it.

'Oh, don't look at me like that,' she scolded with affection. 'I assure you every mother in the *ton* has a list. We can go over the list at dinner so that you are not "ambushed". I think you'll see the candidates are all quite reasonable. There's room in the Colonel's carriage for you if you'd like to attend tonight. Many of these girls will be there. It would be very efficient and I know how you like efficiency.'

'No. Thank you for the offer, though, Mother. I have some business that requires my attention this evening. You should take Orion.' He shot his brother an *I-am-getting-even* look followed by a lift of his brow that said *You-owe-me-because-I-worked-all-day-on-your-behalf.*

Orion shot him a resigned glare before smiling at their mother. 'I would love to go.' The butler announced dinner and Orion offered Mother his arm. 'Whose lists am I on?' he asked as if he didn't know the only lists he was on were the naughty ones. 'Do you think *I* should marry soon? Perhaps a wealthy heiress?' Orion was the king of distractions and he could make their mother

laugh. For that, Jasper would forgive Orion nearly anything. It had been an invaluable gift in the early days
after their father's death when Mother had been inconsolable.

Despite his earlier dissatisfaction with his brother,
Jasper couldn't help but chuckle to himself as he
watched the two go in ahead of him, their blond heads
bent together, Orion charming, his mother laughing as
she said, 'Oh, not you, not yet, my dear. You needn't
rush to marry.'

Watching them brought fond memories. It had always been this way ever since he and Orion had been
allowed down to dine with his parents. He'd been four-
teen, Orion seven, and he'd been the one to insist Orion
be able to join them, that they should dine as a family when he was home from school. Orion and Mother
made a habit of going in together while he and Father,
the 'men of the house', had lagged behind, talking business about the estate.

He remembered how his father's gaze would follow
his mother in those moments, his eyes soft with content-
ment, shining with love. Some would argue his parents'
marriage had been the best of both worlds—a marriage made on the grounds of mutual respect, but which
had blossomed into an abiding love over time. Then his
father had died and he'd seen how the loss broke his
mother, how she'd cried and wept, how her strength
had deserted her for a time. He did not want that for
himself. Love hurt; love cut deeply. To him, it was the
greatest of illogical ironies that something meant to be
beautiful could turn so ugly.

Would Fleur Griffiths agree with him? His thoughts

seemed to drift rather too easily to her. Wasn't she also proof of the damaging capacity of love? She was so wrecked by grief and anger that even a year later she was still looking for a culprit, someone to pin her loss on, even when empirical evidence already suggested she would not find that someone.

If that was what love did to people, he had no use for it. He was the Marquess. He could not afford to be weak. A weak man could not protect his family. He'd promised his father on his deathbed that he would care for Mother and for Orion always, that the family would go on, would continue to thrive. A weak man could not keep that promise.

No, he was quite certain that love was a luxury that was not for him. He had to protect his family, his people, his lands and for that he had to be strong. He glanced towards the family shield that hung over the fireplace as he passed. *Officio et Diligentia Semper.* Duty and diligence always. Love did not factor into it. Such was the life of a marquess.

Burning the midnight oil, toiling over ledgers and adding up unrelenting columns while everyone else had long gone home to families and hot meals. Such was the life of a news syndicate owner. Fleur sat back from the desk and stretched. She'd been working relentlessly since she'd returned from lunch. Her stomach rumbled in reminder that *that* meal had been ten hours ago. That meal had been a delicious feast for the tongue as well as the eyes, which was the very reason she'd assigned herself a punishing list of tasks that needed completing. If she went home she'd have nothing to distract her.

She'd spend her evening reliving lunch with the all too attractive Baron Umberton. He was exactly the sort of man her uncle had wished she'd married. The amount of thought dedicated to Umberton was a sure sign that she'd been alone too long. Not that she needed another sign. Last night had been proof enough. This afternoon's luncheon was merely affirmation of what she already knew: she was lonely.

You ought to take a lover. That would appease your loneliness.

Her inner voice whispered the wicked temptation. It wasn't the first time she'd thought of it. Nor would it be the first time she'd acted on it. She had taken a lover last autumn in the wake of Emma's marriage. It had been an *adequate* experience. There had been comfort, but not much else. But perhaps it had been too soon. Maybe she'd expected too much, been too desperate. Perhaps with the distance of a year, it might be better.

Fleur walked to the sideboard and poured herself a midnight brandy from Adam's favourite decanter of Baccarat cut-crystal. It had been a gift from Emma and Garrett one Christmas. Garrett had been a staunch believer in investing in Baccarat crystal. The memory made her smile. She raised her glass to the ghost in the room. 'I miss you, Adam.' She took a long swallow, letting the brandy burn her throat, wishing it could burn away the pain, too, burn away the sense of loss.

She felt closest to Adam in this space that had been his office in London where they'd spent most of their time. Like the Newcastle office, the room still bore the marks of him: the cherrywood panelling, the green damask wallpaper, the masculine accoutrements—the decanters, the globe, the paperweight, the heavy furniture and draperies—a shrine to a successful man who'd reached the apex of his career.

Yet Adam had not been perfect. The imperfections that had lingered beneath the surface of their life together, both personal and professional, had bubbled *to* the surface. She'd given up her life for him and in exchange he'd left her the burden of a news syndicate in debt. Revenue was down. Confidence in her leadership was down. How long would the board of directors allow her to continue if she couldn't right their course? She didn't know what to do. She'd tried generating more revenue by selling more ads, by offering subscription specials to bring in new readers, all the usual strategies. But still, circulation remained stagnant.

It was a hard pill to swallow in acknowledging that she was the reason for some of the stagnation. People were leery of a woman at the helm. It helped only somewhat that she was Adam's widow. She understood that she borrowed credibility from him. But she was also honest. It wasn't entirely her fault. There'd been debt before his death and he'd hidden it from her. Discovering the debt had felt like a betrayal.

Fleur felt anger flare. For both of them. Her anger had more than one source. How dare Adam leave her with this burden. Newspaper debt was a fact of journalistic life. It went in cycles. She could tolerate that. What she couldn't tolerate was the secrecy. Adam had *kept* this from her and she'd been ambushed with it. She'd appeared unprepared in front of the board of directors. On a personal level, the betrayal went deeper. The secrecy was further proof she and Adam hadn't been partners in the truest sense, that while she'd given him everything, Adam had two separate lives despite the fact that they lived and worked together.

She shook a fist at the empty room. 'You should have told me. Damn it! Why didn't you tell me?' Had he doubted her? Was that why? 'You set me up for failure,' she said to the ghost in the room. She didn't need any help there. She'd become quite good at failing all on her own. She could not fail him in death as she'd failed him in life. She owed him. It was too late to atone for being a selfish wife, for not kissing him goodbye that last night, for pressing him about a child when he'd been clear he didn't want one. How could she atone if she couldn't do this, couldn't hold on to the thing he'd spent his life building? Saving the syndicate was her last chance.

She'd spent the night racking her brain for a solution. The best she could come up with was that she could sell some of the smaller papers, focus her attentions on the papers in the significant regional cities and the *Tribune* in London. That would keep the business stabilised for a while until she could figure out a way to increase growth. But the choice undermined Adam's mission to bring news to all parts of England and with it to bring literacy to rural villages.

To Adam, news was about information, about sharing power with all citizens and that required the ability to read and the ability to have access to something *to* read. When she'd first met him, she'd been as attracted to that vision as she was the man. Here was a man who felt as she felt, believed as she believed. She'd cherished that similarity between them. Together, they had nurtured those ideals. It would positively gut her to sell off those rural papers. But what else could she do?

Even that decision was not risk free. There would be ramifications to either choice. To sell might be akin to signalling blood in the water. Selling might make investors and subscribers all the more hesitant. But to *not* sell meant she had to find another way to generate subscriptions and funds. Perhaps she should consult with the Duke of Cowden who she knew through his wife, the Duchess, and the charity work on the literacy ball. Cowden had a mind for business and investment. He would have advice about the direction she should go. Meanwhile, she needed a good story, something that would sell papers.

She *had* a good story. There'd been a slight uptick in sales in the north when she'd run the Bilberry Dam articles. Of course, the dam accident was still very much on their minds. In the north, by Holmfirth and York, people lived with the residue of the accident daily. They were still recovering fiscally and physically from the ruins. And of course, Meltham was in the north. Lord Orion Bexley was a person of interest to northerners more so than he'd be a person of interest to someone in Bristol in the west. Perhaps it was time to run another article. If she wanted to bring about justice, she had to keep the pressure on.

Umberton had called her justice vengeance today in that quiet but firm tenor of his, those topaz eyes studious and considering. There was no doubting he was a serious man with serious thoughts. Which stirred her anger. What did he know of it? It was only an accident to him, whereas it was a disaster to her. It had changed everything. She simply could not share the same level of detachment he brought to it. But he could still be her ally. He was the one person in London who'd shown direct interest.

An idea came to her as she finished her drink. He could be the first link in the chain she'd forge, the first of the powerful lords and MPs she could rally to her banner if she could gain an introduction through the right kind of person—and Umberton was definitely the right kind of person.

Not just for politics either. Her inner voice was active tonight. *Perhaps you might have a dual purpose for him? There was more than business between you last night and again this afternoon.*

Perhaps. Perhaps it would be all right to mix a little pleasure with business just this once, especially since there would be no expectations beyond the moment.

Fleur returned to her desk and drew out a piece of stationery with the *Tribune's* letterhead on it and drafted two notes, one to Cowden and one to Umberton, realising as an afterthought she had no idea where to reach Umberton. She stifled a yawn. She'd tackle that in the morning. For now, weariness had found her at last. Thank goodness. Sleep was all too rare for her. The downside was that she was too tired to make her way home. She would sleep on the long leather sofa in the office. After all, what did it matter if she slept at home or here? Either way, she'd be sleeping alone. Nothing awaited her but her dreams. That was her penance. It was no less than what she deserved.

Chapter Six

The letter was waiting for him at White's when Jasper arrived the next afternoon, looking for peace and quiet, none of which was to be had at Meltham House. Today was his mother's at-home, the one afternoon a week when she invited every worthy matron and their eligible daughters to flood her drawing room in the hopes he'd make an appearance. He'd done his duty today, mostly to appease his mother and to make up for not having gone to the Swintons' ball with her last night. He'd spent twenty minutes in the drawing room meeting some of his mother's favourites from the list before he'd made his escape.

Jasper took his usual seat in a club chair at the back of the room. He turned the letter over, studying the crisp, strong hand in which the address had been written: *Lord Umberton, White's.*

A rather simple address that offered not a lot of information other than that it was from *her.* Only Mrs Griffiths would call him that. She'd written, so soon after their lunch. The thought of seeing her again made his blood hum, like a soldier preparing for battle. But that humming was quickly tempered, two thoughts occurring to him before he even broke the seal.

First, she'd been rather ingenious to send it here in her deduction that the odds were decent he was a member—many lords were. He saw, too, that this message was an attempt to balance the power between them. If she could find him, she could level the playing field. Right now, he was the only one with a way to contact or reach her. He knew where she worked. He could contact her at any time. But she could not contact him. Not without some guesswork, which was what this was.

That led to the second realisation. The staff at White's had known he was Umberton. If they knew, did she know? Was his element of surprise up already?

The waiter came with his brandy and the newspapers. 'Stay a moment.' Jasper halted him when he would have slipped away with customary unobtrusiveness. Jasper waved the note. 'How did you know I was Umberton?' It was not a title he'd ever publicly used. It was simply one more thing that had come with the entailment. The waiter looked nervous. 'I am only curious, I mean nothing more by it,' he coaxed the man to relax.

'We didn't know, my lord,' the waiter confessed. 'We weren't sure who to give the letter to, so the manager looked it up in *Debrett's*. We keep a copy downstairs for membership purposes.'

'Very good, I like that. Taking initiative to solve a little mystery,' Jasper complimented to assure him he'd done nothing wrong. 'Thank you.' He dismissed the waiter with a smile, but he was already making a mental note to find a better way, a less *public* way, for Mrs Griffiths to contact him.

He slipped a finger beneath the sealing wafer and read. It was good news and bad. The good news was that she was eager to meet again to start working on a legislative proposal. The bad news was that in her boldness, she'd already concocted a plan. She wanted him to take her to a ball or two for the sake of making introductions to others in Parliament who might be of help. She even had a list enclosed. Jasper sighed. What was it with ladies and lists? Perhaps it was something they were born with.

He scanned the balls she'd chosen. He couldn't possibly comply. People would know him there. He'd be Meltham to them. There were solutions to that, though. He took a swallow of brandy for thinking. One option was to come clean with her. Telling her was inevitable anyway, it was just a matter of when. Timing was important because there *would* be repercussions. Most likely, he would be cut off from further participation in her investigation. She would be furious for what she would perceive as duplicity.

Originally, that hadn't mattered to him. He'd thought to see her once, determine what she knew and what she meant to do with it. That would be it. He'd not planned on there being more to learn, more to do. He wasn't ready to let the association go.

Be fair, his conscience nudged, *you are not ready to let her go. You're attracted to her and her saucy tongue.*

The other option was that he knew where she'd be. He could make sure he wasn't in the same place. Of course, he'd have to persuade her that splitting their attendance at events was in their better interest, that they could cover twice as much ground. He would attend events she could not get invited to and she could continue to cultivate her circles. But to persuade her, he'd have to see her. A letter would not suffice.

He gestured for the waiter. 'Can you send an errand boy to Fortnum and Mason for a tea basket? I need it delivered to the *London Tribune* to Mrs Fleur Griffiths.' He pulled out his pocket watch. 'By three o'clock.' Two hours from now. That should be plenty enough time to gather his thoughts and prepare for a battle of wits, a prospect that was more thrilling than it ought to be.

A thrill ran through Fleur at the sight of the tea basket delivered to her desk by a wide-eyed clerk. *He was coming.* With his topaz eyes, tousled curls and argumentative nature. Her pulse raced. She didn't need a note to tell her that. He'd warned her as much yesterday at the curb. *Next time our meal will be on me.* He'd not liked the idea of 'owing' her. Well, *she'd* not liked the idea that by not giving her a way to contact him, he had seized control of determining when they might meet again. Clearly, her shot in the dark—or at least in the semi-darkness…many lords did belong to White's, after all—had paid off. Her letter had reached him and this was his response: a basket brimming with every possible delicacy and utensil needed for a proper tea right down to a stone bottle of hot water and a pot to pour it in.

How much time did she have? She glanced at her clock. Fifteen until the hour. With hot water on the line, she'd guess he'd be here at three. She set about laying out the tea on the low table by the sofa where she'd slept last night. She unpacked white pastry boxes containing iced lemon scones, ginger nut biscuits and violet crèmes, boxes that contained triangular-shaped finger sandwiches of ham and chicken. There were two hand-painted teacups with matching saucers, linen napkins and two small plates meant for cakes and biscuits, all of which matched the teapot. She wondered if he meant to make a gift of the tea set afterwards? And if he did, what did it signify? Their relationship was still in a nebulous phase where they were neither business partners nor personal acquaintances. A gift at this point would make things…interesting, if not escalated.

Umberton arrived at three, dressed in a jacket of blue superfine and a top hat, a walking stick of blackthorn finished with a brass knob in his hand. He looked like a gentleman out for an afternoon stroll rather than someone making a business call. Is that what she saw because that was what she wished? That this was more than a business call? Fleur smoothed her skirts, suddenly conscious that she was wearing the spare dress she left here for occasions like last night when she didn't go home. It was a nice dress of bright blue cambric patterned with pink and yellow flowers, the short sleeves and scooped neck trimmed in the palest of ivory lace, but it was not a fancy dress, something that had not bothered her until now.

'Your tea has arrived.' She gestured to the table as he took off his hat and made himself at home. 'It is quite lavish, more like a meal than a snack.' She led the way to the sofa, acutely aware that there would be little separating them beyond the voluminous layers of her skirts. Every fibre of her being seemed to be intensely aware of his presence today in new ways. Perhaps that was due to the new thoughts that had plagued her last night.

'I remembered what you said about meals being merely fuel. I guessed you might not be in the habit of fuelling up as regularly as you ought.' His eyes twinkled. 'Am I right? Did you skip breakfast this morning? Perhaps even lunch?' He sat, crossing a long leg over one knee. If their closeness on the sofa was of particular note to him, he gave no sign of it.

'You are very intuitive, Lord Umberton.' She settled her skirts. 'You are close. I skipped dinner last night after our lunch together. I woke up ravenous, but I only had time for a sweet bun and coffee and I skipped lunch.' She waved a hand towards her messy desk in explanation. 'Too much to do. So, yes, I am hungry.' She gave him a considering look. 'I do not know if I find your intuition endearing or downright intrusive.'

'That makes two of us, then. *Your* intuition sent a letter to hunt me down at my club.' He smiled, eyes warm. 'We are two people who value their privacy and yet we've invaded each other's on multiple occasions now.'

'The letter was more deduction than intuition,' she corrected, reaching to pour the tea. 'This is a pretty teapot, by the way. What do you intend to do with it after today?' No time like the present to address that particular elephant in the room. There were others, of course, a veritable herd of them, but she'd start with this one.

He took the cup and added his own cream. Ah, so he liked cream in his tea *and* his coffee. 'I mean to leave it here in case we have tea again.' His eyes were on her over the rim of his teacup as he took a small sip.

'Do you think we will have tea again?' Fleur queried

carefully, understanding full well that after two meetings, today was a watershed of sorts, determining how they would go forward.

'We'll see. I like to be prepared for eventualities.' That was no answer at all. He took another sip of his tea and filled his plate with items from the tray. 'I wasn't sure what you liked so I ordered a bit of everything.' He gave a boyish wink as the food piled up on his plate. 'I'll tell you a secret. I skipped lunch, too. Today is the day my mother hosts at-homes at the town house and I wanted to make my bow and get out of there as fast as possible. Eating would only have delayed my departure.'

'What's wrong with your mother's at-homes?' The reporter in her immediately sensed a story, a point of interest, or was that the woman in her who wanted to know more about this man with the quiet manners and powerful personality? Where was the line between the two roles?

'They're full of women with daughters who want to marry me.' It was clear he said it without thinking and they both laughed. 'I'm sorry, that came out a bit arrogant and unfeeling.' He gave an abashed smile that was all too endearing.

'It was honest.' Fleur reached for a violet crème. '*Do* you expect to marry this year? If it is not too personal to ask,' she added, but she suspected it wasn't and that he would answer since he'd brought it up. Perhaps because it weighed on his mind and he wanted to talk about it—he just needed an opening and perhaps a stranger to tell.

'Do I expect to marry this year?' He shook his head. 'If only it were that simple. I just have to put it on the calendar as if it were another appointment, as if it were as easy as going to Tattersall's and selecting a horse for this year's hunt season.' He gave a self-deprecating chuckle that communicated the opposite—that this was no laughing matter. 'I can't seem to bring myself to reduce it to such a common denominator. Perhaps it would all be easier if I did. My mother has a list, you see.' The spark was back in his eyes.

'Tell me about the list,' she prompted out of some type of morbid curiosity. Was she trying to convince herself this fellow was off limits?

'Well, there's Lady Claudia Shipman, daughter of the Earl of Coventry. She has a horsey face and fortune and nothing in common with me.' He devoured a ham triangle in a single bite. 'Then there's Aurelia Dunston...' The list went on with him regaling her with a brief biography of each of his mother's candidates. He'd make a good news writer, she thought. He had a knack for picking out salient details without going off on a tangent.

He was an entertaining storyteller, too. It had been a long time since she'd enjoyed a conversation this much. Too many of her conversations in the past year had been exercises in verbal fencing, protecting herself against probes into the business and the situation Adam had left her with. She could not afford to give too much away.

She poured the last of the tea, dividing it between their cups. The tea tray was down to a few lavender crèmes and ginger nut crumbs. 'It seems as though your mother has a certain type of woman in mind for you.' Obedient, pretty, young, a blank slate for him to write on, to fill with his opinions and purposes. 'But what do you prefer for yourself?' It was clear from his tone that those things did not appeal to him. They'd not appealed to Adam either, although she knew very well that those traits were greatly desired by most men.

He reached for one of the remaining lavender crèmes and popped it into his mouth. He made a sour grimace. 'Yuck.' He turned aside and spat the morsel into his napkin, taking a swallow of tea to wash away the taste. 'Do you like these? Truly? They taste like…soap.'

She laughed. 'I like them. They're…airy…sweet… floral.'

'I prefer floral in my flowers, not my sweets,' he countered, mischief in his eye.

'Some say if clouds had a taste, lavender crèmes would be it.'

'No, absolutely not,' he argued with a laugh. 'Clouds do *not* taste like soap.' He smiled and retrieved the last crème. 'I guess that means this last one is for you.' He leaned forward, offering the crème. Her pulse quickened at the realisation. He meant to feed it to her. She answered his smile with a coy smile of her own, leaning towards him to allow the liberty, the flirting, the lingering of his fingers at her lips, sending a jolt of awareness down her spine, his own topaz gaze meltingly warm, less teasing now and more tempting. The atmosphere in the room changing with the electricity conjured at his touch.

She should not have pressed, knowing full well the question served a dual purpose. 'You haven't answered me yet. What sort of woman do you prefer?' In the interim since the asking it had become a loaded question and he pulled the trigger.

'A woman who knows her own mind, who has her own opinions—well-formed opinions, of course. Anyone can have opinions. Not all are worthy of consideration.' His voice was quiet with an unmistakable husk to it, proof that he felt it, too, the current of awareness connecting them.

'Those kinds of women can be difficult. Demanding. Determined. Are you sure you wouldn't want an easier woman?' Her own voice was also quiet as if they were exchanging secrets. They were weaving intimacy between them with their words.

'Your husband didn't mind such a challenge, why should I want any less?' It was a bold question with a bold implication—that *she* was the sort of woman he sought. An intimate compliment indeed, with intimate opportunity. He filched a remaining ginger nut hidden among the crumbs and broke it in two, feeding her half.

'Will you tell me about him?' He brushed a crumb from her lip with his thumb. 'We've talked about the women who seek to capture me. But what of you? What sort of man was man enough to win you?' The last was said with a chuckle, but it was asked in earnest. This was no joke.

'A bold man.' She smiled, in part because he'd asked. Perhaps he'd sensed that she needed an opportunity to talk about this as much as she'd sensed his need to give voice to his mother's matchmaking efforts. In part she smiled from memory, recalling Adam's courtship over eight years ago.

'We met at Lady Brixton's first ever literacy fundraiser, which she holds during the Season. Adam was very passionate about literacy and early education for children. He believed no one was too young to learn to read and he was appalled at the conditions of the poor, which prevent any opportunity for education.' She paused. 'Lord Brixton is the Duke of Cowden's son—do you know him?' Her uncle had once hoped for an alliance there—Brixton for his niece. But Brixton had eyes only for Helena Merrifield and Fleur had been swept off her feet by Adam.

'I know Cowden, not so much his son, though. I know Brixton only by name as he won a seat in the Commons recently. Our paths have not had a chance to cross yet.'

'Then we should make a chance. Brixton should be on our list for the dam legislation,' she digressed from the personal, offering them an opportunity to bring the conversation back to business. But he didn't allow her to take it. The second half of the ginger nut popped into her mouth.

'I believe we were talking about you, not Brixton,' he scolded with a tease, his voice a low, intimate tenor. 'So, you met your husband at a fundraiser. Then what?' Was it wrong that she wanted his fingers to stay on her lips? To want those fingers elsewhere—on her neck, in her hair, on her body. God, she was lonelier than she'd ever been.

She gave a small smile, their eyes holding. 'Then he kissed me and that was it.' She wet her lips, wanting to stay in the present, not wanting to be dragged into the past. 'You can tell a lot about a man by the way he kisses.' She made the conversation an invitation. This was not as much about Adam any more as it was about her loneliness. If Umberton kissed as well as he looked, maybe she could drive away the loneliness for a while. She'd be willing to try.

His fingers stroked her cheek and lingered, cupping

her jaw. '*I* would like to kiss you.' His lips hovered beneath her ear, his words quiet but bold, turning her blood from warm to hot.

She turned into his touch, catching his wrist with her hand and pressing a kiss to his palm. 'Not if I kiss you first,' she whispered, reaching for him, her hands in the luxurious dark mop of his hair, pulling him to her.

Chapter Seven

At the first touch of his lips she knew what this kiss was: mutual madness. His mouth was ready for her and the kiss *she'd* initiated was instantaneously not hers any longer, but *theirs*, the product of an afternoon spent building towards this moment when curiosity and want could no longer be contained by an exchange of stories or pacified by the faintest brush of fingers as he fed her sweets. Combustion was the only outlet left.

Yet even in the meeting of mutual want there was also the mutual need to duel, to dominate, to claim control. Neither of them wanted to be weak, to be subdued. It was there in the press of his mouth, the probe of his tongue, the nip of her teeth as they sank into his lower lip.

Fleur gave a breathless moan that was part-pant, part-gasp, sucking hard on his earlobe as his mouth found her neck. The heat within her escalated with the kiss. The kiss was no longer about mouths meeting mouths, but bodies meeting bodies. He was all tastes beneath her tongue and textures where her hands slid beneath his coat, palms running over the silk of his waistcoat, feeling the plane of muscle beneath.

It wasn't enough. It wasn't enough to taste the tannins left behind by the tea, or to feel the muscle of him beneath his clothes and to know it was there. The more she had of him, the more she wanted of him, this man she barely knew, and in fact had not known forty-eight hours ago, this man who had sought her out and now had her nearly writhing for him in her office. That was unacceptable.

Fleur fisted her hands in the lapels of his coat and broke away with no small effort. Her body did not thank her for it. The only consolation was that he seemed to feel the loss of the contact, too. His topaz eyes were darker now, the colour of a tawny port, his breathing jagged as he gathered himself in the aftermath. But his wits had not deserted him. He gave a slow smile, overtly seductive. 'Well? What does my kiss say about me?'

Fleur took the opportunity to create distance. Goodness knew she desperately needed some. She rose from the sofa, smoothing her skirts and donning the exaggerated pose of a professor delivering a lecture. 'Your kiss suggests you are a man who is used to being in control. When you don't naturally have control, you will find ways to seize it. It also suggests you are a bold man, unafraid to kiss a stranger on the briefest of acquaintance.'

He smiled and leaned back against the sofa, looking entirely too at ease for what had just taken place. 'I won't say you're wrong. I am used to being in control. I was raised to it, it's part of my job. My family, my social position, expects it of me.' There was a twinkle in his eye. 'But I must disagree on the last. I am bold, but are we truly strangers?'

'We've only known each other for two days.' She

was aware he was stalking her with his eyes, recording every swish of her skirt, every movement of her hands.

'Is there a required amount of meetings before we are no longer strangers?' he asked with feigned innocuousness. He was baiting her. 'Three meetings? Four? If we go to lunch tomorrow, will we suddenly be friends? I know married couples who have been together for a lifetime and are still strangers to each other. Yet, I feel as if you and I know each other better than you think even on short acquaintance,' he drawled in a quiet tone.

It was always the quiet ones one had to be on guard for. Who would have thought Lord Umberton with his untamed hair, wire-rimmed glasses and quietly stern tone would be so wild underneath? She smiled and shook her head, his words making her feel warm and pleasant because they matched how she felt and there was relief in knowing he felt it, too, that she wasn't alone. There was some indefinable quality about being with him that spoke to her. The French would call it *je ne sais quoi*.

'Is that all my kiss says to you?'

'Are you fishing for a compliment?' She busied herself picking up the remnants of their tea. It was best he leave now. She wasn't sure where they went from here. Kisses were like that. Watersheds that divided a relationship into two time periods. B.C.—before curiosity was satisfied, or 'before combustion' if one preferred— and A.D.—after detonation. It was like eating from the Tree of Knowledge. Now they knew what it felt like to act on the chemistry between them and in the knowing, they would have to decide what to do next. Choose exile? Never meet again? Pursue the knowledge? Or perhaps try to ignore their knowledge by stuffing it back into the Pandora's box they'd opened. Was that even possible?

'If you don't want to talk about my kiss, shall we talk about yours and what it says about you?' His sibilant tenor was utterly inviting and dangerous. Part of her wanted to return to the sofa, sit down beside him and play the little flirtation game he was initiating, to let it go where it would. But that was an easy out. She knew where it would go with the current climate of the room being what it was. The heat of seduction, the desire for more, the craving, was still here.

If she sat down beside him, she knew where this would lead. She knew, too, that she would regret this. He was the one lord she'd connected with so far who supported her work on the dam. Conflating business with pleasure might jeopardise that connection and, if word got out, it might jeopardise the project's credibility and hers. This was not a decision to be made in the afterglow of a passionate moment. If she was going to sleep with him, she needed to give it some thought and if he wasn't going to leave, she'd have to make him.

'I don't need you to tell me about my kiss. I already know,' she said briskly, piling the linen back into the basket to be returned to Fortnum and Mason. 'My kiss is the product of desperation, of a woman who occasionally suffers bouts of loneliness because she misses her husband and the intimacies of their marriage, both physical and emotional.' She shut the lid of the basket and held it up. 'The basket is ready to be returned. Thank you for the tea.'

He stood slowly, the heat of his eyes cooling as he

registered the dismissal. But by no means was he willing to cede the field. 'Are you saying you used me for sex, Mrs Griffiths?'

'Not sex, Lord Umberton. It was just a kiss,' she corrected, but his words had done their damage, creating images of what might have been—a floor covered in abandoned clothes, bodies entwined on the sofa seeking completion, seeking distraction from the real world, from their individual worlds. They'd not been far from taking that step and perhaps they would have if she'd not called a halt to it.

'And was the kiss successful?' he asked, taking the basket from her, fingers brushing hers where they met at the handle, perhaps on purpose, knowing full well the jolt such contact would send up her arm, a reminder that she could banish him from the room, but not from her thoughts or from her body.

She gave him a cool smile. 'Tut, tut, Umberton. You know better than to ask. A lady never kisses and tells.' Especially when he already knew the answer. He was not oblivious to how she'd roused to him. 'Good day.'

Good lord, what had she done? She watched him exit on to the street and step into his coach, her thoughts in a riot over what had happened and how she felt about it. She'd kissed a man in Adam's office and it hadn't been just a kiss, a physical connection of mouths. She'd *enjoyed* it. It had electrified her because it had electrified *him*. They had been falling *together* on the sofa, their bodies answering one another. It had not been like that before when she'd sought comfort. This had been different. Did she dare pursue it? Did she *deserve* to pursue it while Adam's newspaper foundered and her leadership along with it? Or was this just another way she'd fail Adam?

She'd have her chance to find out. She'd have to see Umberton again. They hadn't done the one thing that they should have. They hadn't discussed business or next steps. At least not next steps with the dam legislation. Which meant two things: she'd have to see him again, and it looked as though she'd be attending the Harefield ball on her own. Lord Harefield was an avid politico with an eye to a cabinet position. He'd be sure to invite guests who could grease the wheels of his own political advancement and she meant to make use of it.

'Mrs Griffiths?' A clerk poked his head in. 'This note came for you. A man in the Duke of Cowden's livery brought it.'

Ah, yes, the other letter she'd sent. It took a moment to bring her thoughts fully back to business. She crossed the room and took the note, smiling as she read the contents. Cowden would see her tomorrow. At least that was one thing that was going right today. She looked up at the clerk. 'Thank you. I have to pick up my gown for the ball, so I'm going to step out and then head home.' He nodded as if he and the staff weren't aware she'd slept here last night. At least they couldn't doubt her dedication. No one could say the paper failed while she danced the night away.

He knew where she'd be tonight. Dancing at the Harefield ball. It had been at the top of the list she'd given him. Jasper stared idly at the pages before him, unable to concentrate on the latest report from his steward at Rosefields, the estate in Meltham. He'd gone back to the town house after tea, confident that his mother's at-home would be finished, the premises safe for unmarried bachelors once more.

He'd had every intention of doing a couple of hours' worth of work before supper, but other than sitting behind the desk in his study, he'd not made any progress. Instead of crop yields, his mind wanted to think about the yield of her lips beneath his, only Fleur Griffiths hadn't yielded for long. It had been a mere strategy before she'd launched her own attack on his senses. Even now, the echoes of her touch reverberated through his body: the caress of her fingers in his hair, the tug of her teeth at his ear, her hands, palms flat, pressed hard against his chest as if they'd prefer to rip the shirt from his body and press against the heat of his skin. His mind and body liked the image of that. He wouldn't mind removing a few of her clothes either. He did, however, mind her motives for it, though.

Jasper played with a pen. The thrill of the kiss, of their interlude, had been tempered by the ending. Reality had a way of dousing even the most heated of passions. She'd been feeling lonely, and he'd been a handy substitute. It was a bit lowering to realise that he'd been nothing more than a tool, a means to an end, an external end, one that had nothing to do with him specifically if she was to be believed. It raised the question of whether or not she'd assuage that need with just anyone?

Jealousy pricked at the idea of Fleur Griffiths kissing another. Perhaps that was just him being proprietary, or, in her words, controlling. He didn't like to share. Or perhaps that was his ego being bruised over the idea he might merely be an interchangeable part for her. *He* certainly did not feel that way about her. He knew that she roused him especially, uniquely.

He couldn't deny that he'd not been roused like this for ages, not since his one early and foolish foray into the realm of amour, his single lapse in Baconian-driven good judgement when he'd let emotions lead the way— nearly to disaster. Between that disaster and his father's death, he had good reason not to indulge again and he hadn't up until he'd met her. He'd had occasional affairs, yes. He wasn't a rake, but he wasn't a monk either. Passionate indulgences though, no. But he *had* indulged today with that kiss.

Truth be told, he'd been indulging since he'd met her—the flirting at the theatre, the lunch that had veered far afield from a discussion of shared business. She'd tempted him from his usual path and he'd allowed it. That bore examination. Why her? Why now? It made little sense. She was not a logical choice for attraction.

You do see the contradiction, don't you? His conscience laughed at him. *You want to logically select a compatible wife and yet you can't bring yourself to select a carefully curated girl from your mother's list and be done with it.*

But just picking a wife from a list wasn't necessarily a good application of Baconian logic either. That damned list assumed his mother knew what he needed and that was a dangerous assumption to make.

Who knew better than he what he wanted in a wife? A partner, a strong woman with strong opinions unafraid to gainsay him when required. A woman who would help him with Rosefields, who would raise his children with him instead of consigning them to the nursery until they were 'interesting'. A woman who saw more than a title and power when she looked at him. A woman who saw *him*.

It wasn't the fault of the girls on his mother's list that they fell short in his categories. Debutantes weren't raised to view a man in that way. How could he expect something of them they weren't able to give? To see? The more powerful the man, the harder it was to see those things.

And so instead you rouse for Fleur Griffiths, who wakes your primal man, and you answer to it. You like it even though it flies in the face of your precious Baconian code. The attraction makes no sense. She's the enemy, but you cannot get enough of her. Why?

Fleur Griffiths had not been daunted by his power or position. Perhaps because she was aware of her own. *She'd* bought *him* lunch, she'd initiated correspondence with him, she'd initiated their kiss and there'd been a few moments on the divan when he'd thought she'd might initiate more than that. She'd asked meaningful questions this afternoon about him. She'd listened when he talked about his mother's list. It was no wonder he didn't feel she was a stranger even after so few meetings. When they were together they spoke their minds. They argued as freely and fiercely as they kissed.

An interesting conjecture began to take shape: had she really meant it today when she'd claimed to have simply used him to assuage her loneliness? It was certainly plausible. He did not doubt that she was lonely. She was not made for loneliness, for a passionless life.

Was that *all* today had been? Was there no part of her that had kissed him just because she wanted to for herself? For the sake of satisfying the curiosity of exploring the spark between them? Because their attraction to one another was unique, despite her claims to the contrary?

It was a hypothesis that would be interesting to test. Testing it would require more research, more observation, more gathering of data. All of which could be done at the Harefield ball. Could he do it without giving himself away? It wouldn't do now to be exposed as Meltham, not when there was so much yet to learn about her.

And learn for Orion, came the sharp reminder.

What was he thinking? This was what happened when one gave passions free rein and forgot logic. This was not all for pleasure, it couldn't be. He needed to remember his original purpose, the only purpose that mattered. No matter how intriguing Fleur Griffiths was, her newspapers were putting his brother in jeopardy with their claims. He could not lose sight of that. Going to the Harefield ball was first and foremost for Orion. For the family. He needed to plan carefully.

His sluggish mind, which hadn't been able to focus on crop yields, was suddenly vibrant and alive with planning. If he arrived late, no one would pay attention to his arrival. Even if he was announced, it would be too crowded for anyone to put a face with his name if anyone noticed at all. Arriving late also meant he could take advantage of others being already involved in their own evening contretemps to pay attention.

She would be none the wiser if he was introduced as Umberton or Meltham. Harefield's would be a crush. The crowd would allow him to be anonymous among them, to have total control of when she saw him and when he approached her. He could waltz with her, take her out to the garden. They would definitely skip supper. That was too risky. He could suggest they have that discussion about business which had eluded them today. What had happened to that discussion anyway? She'd produced her list, and, oh, yes, then he'd produced his and they'd ended up talking about his mother and marriage. They'd never got back on track after that.

He hummed as he headed upstairs to change into evening attire. It was amazing what the prospect of the unusual, a little derring-do, could accomplish in livening up a normal *ton*nish evening. His inner voice wasn't done with pricking, though, as it whispered the dangerous thought, *Maybe it wasn't the derring-do. Maybe it was a woman.*

Chapter Eight

A woman unescorted in a ballroom had to be careful to cultivate just the right amount of attention: enough to be noticed, but not enough to become too interesting, especially when it was that woman's first ball in over a year. But not her first public appearance, Fleur reminded herself as she steadied her nerves, moving through the receiving line leading into the Harefield ballroom. There were other reminders she gave herself as well: being out alone was not new to her. She was used to being on her own in boardrooms and business offices, at the theatre. She was used to managing the precarious balancing act of attention. Tonight would be no different.

In the year since Adam's death, Fleur had mastered the art of attraction. Her position as the head of the newspaper syndicate had left her no choice. She didn't have the luxury of becoming invisible. She was expected to lead. The syndicate would never have survived if she hadn't. And yet there were other expectations for her as well. Society expected her to mourn, to behave as a decorous, circumspect widow for the entirety of a year.

Business and society hadn't stopped to wonder how those differing expectations might co-exist, how she might manage to straddle those obligations, or even unite them. Yet she'd found a way. Her theatre box had remained empty for a year, but not the chair at the head of the long table in the *London Tribune's* conference room. When board members had questioned her decision, she'd reminded them that it was perfectly acceptable for the public head of a household—she did not dare use the term 'man' here—to discreetly carry on business affairs while in mourning. Her case was no different.

Fleur pressed a hand to her stomach in a quiet, steadying gesture. She had mastered boardrooms, but ballrooms were a different matter. Ballrooms held different memories—personal memories—and it was those memories that were with her now: intimate memories of dancing with Adam, of waltzing with him while he whispered interesting titbits about the guests in her ear that made her laugh and promises about later that made her burn, made her forgive whatever difficulties the day had held.

She reached the front of the reception line and offered her hand to her host. 'Mrs Griffiths, it is a delight to see you this evening.' Lord Harefield bowed over her gloved knuckles.

'I thank you for the invitation. It is time I started circulating in society again. My husband would have wanted me to be abreast of all the political happenings first hand.' She gave the little speech she'd rehearsed in front of her vanity mirror this evening. Two sentences were all she'd have time for with her host and she wanted those sentences to convey a strong message that she was firmly at the helm, carrying out business in a way Adam would approve of, and that she was personally involved in cultivating the high-quality news coverage people had come to associate with the *London Tribune*. She was fully back in circulation and it was business as usual.

'I am working on a piece about dam infrastructure. I was hoping you could point me in the direction of a few members of Parliament who might be interested in commenting.'

'Mr Elliott from Somerset.' Lord Harefield nodded in the direction of a tall, blond-haired gentleman. 'He'll be eager. It's his first term in Parliament,' he explained in a low voice. 'I'll walk over with you and make the introduction.'

It was the beginning of a long evening. Fleur smiled, she chatted, she asked pertinent questions, she let the blond Viscount from Somerset lead her out on to the floor for a dance and then introduce her to a circle of his friends. More dances followed, more chances to make polite conversation. It helped to think of the evening as business. She was dancing as a means of building her support base, of establishing a network of those who might be called on to promote legislation regarding dam oversight. But all the reasoning in the world could not stop the hunger that was unfurling inside her.

These dances, these touches, meant nothing. They were empty and perfunctory, required for the activity of the dance and nothing else. It had never been that way with Adam and the absence of that heat only emphasised her loneliness all the more. *There'd been heat with Umberton*, came the reminder. Their kiss was proof that heat, that passion, with another was indeed possible for her.

It was something she'd wondered about after the disappointment of taking that first lover. She'd thought perhaps she was doomed to never feel such things again. But she'd felt something with Umberton, something wild and reckless and wonderful. But Umberton was not here. Maybe that was for the best. Adam's empire was on tenuous ground. The last thing she needed to invest her time in was a personal affair. It was Adam's empire that required her attentions. But quelling her need was easier said than done.

By eleven o'clock she was feeling worn out from the effort of useful conversation and she was feeling keenly vulnerable in her craving for meaningful interaction, something, *anything* that would fill her. It wasn't the first time since Adam's death she realised how empty she felt. Until now, she'd attributed that emptiness to the isolation that came with her position at the paper and being in mourning. She'd assumed once she re-entered society social interactions would fill that emptiness. She'd been wrong. She could fill her days with work and her nights with entertainments, but quantity was no substitute for quality.

Fleur detached herself from the group she was currently with and made her way to the garden. The cool air felt good on her cheeks and helped to settle the riot of her thoughts. She found a quiet bench near a fountain and idly fanned herself. She missed Adam, imperfections and all. At least with Adam she'd never been lonely. If Adam were here…

'Shouldn't you be inside dancing?' Pleasant, familiar tenor tones teased from behind her and she felt the tension in her shoulders ease.

She turned, taking in the welcome sight of a familiar face, her thoughts tripping over just how welcome Umberton was. How was it that he'd come to claim such a coveted spot in such a short time? Hadn't they just been arguing over that exact thing today and here she was feeling as if she had a partner now, someone to face the evening with. 'Umberton, this is a surprise.'

He came around the bench to take the spot beside her, looking well turned out in his dark evening clothes, not unlike the way he'd looked the night at the theatre. 'A pleasant surprise, I hope?' he asked with a smile that managed to communicate a little humility on his part, as if he wasn't sure of what his reception might be after their afternoon developments. She liked a man who knew the limits of his arrogance.

'Yes, a pleasant surprise,' she assured him. She would have to explore later exactly why she found his presence so pleasant. 'I didn't expect you. Why have you come?'

'Because we have unfinished business.'

Literally, figuratively. He'd not been able to stop thinking about her. Jasper let his gaze linger, taking in the loveliness of her as his mind continued the unspoken answer to her question.

Because you're here. Because I didn't want to wait to see you again. Because I may not have you to myself much longer due to our circumstances. Because I wanted one night with you before things got complicated.

That last was debatable. It was already complicated.

She gave a soft laugh in the darkness. 'I realised after you left that we never got around to making any plans.'

'Perhaps if you walk with me, we could make those plans now. The Harefield garden is quite pretty for a town garden.' He'd love to show her the gardens at Rosefields in full summer bloom, to walk the gravel paths while trying to match the scent of her to one of the many flowers there. But that was a fantasy. In all likelihood she would not be speaking to him by then. He wasn't supposed to care about that when his charade had begun. He was to care only for his brother's reputation. But now he cared for both and wasn't sure how to reconcile the two, or even if they could be reconciled.

He rose and held out his arm for her to take. 'May I say you look lovely tonight? Green becomes you.' The deep summer-green gown brought out the jade of her eyes, the auburn of her hair, the cream of her skin. She'd looked like a painting when he'd spied her in the garden. He'd stood back a few moments when he'd arrived to simply take her in: the curve of her jaw in profile, framed gently by the soft length of an auburn curl draped over her shoulder. He'd taken in more than her beauty. He'd noted a sense of resignation.

Something in the evening had saddened her. Was it that she was alone? Or was it that she *wasn't* alone? Had being among people brought it all back? His mother had once told him after his father died that it had been difficult to go out and do the things she'd once done with his father. Those activities seemed empty without him.

The poignancy of Fleur Griffiths's sadness mixed with her beauty had stolen his thought, his very breath. He'd needed the moment to gather himself, to remember why he was here. Reconnaissance. His brother was counting on him, the family's reputation was counting on him and she was a threat to that. Although it was hard to believe it when he saw her as she was now, alone, sad, fragile. Perhaps because he didn't *want* to believe it.

'I appreciate the compliment.' She smiled and took his arm. 'I admit that I was out here feeling sorry for myself. It was harder than I thought to go to a ball alone.'

'You're missing him?' he said quietly, digesting her confession and what it meant. 'It's your first ball?' He should have realised based on what she'd shared about her outing to the theatre. For all the external toughness Fleur Griffiths displayed with her sharp wit and quick temper, there was a softness, a vulnerability beneath that she kept well hidden. Did he dare believe he was the only one allowed to see it? Best not to be taken in by it, though. Empathy was an emotional response.

She gave a sigh. 'Yes, to both questions.' They stopped beside one of the small fountains in the garden and she trailed a hand in the basin. 'As long as I think about tonight as work, it's not so bad. I have made some connections. We will make more tomorrow night. I thought we could attend the Langston rout. It attracts the political crowd.'

'You should go.' He headed the suggestion in a different direction. The sooner she was disabused of the idea that they would go places together, the better. He could sustain his ruse a while longer. 'I'll go to Lady Elmore's.'

'Divide and conquer?' She slid him a considering look, but he heard a hint of disappointment in her voice.

He liked to think she would miss his company. He would miss hers.

'I think it's our best hope of moving quickly and of avoiding any speculation that we might be conflating business and pleasure. I would hate for legislation to suffer because someone misunderstands our association.'

She arched a slim auburn brow. 'Or perhaps you're worried about your reputation suffering? Perhaps you've realised that you should not be too closely linked with me. I am hardly of your set and, as you say, people will talk, especially when unattached men and women are together no matter what the reason.'

It sounded awful when she put it that way. 'You make me out to be a snob.' It also sounded like something his mother would say. That Fleur Griffith was wealthy because her husband had *worked* for his money. 'I am not embarrassed to be seen with you, if that's what you mean,' he replied. If she knew who he was, it would be she who would be embarrassed to be seen with him.

'It's just a fact. It's how the world is. I know it first-hand.' She gave a rueful smile. 'I was raised by my aunt and uncle. My uncle is an earl's second son and they had no children of their own. They had aspirations for me, primarily that I marry a title of my own. Brixton, in fact, was their grand hope. If not Brixton, then the young heir to the Taunton viscountcy. Taunton hadn't any money, but he had a title and that was all that mattered.'

She sighed and gave a shake of her head. 'But I fell in love with Adam and I refused to be swayed. My aunt and uncle were all the family I had, but they couldn't get past their disappointment in me. I'd failed them by choosing my heart. They didn't come to the wedding and I haven't seen or heard from them since.'

'I'm sorry.' Jasper reached for her hand in an offer of comfort. The confession had saddened her. He'd not intended for that. He *was* sorry. Sorry that her family had disowned her, sorry that she still felt she'd failed them because she'd made her own choices instead of following theirs. 'Do you have regrets?' he asked softly. Had losing her family for what amounted to eight years of marriage been worth it? Had Adam Griffiths, kisser extraordinaire, been worth it?

'Regret not marrying Brixton or Taunton?' She gave a little laugh. 'Brixton never looked my way and I hear Taunton is trying to put funds together for a risky venture to import alpacas.' She shook her head. 'I don't think I would have suited either of them.'

Thank goodness, Jasper thought, because she suited him quite well. 'You gave up more than your family, though. You gave up a lifestyle. You could have been a duchess or a viscountess.' Marrying Adam Griffiths had taken her out of the peerage, out of the life she'd been raised in: the Season in spring, grouse-hunting in the autumn, Christmas at country houses and back to town when the roads cleared to do it all over again. Adam Griffiths was a businessman, a man who worked every day on Fleet Street, who was wealthier than many, but still carried ink stains on his fingers.

'It might surprise you to know that all I ever wanted was to be a storyteller. In a way, I got to be that with Adam. I wrote features for the papers. After the flood, I collected stories from the survivors and had them printed. I never aspired to a title.' She gave him a strong look. 'I like to decide for myself who a person is. Titles are not people and people are not titles.'

Jasper hoped she'd believe that once she knew who *he* was. Inside, a waltz began, its strains drifting out to the garden through the open doors. He held out his hand in an uncharacteristic burst of spontaneity. 'Dance with me.'

'Why? What has brought this on?' She laughed, something flashing in her eyes that alerted him to danger. He needed to tread carefully. She was vulnerable tonight and he was intoxicated by her, by her stories, the glimpse into her life. He already knew how want and need could flare between them, how it tasted, how it begged for more.

He flashed a smile as she gave him her hand. 'I want to prove to you I don't mind being seen with you.' He was playing with fire as he swung her into position, his hand at her waist, her hand at his shoulder. 'We're as proper as Almack's. See, nothing to worry about.' An absolute lie although he wanted to believe it. There was *everything* to worry about. This woman was magic. He could have listened to her stories all night, asked a thousand questions, so immersed had he been sitting beside her at the fountain. Had Adam Griffiths known what a wife he'd had? Had he guessed the depths of all she'd given up for him? He'd like to think he wasn't envious of a dead man, but he wasn't sure he wasn't.

Fleur looked up at him with a bit of mischief in her eye. 'I'm not sure a waltz in the garden proves that. We're virtually alone out here. There's little chance of us being noticed.'

He gave a low chuckle as he turned them about the fountain. 'It's all the more scandalous then, isn't it? If someone notices, it's a much bigger deal than if everyone is watching in the ballroom.' Never mind that he couldn't afford either type of notice at present. 'This proves I am willing to take the risk.' He was getting caught up in the moment, the heat of the afternoon's kiss flaring within him. She was worth the risk. This moment was worth the risk. Perhaps it was worth it to her, too. Perhaps, while the music lasted, they could both find what they were looking for.

She was easy in his arms as if she was made for them, her movements fluid as they glided over the stone pavers of the garden, their steps as light and sure as if they danced across a polished floor. The Harefield fountains burbled against the strains of the music as he turned her at the top of the garden, taking the opportunity to hold her closer than he might have otherwise in a ballroom full of watchful eyes. It gave him an excuse to breathe in the exquisite scent of her. 'What is it that you wear for perfume? I smell jasmine and vanilla, but there's something else, too.'

She laughed up at him, giving a toss of her hair. Some of the sadness she'd admitted to had dissipated as they'd danced and that pleased him. 'Ylang-ylang. It's a flower grown in the South Pacific.' Provided no doubt by Popplewell and Allardyce Enterprises, her connection to the South Pacific, he thought, recalling her friend Antonia, and then marvelling that he could make such a connection, that he could have such an understanding of her in such a short time.

'It suits you.' He smiled down at her. 'Dancing suits you.'

'Dancing with *you* suits me,' she amended, a daring

wickedness flaring in her eyes. His own body surged in response to it, forgetting this was to be only a dance. He'd had a taste of that wickedness this afternoon for better or worse and his body was hungry for more despite the contentious words they'd exchanged at the end. They were waltzing in shadow now, far from the shafts of light coming from the ballroom, the music barely audible.

They did not need the music. Their bodies were as close as clothes allowed. If anyone saw them, it would be a scandal, her hips against his, the fullness of her skirts flattened where they met his trousers, her breasts pressed to his chest so that every inch of him could not help but be aware of her. Her arms had moved to his shoulders, his neck, so that both of his hands rested at her waist, their dancing nothing more than a slow swaying in the shadows, away from moonlight and prying eyes.

Her gaze was green-flame-hot as it looked up at him, her tongue flicking over her lips. 'Do you know what else would suit me? This.' Her last word feathered over his lips a fleeting moment before her mouth took his in a slow, lingering kiss that struck him like a match to a length of fuse, his body left roused in its wake. Her hand dropped to the front of his trousers, hidden between his coat and her skirt, moving over the length of him, moulding him to her touch until he groaned.

'What do you want?' he whispered. He knew what he wanted—he wanted to wash away her sadness, wanted to bring her to life, bring her to happiness. He wanted to wash away the hardship of her year. Whatever she wanted, he would give her. He was already dancing her backwards to the garden wall, some part of him aware that their bodies had reached an answer to what their minds had yet to decide.

'You. I want you,' she whispered into his mouth. 'I want obliteration.'

Chapter Nine

Obliteration was neither a safe request nor a flattering one, if he thought too much about it, which he didn't. He knew very well as he pressed her to the garden wall that she was using him. He would have to grapple with that later. Yet he did not think she'd made the request lightly. Still, good sense argued he ought not to grant it. But he was too far beyond what he ought to do. He was here, wasn't he? If 'ought to dos' held any sway he wouldn't have braved Harefield's to begin with. He was very much the Montague at the Capulet ball.

If she knew who he was…well, that was all the more reason to put an end to her hand on his cock, his mouth at her neck, his own hand at her breast. But for once, he was not listening to any of that logic. In the grips of intense passion, he was content to deal with the aftermath.

She had got his trousers open and her hand wrapped about the hot length of him, no more fabric between them, no more pretence. He knew exactly what she wanted, what she needed and what he needed to achieve the obliteration she asked for. She raised a leg to hook at his hip, skirts quashed between them, as he brought his hand up to skim the silken skin of her thigh, then higher to skim the damp curls that guarded her womanly gate, their dampness a prelude to the wetness he'd find within. Such readiness nearly undid him.

What a treasure she was, a woman confident enough to own her need and claim her passion. Her teeth gave a fierce nip at his ear as if scolding him for being too slow, for lingering and he laughed against her neck.

'Patience, my dear.'

'Patience is a virtue. I think we're well past virtue here.' Her voice was a smoky rasp, low and throaty.

He could not argue with that even if he had been capable of thought. At the moment he was capable only of responding to the primal urges of his body and of hers, his only thoughts revolved around giving her what she needed. He lifted her and thrust hard to their great mutual satisfaction. Her head went back against the fence, her neck arching, the heat of her gaze meeting his for the briefest, most beautiful of seconds when the intensity of connection rocketed through them before her eyes left him, fixing instead on the dark night sky above. He thrust again, more deeply this time, as if he could *make* her look at him. He wanted her eyes back, wanted those green flames on him when the critical moment came.

His own body tightened even as the truth of obliteration came to him too late. Climax would find them shortly; his body was already gathering for it as was hers. When it came it would be explosive, shattering, and for a few precious moments there would be blessed nothingness. Only, she would not be there for it. Oh, her body would be there for it, but *she* would not, not the part of her that mattered. Her mind and soul were already somewhere else. With someone else.

Her hands tangled in his hair, her hips moved against his, pushing him, pushing them both to grand heights, gasps of encouragement purling from her throat. Her eyes were shut now as she rocked against him, her expression fierce and unguarded. Her breathing came hard and fast as release swept her, her body giving a visible, violent tremble. Sure of her pleasure, Jasper claimed his own release outside her body, his physical satisfaction diminished by the knowledge that he'd been a stand-in—quite literally given their current location—for the man she couldn't have.

He held her steady against the fence, giving her time to savour the obliteration she'd so desperately sought. Her eyes were still closed, but her breathing slowed and the fierceness ebbed from her face. There was a satisfying softness to her features in these moments, a softness he'd seen hinted at in unguarded moments. A stab of envy pricked at him. Her husband had seen her like this. Damned, dead Adam, who'd stolen Jasper's pleasure from beyond the grave. Jasper didn't even know the man and he was jealous. It was a ridiculous reaction for a man who prided himself on being logical. There was nothing logical about jealousy. Envy was a weakness. Covetousness a sin.

But I was the one she wanted tonight. I was the one she chose for obliteration.

At last, she opened her eyes and he set her down. 'Welcome back.' He smiled, reaching in his coat pocket for a handkerchief for her.

'Thank you.' She took the handkerchief and Jasper turned away to give her privacy. Was that a thank-you for the handkerchief alone or for everything else? Not just for being the provider of the act, but for something more? He knew he hoped for the latter. Did she understand that *he* understood what she'd been looking for? He tucked his shirt into his trousers and straightened his clothes along with his expression before turning back to her.

'I think I will leave.' She smiled gently at him and gave a low, throaty laugh that had him rousing once more. 'I'm not sure I could pass muster if I went back in now.'

He reached for a loose curl and tucked it back behind her ear. 'You're probably right.' She looked beautiful, peaceful. The sadness was gone. That was something at least. Perhaps his own disappointment was worth that. Her lips were puffy. They'd lost their elegant colour just as her hair had lost its perfect curl. But it was her eyes that betrayed the most. They were dreamy, far away. One close look at her would give it all away. 'This gate will take you around to the front,' Jasper suggested. 'I will go through the house to fetch your cloak and make your farewells to the hostess. I will see you at the curb in ten minutes.'

Some of her softness faded. 'I intend to go home alone.'

He inclined his head respectfully. 'I understand that.' Too well, in fact. It was further proof he'd been a stand-in for another. 'I mean only to facilitate your departure in a discreet manner. I do not mean to accompany you.' The last thing he wanted was a *ménage à trois* with a dead man. There were limits to what he'd do even for a beautiful woman.

She reached for his hand and gave a sincere squeeze. 'Thank you.'

He cleared his throat. 'At any rate, I need to go back in and dance a few times.' The comment bordered on caddish. He wondered if subconsciously he was trying to stoke her jealousy.

She lifted an eyebrow. 'With girls on your mother's list?'

'Yes, exactly so.' Girls he'd never dream of making love to against a garden wall, never dream of seeking obliteration with. That woman was going home with her husband's ghost.

The wry ghost of a smile played at Fleur's lips as she set down the morning papers. How ironic. If only she'd stayed a little longer. The Marquess of Meltham had made a late appearance at the Harefield ball and the society pages had jumped all over it. Everyone was sure this would be the year he married and the matchmaking mamas were lining up their daughters. If she'd walked through the ballroom on her way out, she might have met him coming in, assuming she'd recognise him. Perhaps it was best she hadn't seen him. It would have ruined a perfectly good night.

She reached for her coffee mug and took a hot swallow. Despite the late night, she was back at her desk this morning at the *Tribune*, writing letters and following up on last night's conversations while they were fresh. She had a busy day, including a meeting with the Duke of Cowden. There was too much to do to lie abed spending time staring at the ceiling and thinking of last night. Of Umberton. Of what had transpired in the garden. And yet, every few minutes, her mind went back there, unable to stay entirely focused on the work at hand.

Perhaps she should write to him this morning, too? What would she say? *Thank you for sex against the fence?* No, that sounded too much as though he'd done her a favour. Or something more conciliatory? *I am not in the habit of such actions.* No, that made it sound like an excuse for acting outrageously or, worse, that she now regretted her decision.

Regret would be a lie. She did not regret the fence in the least, although she did wonder if he did. There'd been something in his eyes afterward she'd not been quick enough to decode. Misgiving? Pity? Understanding? She wasn't comfortable with any of them. She didn't want him to see too much. She'd just wanted sex, obliteration. She'd not wanted any of the other things that came with it: concern, caring, connection.

She did not want Umberton's concern or Umberton thinking there was a connection between them that went beyond the business of legislation. If he thought there was more, he'd want more. She could not reciprocate. Her heart, her soul, were off limits. She could not give them again. She'd given them to Adam and now Adam was dead. Dead before she'd had a chance to make amends. Did she even deserve a second chance at love since she'd failed at it so spectacularly the first time?

Was I worth it, Adam? Do you regret marriage to me? Was I too difficult? Too headstrong? Would you have been happier with a biddable wife?

These were the dark questions that had followed her guilt over that last night in Holmfirth. That fight had been one of many. Too many? She could not regret that fight without thinking of other fights. How much time had they wasted arguing? And yet she could not be the sort of woman who agreed to everything just for the sake of peace. Compliance wasn't peace, it was conformity, and conformity bred all nature of illusions: agreement, accord, co-operation, uniformity where there was none. Newspapers protected against such illusions. It was one of the many things Adam liked about them.

Perhaps that was why she'd chosen Umberton last night. He was no risk to her. He needed to marry a girl who met his mother's specifications. She met none of them. She'd be a walking scandal for a man such as he and they both knew it. The only risk she posed was to his honour. Bold women didn't fit comfortably into the code gentlemen were raised by. For them to be gentlemen, women had to be helpless, had to require their protection. Such women didn't run newspapers or seek justice for murders. Neither did they boldly take lovers.

Umberton had been very good at his job. Much better than her previous lover. It had almost been embarrassing how much better. She'd nearly lost herself with him, in him, shattering *for* him, which was very different than using him to seek obliteration, blankness. She'd been acutely aware of him, of gripping him as if he were an anchor amid a stormy sea, of riding him hard in order to have all of him within her. With each thrust, she'd wanted. She'd panted and writhed for him. A nearly inexplicable reaction on her part and a dangerous one, too.

If this were to happen again—and that in itself was still an if—she'd have to proceed with more detachment before she ended up investing too much of herself and risking real hurt when it ended, because it would end. That was the beauty and the curse of choosing Umberton.

There was the business aspect, too. If an affair between them came to light, their plans for legislation might be compromised as well as her reputation in the eyes of the board of directors. There were plenty of reasons not to engage with him again as they had last night, yet parts of her felt those might not be reasons enough.

The little clock on her desk chimed. Time to stop wool-gathering. Time to stop fantasising about Umberton. Time to go meet with Cowden and figure out how to save the syndicate without reducing it.

'My dear, you seem distracted today. Forgive me for saying so. It's not like you.' The Duke of Cowden sat back in his red Moroccan leather chair and laced his hands over the slight paunch of his stomach. Approaching his upper years, Cowden was silver haired and sharp eyed, father of three sons, had four grandsons and was the head of the Prometheus Club, a group of investors who'd generated spectacular wealth for themselves and for England. Nothing got past him, Fleur realised belatedly.

'It was a late night last night. I attended the Harefield ball. The first one,' she confessed, 'since Adam passed.' Then she smiled brightly. 'But business must go on and there were people to meet.'

Cowden nodded and she felt encouraged. Best to keep the conversation steered towards business lest Cowden ask anything too personal. He was known to pry lovingly into the lives of those he cared about and he'd cared about Adam and Keir and Garrett. By extension, he now felt a need to watch over their widows. He'd been one of the first to help Antonia when the department store had burned.

'I am making progress with the dam legislation. I think there will be a law to put before the House perhaps before this session is even out.'

Cowden gave another nod, his eyes keen. 'I will look forward to supporting it when it's ready. And the investigation? You've hardly mentioned it.'

Guilt twinged. She'd not given it the usual lion's share of her attention since lunch at Verrey's with Umberton. It was much more pleasant to think about the baron and the baron did not favour re-opening the investigation. 'I've been busy and I've met someone.' She blushed at the admission. 'No one I care to share about at present,' she added rapidly to stave off Cowden's inevitable inquiry. 'But it's definitely still at the top of my agenda.'

Cowden grinned. 'Well, don't let him, whoever he is, distract you.'

'I won't,' she assured him but Cowden's playful teasing stirred a concern. Is that what Umberton was doing? Distracting her? The dam investigation wasn't at the top of his agenda. Every time she meant to discuss it with him, another topic took its place. Was that a coincidence or something more? A seed of suspicion took root. Had Umberton used their attraction and their agreement upon legislation as a means of distracting her? Refocusing her attentions? Other than his philosophical objections, which he'd voiced eloquently at Verrey's, what would his motive for that distraction be? What purpose could he have? Or what did he stand to gain? These were worrisome questions she'd be wise not to put off any longer.

'I hope you're not too busy to re-join my daughter-in-law's committee for the literacy ball? And my wife would love your help for her Christmas charity ball as well.'

Fleur rose, understanding this was the end to the interview. 'I will look forward to returning to their committees. Tell them thank you for me and thank you also for your support of the legislation. It means a great deal.'

She left Cowden house with mixed feelings. On one hand, she was thrilled to have recruited a second ally for the legislation and possibly a third given that if Cowden was on board his son, Lord Brixton, would be, too. On the other hand, she was becoming concerned about the wisdom of Umberton as an ally.

'Where to, Ma'am?' her coachman asked as she settled into her seat.

She opened her mouth, intending to give instructions to go to Lord Umberton and then realised she couldn't. She didn't know where to find him. She couldn't go to White's herself without drawing undo attention, the very last thing she needed. 'To the office.' Concern escalated. She'd have to wait for him to come to her on all accounts. She did not like that he held a certain power in being the one who chose to call and that he could keep her waiting. She wasn't very good at waiting.

Waiting called up fragments of last night's conversation. 'Patience,' he'd whispered when she'd reached for him. Patience was a virtue, she'd replied, something she'd been beyond in the garden and she definitely remained beyond it today.

Chapter Ten

Apparently, Cicero was right. Virtue was its own reward. Umberton was waiting for her at the office. She would have missed him if she'd gone to White's. He was lounging on the divan and dangling a tumbler from his hand with the casual nonchalance of one who felt at home in his surroundings. He rose when she entered.

'How was your meeting with Cowden?'

'Cowden has offered support for our legislation when it's ready. That's good news.' But her original excitement over that was diminished by practicalities. Mainly, she wasn't sure how she felt about him being here as if he could come and go at will when she had no way to find him on her own. 'How did you know that's where I was?'

'Your clerk told me. He let me in.' Umberton looked well rested for one who'd danced the night away. 'It's good news about Cowden. He'll be a formidable ally.' He waved his tumbler to indicate the room at large. 'I hope you don't mind me waiting in here?' he enquired with such sincerity she nearly forgave him for the inconvenience of his lack of address.

'I don't mind too much, but I do mind the inability to

reach you. I realised this afternoon that I couldn't even send you a note to tell you about Cowden.' She slid him a meaningful look. 'I do not think I like *you* having all the power to guide when and how often we interact.'

She went to her desk, her point made, and gathered together all the loose sheets she'd left out, wondering if he'd looked at them and if it mattered. What would he have seen? Would it have meant anything to him? She hated the suspicion that had taken root since her meeting with Cowden. She looked across the room at him. He wore a blue jacket and buff trousers today, with a striped-blue waistcoat beneath, his jaw clean shaven, eyes clear, wavy hair in its usual state of tousled decadence. He looked handsome and harmless.

No, not harmless. He would never be harmless. Inviting was the word she was looking for. Those eyes, that smile, invited a woman to reveal her secrets, to lay those secrets and perhaps her head on those broad shoulders. He was a safe place for a woman to land. She'd taken advantage of that last night. She hoped she hadn't been wrong. Well, the only way she'd know was if she voiced her concerns. She'd never shied away from difficult conversations. She wasn't going to start now.

'I want to talk to you.' She sat behind her desk, letting the big piece of furniture be her source of power and protection. She needed distance for this conversation. She could not have it sitting side by side on the sofa where'd they kissed yesterday, where she'd be reminded of his touch, of the clean scent of him, of all the things that had led her to seduce him last night. She would not mince words with herself. She *had* seduced him.

'Is this about last night? If so—' he said, but she interrupted.

'No, it's not about last night. It's about the enquiry on the dam.' She drew a breath and counted to three. She wanted to deliver this next sentence with even tones, with no hint of anger. 'I want the truth from you.' She fixed him with a hard stare and watched him stiffen in alertness.

'Of course, always.' But he was wary.

'Have you deliberately refocused my attention away from it by pushing the legislative end of things and by...' it was hard to say the last bit '...by conflating business with pleasure?'

His eyes went wide. 'You mean by seducing you?' He gave loud chuckle. 'I believe you were seducing me last night. And our kiss yesterday afternoon seemed fairly mutual to me. So, I think you'll have some difficulty selling that argument.'

'I think you are having difficulty answering the question,' Fleur said firmly. She would not let him distract her with talk of romance and who had seduced whom.

'Why are you asking? Are you having trouble coming to grips with last night? Perhaps you're looking for a scapegoat and would like to blame me?' He rose from the sofa, pacing his corner of the room. 'What is this about, Fleur?' His use of her given name threw her for a moment. 'I would think after last night we could at least call each other by our given names,' he said, reading her hesitation, 'My name is Jasper, by the way.'

Like the stone, she thought. The name suited him. Jasper, the stone of protection, of strength. She tried not to think about other things his comment pointed out, like the fact that she'd engaged with him so intimately without knowing his name, only his title. After her protest to Cowden this morning, there was some irony in that.

'Did you use our attraction to manipulate my agenda? You made no secret at Verrey's as to how much you disliked the idea of re-opening the investigation.' The idea that he had prevaricated in the past and was prevaricating now seemed to affirm her alarm was not unwarranted.

'Do you think I am that sort of man?' he shot back. 'This conversation does not paint me in a favourable light. But I'd be very careful about what I was asking if I were you, Fleur. If you think to pillory me for using sex as a tool, you'd best look in the mirror first.'

'What exactly are you suggesting?' She'd not wanted to talk about last night, but somehow the conversation had gone that direction anyway.

'If anyone was using anyone for sex, it was *you* using *me*.'

She met his gaze evenly. Was that a reprimand she heard in his voice? 'You were not unaware. I told you exactly what I wanted.' She'd wanted him and an escape from the loneliness that had driven her from the ballroom. He'd managed to give her both. 'It seemed to me that you enjoyed it last night. So, I am mystified as to the source of your irritation today.'

He broke from his pacing and approached the desk, leaning over it, palms flat on its polished surface. His eyes glittered with dangerous warning. She should *not* find that arousing. But she did. Or maybe it was the fight she found arousing. She hadn't had a good fight for a long time. Not since… No. She put a full stop to her thoughts. 'You talk about the mutuality of our "activity" last night, but you were not there with me in the end. That's not fair.'

Oh. So that's what this was about. She was surprised he had even noticed. She doubted many men would care enough at that point, too lost in reaching for their own release to note their partner's. 'I told you I wanted obliteration. It's not a state of togetherness. You gave me exactly what I asked for.' But he'd wanted something else, been searching for something else and he'd not found it. It was something of a revelation.

'You were lonely, too,' she said softly, the tension between them gentling with the realisation. But they'd used different means to assuage that loneliness. She'd sought obliteration and he'd sought togetherness. Both of them temporary variations for the real thing.

He fingered the heavy glass paperweight on the desk. 'A lord is always lonely, especially when he's expected to marry. Perhaps that is when he's at his loneliest, knowing that everyone is circling, waiting for him to commit, to give in and choose someone.'

Something in his voice touched her and she reached for his hand out of an innate need to offer comfort. 'You make it sound like surrender, capitulation. A defeat.' Those were not characteristics she'd come to associate with this man.

His gaze held hers, sharp and all-seeing but his voice was soft in its reflectiveness. 'My father once took me to Scotland for hunting. We tracked a herd of elk for miles. There was an older stag with them and our hounds culled him from the herd, separated him from the others until he was alone. The first shot missed and, by missed, I mean it wasn't fatal. It merely slowed him down. We followed him until our hounds surrounded him. He was on his knees in a clearing when we took him.'

He sighed and gave a shake of his head. 'I didn't like it. I suppose it's not manly to admit such a thing. My father assured me it was all part of the circle of life.'

'You were close to your father?' She ventured the personal question. 'Whenever you talk of him or your mother, it sounds as if your family was close.' Was that quite the right word? 'I mean, "is" close. Your mother is still alive.'

'My father was a good man. He taught me about honour and what it means to be a good man. I try to live up to his standards. I loved him and I miss him every day.' He smiled and something warm fluttered in her stomach. 'I love my mother, too, despite her list.' He gave a wry laugh. 'But I think of that story every time my mother drags the list out.'

He chuckled, but it wasn't an entirely happy sound. 'I'm like that bull elk. Each year, all the matchmaking mamas separate those of us who should marry from the herd and do their best to bring us to our knees.' There was another sigh. 'It is an illusion that a man goes courting, that he somehow is in pursuit. I think it's the mamas who are in pursuit. We poor bachelors are all stags on the run.'

She completed the thought for him. 'While the mamas circle and wait to pounce and bring your carcass home for their daughters.'

'Yes. Am I terrible to think that? Nobody puts that in their love poems.'

'No, they don't. It's all roses and blushes. Virgins and unicorns. No one seems to understand that the unicorn horn in the virgin's lap is a symbolic penis.'

'Is it?' He looked astonished. 'I didn't realise…' He cleared his throat. 'Well, that certainly puts a different take on things.' He furrowed his brow. 'I studied Classics at Oxford and I don't think that's quite right. The unicorn is a symbol of purity in Raphael's *The Virgin and the Unicorn* and I am sure the unicorn was used in the Renaissance to depict chastity.' He paused. 'Are you laughing at me?'

'Laughing *with* you. I was quite enjoying the lecture, Professor.' Fleur came around the desk. 'I like my version better. It took your mind off things, didn't it?'

'Yes. My apologies. I was being maudlin.' They made their way to the divan and sat, but Fleur had not entirely forgotten the roots of their quarrel.

She hesitated to revisit the topic of that disagreement after such a nice moment. It had been quietly intoxicating to listen to his story, to know he was sharing something deeply personal and simultaneously troubling to him. But she needed her answers. Perhaps she'd do better with sugar than vinegar. She'd been bold and confrontational earlier and that had resulted in a quarrel. Maybe if she was less direct she'd get a better response. Part of her was very much aware that on at least two occasions they'd meant to talk business and had ended up not discussing anything resembling business. She could not keep letting those opportunities slip away or it would be August and another summer would have come and gone with nothing done.

'If I ring for tea, will you let me show you something?

And will you listen with an open mind? I want to share with you the case I have against Lord Orion Bexley.' It would be the ultimate litmus test for him. It was time for him to prove his worthiness.

He did not want to hear it. His damned brother had messed up a lot in his life and now he was going to mess this up, too, whatever 'this' was that sparked between him and Fleur Griffiths.

'Fleur, you know how I feel about that,' he reminded her in an attempt to dissuade her from showing him.

'Yes, I know exactly how you feel and because of that, is it any wonder I *feel* derailed any time the subject comes up? I want legislation but I also want this: justice for those who died.'

Coward! His inner voice snapped. *Let her show you. This was your whole plan all along, to earn her trust enough to learn what she has on Orion. This is what you came for, what you'd started this whole association for. You ought to be thrilled. You will finally have your answers, finally know how to protect Orion.*

Yet, the only thought that came to the fore as Fleur called for tea and retrieved a file was that he ought to stand up and walk out of the office, that he didn't want to know. Didn't want her to tell him. He didn't want to be reminded that this was business, and she was the enemy. That he'd shielded his identity from her in order to gain access to her world, that he'd misled her about the motives for his interest in her project.

If she knew, she would hate him for it. From her perspective, these were not the behaviours of a man of honour. Yet he could argue from his perspective—the perspective of a man who must protect his family and name—these behaviours were warranted. They were omissions only, none of them outright lies. He could hear his father in his head alongside his own inner voice.

Family first. Your mother, your brother, will need you when I'm gone. You will have hard choices to make.

She spread the papers from the file out on the low table. 'The troubles begin in 1846 when the Holmes Reservoir Commissioners were found to be in a state of insolvency, having spent Parliament's allotment for the reservoir project, but also owing several outstanding debts.' She passed him a sheaf of papers. 'This is the testimony of Charles Batty, who was the drawer for the commissioners, and these are copies of outstanding bills the commission owed. The Huddersfield Banking Company was owed two thousand pounds, money was owed to clerks who worked for the commission and monies were owed to companies who worked on the dam. These are no small sums and the fact that one of these bills ended up in Chancery speaks to the depth of dysfunction in the commission.'

Jasper fished his eyeglasses out of his inner coat pocket and studied the papers. 'If I may play the devil's advocate?' he said after a careful perusal. 'I feel as if this only affirms the original findings that no one person was culpable. There was unfortunate disarray up and down the line when it came to the Holmfirth Reservoirs Act. This notes only that Lord Orion Bexley was on the commission at the time.'

'The debt is curious, is it not? Where did all the money go if the dam was never repaired? What this establishes is the insolvency and that the money set aside for repairs was gone. It allows us to ask—where did the money go? I propose it went into Lord Orion Bexley's pockets by way of a very careful, very expert sleight of hand.' She handed him another sheet of paper.

'What is this?'

'This was issued by the commission on August 26, 1846. It's an order to improve the waste pit so that water could be safely processed and filtered through the dam.' She summarised as he scanned the paper.

An opening should be made in the waste pit of the Bilberry Dam reservoir at the height of eighteen feet above the clough or shuttle and Mr Littlewood authorised to see the same forthwith carried into effect.

He looked up to meet her gaze, waiting for the blow to fall.

'That repair was never made. In fact, although it was authorised, Mr Littlewood testified that he did not know about the request and, in fact, no engineer or construction manager on the project after that date reported knowing about the request or any later requests to carry out that work.' She reached for another stack of papers. 'This is the testimony of those men: Mr Littlewood, Mr Leather, Jonathon Crowther…the list goes on.'

Jasper scrubbed a hand over his face. 'Why would the blame for this, the pocketing of the money, be laid at Lord Orion's feet? Why not one of the other commission members?'

'Two reasons. Because he was one of three men assigned specifically to the Bilberry Dam Reservoir. It was the commission's practice that those members residing nearest a dam took over supervision of that dam. He was one of three who submitted the order.' She paused and said with emphasis, 'It was Bexley's job to ensure that order was carried out.'

'His job and that of the other two men with a particular interest in the Bilberry Dam.' Jasper racked his brain to remember who those other two might have been.

She shook her head. 'Those positions are reappointed every year. Those men left and new men took their places. Bexley is the only returning figure, the only one who could provide continuity. The only one who had knowledge of the order to work on the waste pit and he *never* acknowledges that it wasn't acted on. He never calls attention to the fact that the work order—*his work order*—was placed and nothing occurred.

'That waste pit and its inefficiencies were the cause of the fatal accident. Listen to Mr Leather's testimony.' She proceeded to read slowly and carefully aloud. *"'My opinion as to the cause of the breaking of the embankment on the fifth of February is that it arose from overflowing and washing away the outer slope...if the waste pit had been seven or eight feet below the embankment, the inference is that the embankment would have stood...if the order of the Commissioners in 1846 had been carried out and a hole made... I think it very likely it would have prevented the accident. Had I been consulted I should have recommended such a course of action."'*

Jasper listened intently. He saw the argument she was making in his mind. Orion had submitted an order for repairs, pocketed the money for himself and the repair had never materialised. The lack of that particular repair bore full responsibility for the accident. Had Orion seen the work carried out, the accident would have been prevented despite all the other mismanagement by the commissioners. Fleur's was not an implausible argument, and his worries began to rise. What had Orion done?

Fleur set aside her folder. 'I know what you're going to say—that I don't have proof he siphoned the money. If I had access to his bank accounts, it would be the proof I need.' She gave a little lift of her shoulders, a smile playing at her lips. 'Adam always said to follow the money. Money never lies.'

Jasper was very much afraid of that.

Chapter Eleven

Money never lies. Those words drove real fear into his heart. There was a knock and a clerk entered with tea. She cleared the coffee table, making a space for the tray. 'It's not Fortnum and Mason's…' she smiled '…but it will do. The bakery down the street makes delicious lemon scones.'

How odd, he thought, watching her fix his tea, that everything was still right-side-up in her world when his had been turned upside down. She was calmly stirring cream into his tea while his mind was running riot. What if she was right? What if Orion had pocketed the money? His brother could be tried for manslaughter, eighty-one deaths laid at his door. But Orion was not a murderer. He was a wayward young man with no sense of direction, struggling to find purpose in a world that gave him few options as a second son.

If anything went to trial, his title couldn't protect Orion then. But it could protect his brother now. It could prevent this enquiry of hers from ever getting that far. Would he use his title, though, to obstruct justice? Would he suddenly turn away from his voting record championing free press? To do either of these things would paint him as a traitor to his own beliefs and positions. But perhaps that was the sacrifice required: trading his reputation for Orion's.

She passed him the tea and the warm liquid seeping through the cup settled his thoughts and soothed his nerves. His mind began to work. She had information, she had a hypothesis, but she'd not yet tested it and she didn't have all the research she required to support it. He needed to remember that instead of allowing himself to jump to dire conclusions.

'How would you get a gentleman's accounts? That's very private information.' He hated himself for asking, knowing full well he was not asking honestly, but asking in order to plan his next move, to decide what he needed to do to protect Orion.

Should he need to.

Yes, he couldn't forget that most basic premise. A man was innocent until proven guilty. It was just that in Orion's case, he held out little hope of that. Innocence and Orion weren't the closest of companions.

'A warrant, of course. If the accounts are evidence for a proceeding, they can be acquired.' She took a bite of scone, a crumb lingering on her lips.

'But you'd have to prove that first. I can't imagine banks go turning over gentlemen's personal accounts on just anyone's request.' It might take her a while to get that approval. She'd have to win the argument that Orion's bank accounts mattered in order to have access to them. If her arguments weren't compelling, it would all be over before it began. A good barrister could surely punch enough holes to call her argument into question. It only had to be enough to deny the procurement of those accounts. There was hope in that.

But there was no honour. No ethic. It would be using the arbitrary nature of the courts and his own privilege to prevent an action that might lead to the truth. Or to scandal. There was already scandal enough to upset Orion. The longer this went on, perhaps the more validity it gained in the public eye, the more teeth it had, teeth like a saw blade that cut both ways. He'd not considered that.

He set his teacup aside. 'I think this is a dangerous game you play. If you are wrong, the newspaper could face charges of slander. I think it's been a good idea to scale back publicising this. I know there'd been several articles published in your papers before we met'—for it was thanks to them they *had* met—'but there hasn't been any lately and that is to the good until you are certain of the claims you're making.'

'The board of directors would not agree with you. Safe news isn't interesting. It doesn't sell newspapers,' she said sharply, some of her calm leaving her. This was apparently a sore subject.

'They certainly wouldn't welcome being sued for slander either.' He watched her carefully, a thought coming to him. 'Are you being pressured to pursue this?'

'No, I want to pursue this, but the board would like to pursue it more flagrantly despite the missing pieces.' She crumbled the remainder of her lemon scone on her plate. 'The story sells newspapers, especially up north where people are more concerned with the accident.'

He reached for a scone. 'Do you *need* to sell more newspapers?' This was an additional angle he'd not considered. Francis Bacon would call it a variable. This was not merely a question of his brother's waywardness colliding with Fleur Griffith's grief-driven search for justice as he'd originally thought.

'Quite a few more.' She gave a wry smile. 'It's really not a surprise, is it? There's a woman now at the helm of one of Britain's largest news syndicates and no one knows what to make of it. It's not normal. It raises questions of competence and capability. Subscriptions have declined. As a result, advertisers have pulled back, choosing to advertise elsewhere in other papers where they perceive there is a larger readership. It makes for a vicious cycle. The *London Tribune* needs to prove itself. I need to show everyone—readers, advertisers, the board of directors—that I am personally capable of delivering the kind of news the paper has always delivered.'

She leaned forward in earnest. 'If I can break this story about Lord Orion Bexley, I can do all of that. Additionally, the story will serve as a way to restore interest for our legislation on dam oversight.'

Jasper saw all that she imagined and more. She could vindicate herself and her husband's death in one fell swoop while getting the board of directors off her back. It was a potent vision and it was no wonder she was compelled by it. No doubt, she felt as if her whole world hung by this one thread.

Against his will, his heart went out to her. The indomitable Fleur Griffiths looked quite vulnerable at the moment, her hands clutched about her teacup, frustration vying for defiance in the green sparks of her eyes as she waited for his approval, *wanted* his approval.

Every manly attribute he'd been raised with to protect surged to the fore, urging him to take her in his arms, to offer her comfort, to offer assurances that everything would be all right. But such actions would ignore other aspects in their relationship—that she had used him for sex, made him a stand-in for her dead husband and he had not been entirely forthcoming with her about who he was.

These were not small things. Their relationship was established on the rockiest of foundations, assuming that what they had between them was a relationship at all. It ignored the pivotal reality that for things to be all right for her, things would not end well for him, and vice versa. For him to have the things he wanted— his brother's safety and the family name cleared of scandal—he would have to give up his fascination with Fleur Griffiths and his reputation for equality and reform.

'I see,' he said solemnly. Perhaps for the first time he did see. He saw the complexities of what it meant to be Fleur Griffiths. It was as complicated to be her as it was to be him. Too bad. He rather liked her, rough edges, silk gowns and all. She was unlike any woman he'd ever spent time with. He would have liked to have spent more time with her, but to what end? To what purpose but hurt? This afternoon had shown him how impossible that would be.

Soon, he would have to act on his brother's behalf and she would know who he was and what he'd kept from her. She'd think her suspicions were right, that he'd tried to seduce her to distract her. It would set her against him entirely. She had a newspaper to save and he had a family to protect. There was no option. He had to end this now.

He set aside his teacup and reached a hand to her cheek, cupping her jaw. He wanted to remember her like this—the way she looked at him *before* she hated him—her auburn hair parted and smooth, gathered in a chignon at the base of her neck, her face smiling back at him, a bit of coquetry lighting her eyes. Beautiful, intelligent. A one-of-a-kind woman but not the woman for him, unfortunately. He would go home and throw himself into protecting his brother, and wife hunting, letting the attention on him distract the *ton* from attention on his brother. But first, he'd have one last moment. He drew her close, taking her mouth in a sweet kiss that tasted of lemon and sugar to mark a short interlude that had come to an end.

Fleur knew a goodbye kiss when she saw it—metaphorically speaking. One didn't *see* a kiss as much as *felt* one. She'd definitely felt goodbye in Jasper's kiss.

The days that followed his departure had confirmed her gut instinct as she'd sat on the divan and let him walk out the door, intuitively knowing that he would not walk back through it.

She told herself it didn't matter. She had too much work at present between the Bexley story and arranging to sell a few of the smaller papers to devote time to cultivating a relationship or simply taking a lover. A lover required time as well, which was something she convinced herself she didn't have. But as the last weeks in May blended into early June, he was never far from her thoughts and those thoughts had questions.

He'd simply left. Why? Mixed messages abounded in answer. Their one night in the Harefield's garden had been explosive, both of them matching the other in need and ferocity. As lovers, they'd been a good fit. The kiss he'd given her that last afternoon had been tender, sincere. It was not the kiss of a man who *wanted* to leave. And yet he had. There'd been no note, no attempt to contact her, to explain.

Perhaps he thought she'd know the reasons he'd left. There was no future for them. Class stratification made it an unlikely pairing. A peer with a businesswoman, special emphasis on the woman. Her position was controversial within her own circles. It would be a scandal in itself among his ranks. Titled ladies didn't run newspapers, didn't hold down jobs that required they put in long hours away from home. But she wasn't looking to marry him.

Of course, he needed to marry and that added its own complications. She would not settle for being a married man's mistress. She would not be the wedge between another woman and that woman's husband. Neither did she think he was the sort of man who would have such an arrangement, although she knew many peers did. Such arrangements seemed sure pathways to disappointment and failure.

Perhaps he'd left because he'd realised the relationship was impossible not only romantically but practically. He'd not been comfortable with her case against Lord Orion Bexley. He'd been clear about that from the start and when she'd brought it up again that last afternoon, he'd not been enthusiastic. Her line of reasoning and proof should have excited someone who claimed to be interested in the dam situation.

To his credit, he'd listened as she'd requested. He'd asked pertinent questions and he'd pressed for explanations, but he'd not been imbued with the eagerness she'd hoped solid proof would engender from him. There were even points where she'd sensed he was horrified. At her? At her discoveries? It was hard to tell, further fuelling her suspicion that something was off.

He had softened though, at the end, when she'd shared the situation at the newspaper and how the Bexley story fit into her predicament. But he'd still walked out of her office as suddenly as he'd walked into her theatre box, without warning, without reason.

Fleur paced her office, looking down on to Fleet Street, home to many of London's great newspapers and publishers. It was early evening. Clerks were starting to go home, vendors were working hard to make a few final sales before the day was done. She wondered what Jasper was doing. Was he preparing for an evening out? Had he, perhaps, resigned himself to his fate? Would he spend the night waltzing with girls off his mother's list? Those broad shoulders and tousled hair would be wasted on a debutante. She'd been attending balls in order to carry on discussions and encourage interest in legislation. She spent a large part of those evenings looking over her shoulder hoping to see him. She had not.

Fleur turned from the window at the sound of a knock on her door. 'Mrs Griffiths, this has come in.' The clerk left a large envelope on her desk. In her experience, large envelopes were usually promising. She opened it and sat down to read. It was an offer for a couple of the smaller newspapers Cowden had recommended she sell up north. This was good. The board would be pleased to have such rapid results. It was a sign that their presses were coveted, valued. She looked at the offering price. Yes, definitely valued. The buyer was willing to pay the asking price. No negotiation involved. Was that cause for celebration or for alarm? Who didn't negotiate?

She knew the answer to that: someone who wanted something urgently, no questions asked. But she *would* ask questions. Mainly the question of who? Fleur scanned the document for the name of the party or parties involved, her gaze landing on the name at the bottom of the proposal: the Earl of Wincastle. She could not recall him from personal acquaintance. Perhaps he was an acquaintance of the Duke of Cowden's? How like him it would be to send a buyer in her direction. She glanced at the copy of *Debrett's* sitting on the bookshelf. This was one of those times when looking someone up would be necessary. She could not take this offer to the board of directors uninformed.

Fleur retrieved the tome from the shelf and set it on her desk, flipping to the section on earls and then towards the back to the 'W's.

'Wincastle… Wincastle,' she murmured, her finger running over the columns. There it was.

Wincastle, also a title currently held by the Marquess of Meltham.

Her gaze froze. Her mind raced. Wincastle was Meltham? She knew what this was, an attempt to silence the stories about Lord Orion Bexley, his brother. How convenient for him that he could do just that so close to home by purchasing those presses.

She very nearly did not check the cross-reference. It was enough to know that Wincastle was a guise for Meltham and that Meltham was her sworn enemy. It was nefarious enough, this idea that the Marquess would attempt to covertly silence her, but some inner voice urged her to do it, perhaps out of habit to leave no piece of information unclaimed.

Fleur found the listing for Meltham. It was large and contained a detailed family tree going back several generations. The Marquess of Meltham was a well-established title. Her finger scrolled down to the most recent limb of the tree.

David Harold Arthur Bexley, b. March 2nd, 1782, d. Aug. 19th, 1840. Married to Mathilda...

She hurried past that to their 'issue'. Two sons. Jasper Bexley and Orion Bexley. Jasper... Hmm... A somewhat uncommon name and now she'd encountered it twice in a short time. She read further.

Titles associated with the marquessate: Earl of Wincastle, Baron of Umberton.

She sat down hard on the desk chair, letting the shock sink in. *Jasper* was Umberton. And if Jasper was Umberton, he was also *Meltham*. The realisation of what that meant was stunning, overwhelming on so many levels. That made her lover, her confidant, a man whom she'd understood to be her ally her *enemy* because at the core of it all, he was Lord Orion Bexley's brother.

Common sense argued that it couldn't be otherwise. Brothers would support one another, like Adam and Keir and Garrett had supported one another, though they had been a brotherhood of businessmen, rather than blood relations. Cross one of them and you crossed all three. Hadn't Captain Moody warned her that morning in Newcastle that to tangle with Lord Orion Bexley was to tangle with the Marquess? That was to be expected. But she'd made a miscalculation. She'd also expected everyone would play fair, that the Marquess would approach her directly, that she would see him coming and, when he did, that it would be an approach through an open confrontation, *not* through stealth and seduction.

Oh. *Seduction.* Oh, God.

She moaned, recalling the Harefield ball. She cringed. Shuddered. In hindsight she'd been stupid and careless in her loneliness. She'd slept with him. Well, sort of. A romp against a fence wall didn't necessarily constitute 'sleeping'. He'd been eager to accommodate. Now she understood why. It was a first step towards working his way into her confidence, the first step in binding them together.

And it had worked. She *liked* him. He was handsome and intelligent and intuitive. As a result, she'd been attracted to him and she'd trusted him with her body, with her secrets. She hadn't talked to anyone in depth about what she knew about Lord Orion Bexley, preferring to keep her own counsel. But with Jasper, she'd laid it all out voluntarily. What a fool she'd been!

Now she knew why he'd left. He'd had no reason to

stay. He'd got what he came for. Was he even now laughing at her? Thinking what a prank he'd pulled? Flirt with a lonely widow, listen to her stories, give her a little fun against a fence and she'll tell you anything? Had he taken her information and bolstered his defences so that she'd never get past them? Never get to his brother as Captain Moody had predicted?

Recriminations came hard and fast. Somehow, she *ought* to have known. If it had just been the sex, she might not feel so badly. But it was everything that was attached to it. It hadn't *just* been sex. Beneath the self-recrimination simmered another logic. She might have trusted too soon. But he had betrayed. And betrayal was a far bigger crime than trusting. One ought to be able to trust by default. People ought to be honest as a basic, expected practice. That he'd not been spoke more poorly of him than it did of her.

Later, when her anger had passed, she'd take solace in that. This was the very crime she'd railed at Adam's ghost for. He'd betrayed her, too.

Fury simmered. Her words had no effect. Adam was not here to be scolded. But Jasper was and she would *not* tolerate *his* betrayal. Not when she was so close to justice. Not when she had so much personally on the line—all of which she'd sat here in this very room and outlined for him as if he were a trusted friend. She stood up and grabbed her coat. At least now she knew where to find him: Meltham House on Portland Square. There was going to be a reckoning. No one played Fleur Griffiths for a fool and got away with it.

Chapter Twelve

There needed to be a reckoning. Orion *had* to account for his time on the Bilberry Dam commission, yet, despite knowing how desperately that accounting was needed, Jasper was loath to have the conversation. It was why he hadn't gone straight to Orion's favourite club off St James's and dragged him out immediately after he'd left Fleur's office for the last time.

That reckoning was also why he'd decided to leave Fleur. This was war, this was shame. Neither were conditions upon which a relationship could be built. How could he face her if she was right? That was the shame—that he'd been ignorant of his brother's role in the dam's demise. And if she was wrong, there would be shame on her side, too, or resentment. The scandal would always be between them as a competition one of them had lost.

He hoped it would not be him. He was the Marquess. He was supposed to protect his family and his people. But people had died and possibly because of a position he'd put his brother in by arranging for a spot on the commission. Beyond the shame of what he perceived as his own culpability, how could he possibly consort with the enemy? Whether she was right or wrong, he had an obligation to protect his brother and by extension the family. But as much as he didn't want her to be right, he also didn't want her to be wrong. She had much at stake and he appreciated how difficult her position was.

In the weeks since he'd left her, he'd done what he could for both Fleur and for Orion. He'd had his solicitors prepare an offer for the northern newspapers in an attempt to mitigate publicising the suspicions being raised against Orion. It would help them both; she needed the sale, and he needed the silence.

However, in the interim, Orion had slipped through his fingers. His brother was gone, leaving only a note that said he was lying low until the scandal blew over. Which meant Orion was avoiding not only the scandal, but also him and the reckoning. That was concerning. Jasper felt compelled to see his brother's action as a sign that Orion had something to hide, something he did not want to confess any more than Jasper wanted to hear that confession. Once he knew, he'd have to act one way or the other. But what kind of action could he justify? Baconian logic was of no help here.

He scanned the shelves of Meltham House's well-stocked library until he found what he was looking for, his worn copy of Bentham's collected works. It was easy to spot with its faded red cover amid the sleek, smooth spines of lesser read books. Perhaps he'd find comfort in the familiar pages outlining utilitarianism as a political moral compass. If not comfort, perhaps direction, a prompt for what he ought to do when the reckoning came not only for Orion, but himself as well. He did not delude himself in thinking the scandal would not touch them all if it picked up enough momentum.

Jasper poured himself a brandy and settled in his favourite chair beside the empty fire. He took a moment to appreciate the quiet of the house. It seemed he hadn't had quiet for days between putting together the offer to buy the papers and evenings out escorting his mother to balls, sometimes two or three a night. But tonight, he'd been firm. He was staying in. No balls, no visits to his clubs to talk politics. Tonight was for him, to settle his thoughts and perhaps to come to grips with them.

He was halfway through his glass of brandy and Chapter One when the commotion reached him. He sighed. Perhaps an evening of peace and quiet had been too much to hope for. He set aside his book, listening to the brisk clack of heels and the rustle of skirts in the corridor. If his mother thought to cajole him into going out, she was going to be disappointed.

Strident tones sounded in the hallway. 'I will not be kept waiting so that you can come back with an excuse as to why he will not receive me.' *That* was not his mother. That was… Fleur. His reckoning was *here* in Meltham House. Which meant… She knew *everything*. Umberton. Wincastle. Meltham. He had nowhere left to shelter. Like the old elk of his childhood, he was flushed into the open.

He barely had time to rise and brace for battle before Fleur Griffiths blew into the library, disrupting his calm with the force of a spring storm. 'You are a bastard of the first order!' Her eyes blazed with green fire as she made the accusation.

His butler stumbled in her wake. 'My lord, I am sorry. I asked her to wait.'

Jasper waved a hand. 'It's all right, Phillips. I will see her.' He would face his reckoning like a man. It's what he deserved, but he would also face her with the hope that from argument arises a new truth. That was what Aristotle believed anyway. He wasn't sure Fleur Griffiths shared those beliefs. The higher truth was that, despite their differences, they needed each other in order to get to the bottom of this business with Orion. Tonight would test that hypothesis.

Phillips left them and Jasper took a moment before speaking to drink her in: the flashing eyes, the flush of her cheeks, the heave of her breasts, her breath coming fast in her anger. She wore a plain blue skirt and a high-necked white blouse trimmed in lace, her hair done in her usual sensible chignon. She'd come straight from work. His offer must have arrived and all else had un-ravelled from there. It had always been a risk. Perhaps he'd wanted her to find out, wanted to end the pretence between them.

'Please, come and sit and you can tell me why I'm a bastard.' He used his coolness to calm her storm. He'd learned many things about her during their short time together. One of them was that she liked to fight, liked the heat of argument. Undermining that heat was his best chance of having a logical conversation with her.

'I prefer to stand,' she snapped, taking up a position near the sideboard with the decanters, dangerously near breakable items. He hoped it wouldn't come to that. He resumed his seat, wanting to juxtapose his outer calm with her obvious turmoil. In truth, he had his own turmoil to contend with. In spite of their contentious circumstances, she was the loveliest woman he'd ever seen. His body roused to her anger as much as it had roused to her passion. Challenge was a heady aphrodisiac to a man with power.

'This is not a social call, Lord Meltham.' She nearly growled when she said his title.

'I did not think it was. You are angry because you feel lied to.' Validating anger often took away the fuel for that anger. Fleur's anger thrived on opposition. Just as fire thrived on oxygen. He would take her anger's oxygen from her.

Her eyes blazed. 'Don't do that. Do *not* pander to me by explaining my anger to me. I know damn well why I am mad. You misrepresented yourself in order to inveigle yourself into my good graces.' He didn't usually hold with women using profanity, but it was *damned* sexy on her. It stirred him, made him want to get up from his chair and fight fire with fire. He held on to his composure a little longer. Perhaps she was counting on that. Perhaps she was trying to melt his ice even as he tried to cool her heat.

'I *am* Lord Umberton. I did not lie about my identity. I will own that it is not my highest-ranking title. But it's right there in *Debrett's* for anyone to find. You could have looked it up.'

Her eyes narrowed. 'That's ironic advice from a man who claims he wants to be known for himself. *Now*, you want your titles to speak for you. As it happens, I prefer to let people prove themselves. I did not look you up because I wanted to form my own impressions.'

'You liked those impressions. You liked the man you

saw,' he reminded her, even as his body reminded him that he liked her, too, differences aside.

'I did,' she confessed bluntly. 'My instincts are not usually so wrong.'

There was condemnation in her eyes. Not all of it was for him. There was plenty for her as well. She blamed him for misleading her, but she also blamed herself for being taken in and he hated that. He also disliked, that she saw this as a personal failure at a time when she shouldered so many other burdens. He had inadvertently added to those burdens and he'd put a chink in the armour of her confidence when she could not afford it. That was not an intended consequence. He wished he could erase that. Since he could not, he could perhaps explain it.

'I am all those things. I *am* interested in dam legislation. I *am* interested in preventing accidents like the Bilberry Dam in the future. I am also interested in you—just you—although I am not sure how we separate that interest from our circumstances.' He softened his tone and allowed himself the luxury of letting his eyes rest on her. 'Nothing I did with you, nothing I *felt* about being with you, was a lie.' Those few days were some of the most vibrant he could recall in recent history.

'That does not change the fact that you betrayed me!' Fleur railed. His attempt to steal the fuel for her fire was failing. 'You used how I felt about you, you manipulated my trust and then—' she reached for one of the crystal tumblers next to the decanters '—you broke it!' Glass shattered against the hardwood floor. Her eyes blazed.

'Fleur!' He was out of his seat, but she was faster. She grabbed another tumbler and smashed it.

'How do you like that? How does it feel to have something broken?' she raged, smashing another. 'You lied to me, you had sex with me, you pretended to care about me! You are a cad of the highest order. You betrayed me on all levels.'

The hell he had. His self-control was gone now. He gripped her by the forearms, wresting the last tumbler from her and dancing her back to the wall, out of reach of shattered glass and things that could be converted into shattered glass. 'Stop it, Fleur!'

'You didn't betray me?'

'Be fair, you betrayed me that night at Harefield's,' he growled. '*You* used *me*, *you* pretended I was Adam.' The gloves were off now. 'No man likes being a stand-in for a dead husband.'

'Maybe I did use you,' she sneered. 'It doesn't mean I deserved to have you lie to me.'

They were pressed against one another, his body trapping her, keeping her from the rest of his glassware, their chests heaving with the exertion of their anger.

He seized her mouth in a hard, bruising kiss, to stop her words, to stop the anger, to make a different argument, to prove to her…something. He shouldn't have done it, but he wasn't thinking clearly.

She bit down hard on his lip. 'Ouch!' He drew back, wiping his hand across his mouth and coming away with blood. 'What the hell?'

'What the hell is right! How *dare* you kiss me, when you know damn well what it's like with us, how we spark, how we burn and look what that's got us!' She pushed him and stepped around him. It had got him a virago in his arms and a shattered crystal tumbler set on the floor. 'There are weighty considerations between us that we cannot shove aside or solve with a kiss. There is the issue of *your* duplicity and there is the issue of your *brother's* culpability.'

No, she didn't get to do that. The issues of fault weren't entirely all his. 'Don't forget there is also the issue of your newspaper's marketability and your voracious tenacity for justice, which may be misplaced,' he said quietly, his own calm reasserting itself. 'Not all of the issues are on my side of the equation.' She could have her anger, but he wanted to make sure she understood it accurately, truthfully.

He gestured to the chairs beside the cold fire. 'Will you come and sit now and sort through it all with me, see what can be salvaged?' He picked up the last remaining tumbler and poured her a drink to match the one he'd left beside his chair.

She scowled, but she took a seat and the drink. If it wasn't exactly peace it was at least *détente*. They sat in silence for a short while, each one assessing, measuring the other. He braved the silence. 'Have you thought about why I would introduce myself as Umberton?'

She slid him a disapproving look. 'To get close to me, to earn my trust so that I might share with you what I have on your brother. You would be able to thwart me. Perhaps even try to talk me out of it with arguments about doing what was right, about considering the consequences and the purity of my own motives even while you sat there knowing full well the impurity of *your* own motives. You did not seek to guide me with good counsel, but to protect your brother.'

That last stung. She was referring to the arguments

he'd made at Verrey's and she wasn't entirely wrong. He'd made those arguments in the hopes of forestalling more articles naming Orion as the guilty party as much as he'd made them out of common sense. 'They were and are still valid arguments,' he said.

'Arguments that you have vested interest in and you hid that,' she replied.

'Careful, Fleur. Can you say *you* have no vested interest in pushing this story, this investigation out into the public?' he queried.

'I am doing it honestly. I am not hiding behind any pretence. I am not fabricating evidence to fit my own needs. If your brother is innocent, I'll admit that. At least I will have got to the bottom of it. Either way there will be closure for myself and for others who lost loved ones and are still searching for some reason, some understanding behind it,' Fleur said earnestly.

'Even if the board of directors would prefer another outcome?' Jasper nudged the argument a little further along. She might believe she was merely on a quest for the truth, but sometimes the truth didn't sell newspapers.

'Of course,' she snapped. 'I am insulted that you would think otherwise.'

'Just as I am insulted you would think me a charlatan,' he scolded. 'Have you stopped to think how you would have responded if I'd entered your box that night at the theatre and announced myself as the Marquess of Meltham? Would you have listened to me? Would you have allowed me to meet with you at your offices? Would you have shared your information with me? Or allowed me to help with the dam legislation?'

He studied her profile as he waited for an answer, watching the first hint of a smile curve her cheek as she stared into the empty fireplace. In those moments he wished it were autumn so that they might have reason to sit beside a warm fire together. It was a potent domestic fantasy he needed to handle with care.

'You know I would not have,' she admitted.

'Correct, because you were at war with Meltham. But you were not at war with Umberton. He had a clean slate, from which real discussion took place. Is it any mystery I took that option?' He leaned towards her. 'Are we not the better for it? Instead of sworn enemies, we are now friends who can decide how they want to handle these circumstances.' At least that was what he hoped.

For once in her life, Fleur didn't know what to say or even to think. She ought to find the suggestion that they were friends ludicrous in the extreme. It was an extraordinary idea, one that was matched only by the extraordinary circumstances she found herself in— sitting in the Marquess of Meltham's library rationally discussing his brother's culpability in her husband's death.

This was not the encounter she'd expected when she'd stormed out of the office and into his town house. She'd expected a fight, expected to throw things—hot words, a glass or two, to give full vent to her spleen, to her sense of betrayal. And she had. But as a result, she'd expected to be bodily removed from the town house. She would have written about that and painted Jasper Bexley, Marquess of Meltham, with the blackest of brushes, an obstructor of justice, a man who was above the law, who threw his title around to protect a guilty brother.

Instead, he'd asked her to sit, to voice her grievances and he'd answered them, explaining his perspective while holding himself and her accountable. It definitely had her off-kilter but not so far off that she'd forgotten what she'd came for.

'I will not let it be that easy.' She gave him a strong stare, although it was difficult to look at him and not see Umberton, not see her lover, a man she'd trusted with her body and her mind. 'You cannot justify your deception because you feel the consequences were worthy. One cannot say bad behaviour is suddenly good because something good came from it.'

She'd had enough of men making that argument. Adam had kept the state of the newspaper from her, no doubt thinking to protect her from worry. And now, Jasper Bexley had deceived her, too. 'Besides,' she added, 'you did not deceive me with the intent of friendship in mind. That was an accident.'

'A *happy* accident,' he countered. 'As I said, we get to decide how we go on. What shall it be, Fleur? Shall we go forward with forgiveness and friendship or with fear and mistrust?' There was no true 'we' about it. He was leaving the decision up to her and she thought it rather unfair that he made it her responsibility to end things when he'd been the one to walk out.

'There is no decision because there are no choices.' Which was probably for the best. The way he was looking at her now, those eyes of his steady on her, his interest, his want, naked in them, there for her to see, made her wish it could be otherwise. But 'otherwise' was not practical. 'The issues between us are too large, they divide us too thoroughly. And even if they didn't, our association would undermine our individual credibility.' Even without the issue of his brother between them, she knew better than to think they could be friends.

He took a swallow from his glass for the first time since she'd sat down. 'I think I'll need you to explain all of that to me. You must excuse my denseness. I'm not a man used to being without options.' He was half teasing, half serious.

'You will be inclined to protect your brother. I can understand that even if I can't support it. On the other hand, I cannot let the truth go unpublished for the sake of...' She groped for the words. She'd been about to say for the sake of a lover. 'For the sake of someone I care for. I cannot be driven by my emotions, or the truth becomes subjective.'

She sighed. 'The chasm is too wide. Either I will be right, or you will be right. Either way, there will be consequences. Which leads me to your idea of friendship. I do not think friendship can survive such pressures. Aside from that, us associating together—the Marquess of Meltham, brother of the maligned Lord Orion Bexley, and the widow of a prominent man killed at the dam Lord Orion Bexley oversaw, will not build credibility for legislation. People will suspect a conflict of interest and neither of us will look well. Perhaps me most of all, since it impacts my ability to be taken seriously at the newspaper.'

Especially if they were found to be friends and Lord Orion Bexley turned out to be innocent. People would wonder what had driven that conclusion and if she'd arrived at it honestly or if it had been kissed out of her. It was a double standard that one always asked such things of a woman, but never asked them of a man.

He nodded, his hand cradling his glass. 'A man you care for? I am honoured by the description. It gives me hope,' he said in a soft tenor. 'I care for you, too, Fleur, despite our differences.' He reached for her hand and the warmth of his touch sent a delicious shudder through her as he lifted her hand to his lips, his eyes intent on her.

'I must disagree with you, though. This difference needn't keep us apart as I once thought. The day I left you in the office, I meant that kiss to be goodbye. I thought there was no way through it. But that's not true. Lately, I've come to believe that we need each other to see this done. Where you see a chasm I see commonality, something that brings us together instead of setting us apart. We are both searching for the truth about my brother's involvement in the dam accident. We both claim honest intentions to see right done, whatever the outcome. Why not work together?'

He gave a small sigh and she saw how much the proposal cost him. Despite his usual confidence there was worry she might refuse. It was a refusal he would take personally.

'If Orion is guilty, I want to make reparations. I want to see that the families are taken of. It can never bring loved ones back, but it can bring practical ease, a way for them to move forward.' His brow furrowed and she felt his grip on her hand tighten. 'Discovering the truth scares me, Fleur. Part of me doesn't want to know.

'For the past year, I've not questioned the original report's verdict that this was a comedy of errors, all conspiring to create the circumstances of the accident. But you've shown me it could be different, that one man could be at fault. Now that I know that's a possibility, I can't ignore it. If I did ignore it at this point, I'd be guilty, too. I could not live with my conscience. Although, I hope it doesn't come to that. It's a damnably awkward position to be in to choose what is right—protecting one's family or protecting the truth.'

She nodded. She felt for him, she really did. His stance on the issue was admirable in the extreme. Not all people would face such a dilemma head on with such integrity. She found that integrity appealing. Adam had been such a man, always standing up for what was right, standing up in print for those who couldn't stand up for themselves even when it was unpopular with those who funded newspapers.

There was no doubting the sincerity of Jasper's confession or her response to it. She wanted to believe him, wanted to join forces with him. His argument was persuasive. It made sense that they work together. Too much sense. She should not accept it at face value.

When an answer sounded too good to be true, it probably deserved more consideration. Was working together simply the 'easy' answer? The answer that allowed them to pursue not only the truth of Orion's involvement, but also the chance to explore the truth of their personal attraction? More time together meant they could continue what they'd started in Harefield's garden.

That posed its own delight and its own danger. To continue their affair would personalise the context of their interaction—there was the risk of emotions and growing attachment forming, emotions that could potentially colour their quest. She could get hurt if that was the case. Jasper was a hard man not to like with his integrity, sincerity and tousled good looks.

Was he counting on that? The woman in her who fully understood how the world worked was wide awake now. Did he think to use her emotions against her if Lord Orion was as guilty as she thought he was? Did he think she would give up her quest for him?

'I want to be clear. I will print what I find, feelings for you notwithstanding.' Best to air that right now before things went further even if it meant 'things' didn't go further. After all, a man who manipulated a woman with sex was a man for whom integrity was merely a façade. *That* was not the man for her. That was not her idea of working together. It still stung that Adam had not told her about the debt. That had been a betrayal of their partnership. She would not set herself up for another betrayal.

Anger flickered in Jasper's eyes. She'd attacked the bastion of his honour. But she had to know. 'Do you think that is the sort of man I am? To use a woman for sex? To manipulate a person's feelings for personal gain?' There was no denying that he'd been honestly engaged in Harefield's garden, present in their pleasure body and mind as far it went, while she had not. She didn't like the idea that she'd dealt him some hurt that evening, even if unintentional.

'Can you blame me for thinking it when you've offered to buy the northern newspapers? If you were looking to protect your brother, it's not a bad strategy. Buying them ensures stories of your brother's perfidy won't be printed. The populace may never hear of it.

Then, seducing the head of the *London Tribune* could be a means by which to silence the printing of her findings in the largest city in England. Out of devotion to you, perhaps you think she'd forgo the story,' Fleur described the scheme bluntly.

'You do know how to wound a man, Fleur. It's a plausible plan except for one thing: the head of the *London Tribune* would never allow herself to be swayed by such sentiment.' He favoured her with a smile that warmed and complimented. 'I am as sure of that as I am of the sun rising in the east tomorrow. I know such a strategy would never work with you. Integrity will be the saving of us, both yours and mine.'

'And trust,' Fleur added. 'We're trusting each other to know our boundaries, to know the cost of the kind of relationship we want to pursue, to accept limitations, and most of all, to keep our promises when circumstances might tempt us to rethink them.' There was no might about it. Circumstances would evolve that would put that temptation right in front of them. 'So, I ask you again. If not to protect your brother, why did you offer to buy the northern newspapers?' There was no time like the present to test their promises of integrity and trust. This partnership might be over before it began.

Chapter Thirteen

Fleur wanted to stop time. She didn't want to hear his answer. Earlier he'd said he was frightened of the truth and what it might force him to face. He was not alone. She was scared of the truth, too. She didn't want to believe this tawny-eyed man, who could heat her blood with a touch, was guilty of deliberate censorship, that he would seek to buy out her newspapers in order to protect his brother. She sat on the edge of her chair, braced to face one more betrayal.

'I wanted to help you.' She'd not expected that. For a moment she was speechless in his presence, yet again. When she said nothing, he gave an elegant shrug of his shoulders. 'You were selling the papers anyway. I thought a quick sale would be helpful to you, to show the board of directors the papers had value.'

She nodded. She'd initially thought the same thing. 'But you if owned the papers, you could also choose to not print any news about the investigation.' She voiced the concern with a certain amount of tentativeness. Here was another answer she didn't want to hear.

He answered slowly, thoughtfully. 'I could and, to be honest, I would probably not print any stories that continued to make my brother appear to be the lone villain until the links were ironclad. I know you would find that disappointing. However, if he were indeed guilty of taking money and not making the repairs, I would not stop the story from running. In my mind, *that* would be undue and intentional censorship.' She felt she could breathe again. It might not be the way she would do things, but it was a tenable compromise, one that was honest and fair.

'Thank you. I appreciate your candour. But I must offer some candour of my own. I do not know how open the board of directors will be to an offer from Meltham, given the…um…circumstances with your brother.' Perhaps that had been another guiding reason for him offering as Wincastle. Now that she had time to think, it was possible that choice hadn't been all about tricking her. He'd been trying to help her as best he could.

'Well, I tried.' He gave a wry smile before sobering. 'He's gone, you know. Orion left a note saying town was too hot for him at the moment.'

That was news. Not that it mattered if he was in town or not. The stories could run with or without him. But she could see his brother's absence bothered Jasper. 'I suppose you blame me for that.'

He gave a short nod. 'I do. The stories in the *Tribune* have called him out as a prime suspect in the "new" investigation the *Tribune* is single-handedly running. It's called enough attention to him that he feels it is difficult to go about in society.' He shook his head. 'He can't go home to Meltham because the story has run in your regional papers up there and it's called him out in front of our people. I don't know where he's gone. I hope he'll resurface. He left before I could talk with him.'

Fleur slipped her hand from his grasp. 'I'm sorry.' She sincerely was. Sorry that he was hurting. Sorry that his brother was gone. Sorry that she was part of it. Through her choices, she'd hurt him, this man she cared for.

He fixed her with a firm stare. 'I did not tell you so that you'd be sorry. I told you so that you would be aware. Your quest has real, concrete consequences, not just for a single individual, or for yourself, but consequences that will spread like ripples on a pond. When you act, you are not choosing those consequences just for yourself, but also for others.'

There was much left unsaid there—that she would be choosing for him. Choosing for his mother. Choosing for Lord Orion. Choosing for all the families affected by the accident. Lord Orion Bexley's leaving was a tangible consequence, no doubt, the first of many that she would be responsible for.

She gave him a solemn nod. 'This quest is indeed dangerous for both of our reputations. I admit that I've printed a story that has caused your brother to flee the town to escape social persecution. But you must also admit that fleeing certainly lends itself to believing he has something to hide, that he is indeed guilty.'

She was silent for a while, letting them both digest that. Neither side of that coin was particularly pleasant for either of them to contemplate.

'You may have the right of it. With so much at stake, this is best undertaken together.' At least for as long as an alliance could last. She did not delude herself in thinking that it would be an indefinite association. If his brother was guilty, Jasper's loyalty would be sorely tested no matter what he said tonight. How would he truly feel when that moment came? Would his integrity and trust withstand that test? It was an enormous leap of faith for her.

'I think to undertake our investigation, we must leave the city,' Jasper said.

She gave him a questioning look. 'What are you suggesting?'

'I am suggesting we go back to the scene of the accident. What we really need to find, we'll find there or not at all. My family seat is not far from Holmfirth. Tomorrow, we leave for Meltham.'

Another woman would have baulked at such a speedy departure for what might appear to be a spontaneous trip to the country in the midst of the Season. But not Fleur. She spent the night packing, writing out instructions for the paper, rescheduling meetings and sending notes of regret cancelling her attendance at a few upcoming events. This trip pre-empted all else because it decided all else. This trip was not as much a spontaneous occurrence as it was an inevitable one. The events of the past year had been leading up to this. This was the way forward.

Fleur closed her travelling trunk shortly after one in the morning, letting the enormity of the trip overwhelm her at last. When she came back from Meltham, it would all be over, the search for justice settled. She was both excited and terrified by the prospect. To have closure, to know for sure, would be a blessing and it ought to bring peace, but she wondered if it would. It couldn't bring Adam back; it couldn't resolve the differences their marriage had ended on. It could not absolve her of the guilt she carried. But it could help the paper, it could solidify her position and her ability to hold on to Adam's empire.

She had slept very little that night, her thoughts in turmoil. She rose early and dressed in a blue travelling ensemble that she liked for its simplicity, then left the house. Better to do her waiting at the station than roaming the house and checking the clock every two minutes. This way she could feel as if she was doing something.

Alone at the station, she had another set of nerves to contend with. She could not ignore the other facet of this trip. She was going away with Jasper. Not the Marquis of Meltham, or Lord Umberton, but with *Jasper*. A man whose touch made her tremble, whose gaze made her warm, made her feel seen. A man who had kissed her, made wild love to her and danced with her beneath the moonlight. A man who made her feel alive, even though he was poised on the opposite side of the business between them.

How might that play out? He'd said they were friends last night. Was that all there was for them? Whatever there could be between them would always be short term, but Meltham offered a certain freedom to explore that potential, away from society's eyes. Away from his mother's list of debutantes, away from politicos and a prickly board of directors who might find their association a conflict of interests.

She caught sight of his tall, broad-shouldered form

cutting through the crowd coming towards her, her pulse quickening at the sight of him in his buff trousers and blue coat. She rather wished her pulse wouldn't do that. It made her mind ask difficult questions like what would happen if they were just Jasper and Fleur, if they could just be themselves? Was that even possible? Or was the business between them too much?

'You're early. I am impressed.' Jasper smiled, his gaze lingering on her longer than needed, and the conversation lagged into an uncomfortable silence. Perhaps he, too, was nervous. What had seemed like a straightforward idea in the quiet of the evening suddenly seemed more complicated by daylight. Or perhaps, like her, it was simply nerves born of their unsettling attraction to one another. He recovered first. 'Are you ready for our adventure? Our train is over here.'

He dropped a hand to the small of her back and ushered her towards the London Northwestern Railway locomotive, already huffing on the track. They let talk of the journey's details fill the empty space and ease the way. 'I have a first-class compartment reserved for us. We might as well enjoy some luxury while we can. I've arranged for breakfast to be served privately.'

She smiled. 'You're spoiling me. Should I be concerned?'

He laughed. 'We'll see if you feel that way at the end of the day. Not all of our trains will be this comfortable.' They'd take this train to Leeds and then a train to Huddersfield. From there it would be a carriage ride to the seat of the marquessate at Rosefields. 'It will be a long day.' He handed her up the steps into the train car, allowing her to precede him down the narrow aisle leading to their compartment, each gesture making her acutely aware of him, of his closeness, of his consideration even though she could very well be the enemy before this was through.

'I don't mind.' She laughed over her shoulder, catching his gaze. 'It is still a marvel to me that we will be in the west Yorkshire Dales tonight when it would have taken three or four days to make the journey by coach just a few years ago.'

'We're right here.' He gestured to the coupe compartment at the far end of the train car. 'The compartment seats three, but I bought the third ticket so that we needn't worry about any intrusions. Ah, look, our breakfast basket has already arrived. Thank goodness, I'm famished.'

She was famished, too, Fleur realised as their day progressed. Famished not for food, but for care. She secretly revelled in the little comforts he'd arranged because *she'd* not had to do the arranging. Along with that secret came another one: part of her liked being cared for, looked after, having someone else to share the burden for once. Not all the decisions had to be hers alone.

She'd had that with Adam. Mostly. At least she'd thought she had. They'd made decisions about which charities to support, which stories to run, which direction to take the newspapers. Of course, she knew now that it hadn't been perfect. Decisions about the debt had not included her. And when it had come to the biggest decision in their marriage, the decision to have a family, Adam alone had made the choice.

With Jasper she would be certain to ensure this was a true sharing of responsibility. She was well aware that control was hard for both of them to surrender. Until last night, Jasper had controlled when they would meet by withholding an address. But she'd paid for lunch. These were small things, but they did hint at the larger need. They were both establishing their boundaries, protecting themselves. And yet the thought tickled: wouldn't it be wonderful if instead of protecting themselves, they could protect each other. She feared circumstances made that an impossibility, a reminder that even this partnership had limitations.

'Fleur, Fleur, wake up, we're nearly there.' A gentle shake roused her as a soft early evening light bathed the interior of the coach. Sweet heavens, she'd fallen asleep. Jasper shifted on the seat beside her and she realised where she'd slept. On the ledge of his broad shoulder, or from the looks of his once perfectly pressed coat, against his chest in that space where shoulder meets torso. She put a quick hand to her face, hoping she hadn't drooled. It was bad enough she'd fallen asleep on him.

'I'm sorry, I didn't mean to…' She stifled a yawn. 'The late night apparently caught up to me,' she apologised.

He gave a soft smile. 'I didn't mind. Although I was worried it might have been my company that had sent you off into the arms of Morpheus.'

'Not at all,' she assured him truthfully. He'd been an excellent travelling companion today, full of interesting small talk about the countryside they were passing. By tacit agreement, they'd discussed nothing too meaningful, or too personal that would lead them back to their business. Yet talking with him had still been enjoyable.

It was no wonder he was one of the most sought-after bachelors this Season. He knew how to put a person at ease, how to engage them even on the most mundane of topics.

He leaned forward to look out the window, then turned to her with a smile that spoke volumes. 'We're coming down the drive now. You can see the house.' There was pride in his voice, she noted, and relief, too. He *liked* it here. Rosefields was not just the seat of the marquessate it was also a homecoming for him.

And he'd invited her here, into his world.

Fleur's hands clenched in her lap as she took in the sandstone façade of the house. The realisation was a bit overwhelming given that it might shortly become the site in which a horrible truth was revealed. How might that taint his associations with the place? 'It's very beautiful,' she acknowledged.

'I'll give you the tour after supper if you'd like. I thought we'd dine on the terrace and enjoy the spring evening.' He paused, reconsidering. 'Unless you are too tired?'

'Not at all. It would be good to stretch my legs. I am not used to so much sitting.' Or so much comfort, so much spoiling. Was that what he was counting on? They'd sworn to be friends, to be on the same side, but he'd deceived her once. She would be foolish not to think about this from a strategic point of view.

Were today's comforts meant to lull her into complacency? Was being here at Rosefields meant as an attempt to soften her desire to pursue his brother? Was their very attraction to each other meant to also be a tool by which her mettle was undone? She didn't want to think of it that way, but she must. Her station in life required it. A woman alone must always be on her guard. Even at the paper she wasn't safe. The board of directors were always looking to question her decisions.

The carriage came to a halt and the step was set. Jasper jumped out first and handed her down, his grip on her fingers warm and sure, yet a cold, warning trill went down her spine as she looked up at the majestic façade of the house. What had she walked into?

She was on the Marquess's ground now and she was alone.

Chapter Fourteen

This felt *right*. Whenever Jasper had imagined bringing Fleur to Rosefields, it had been just like this: walking with her through the grounds at sunset, the June evening wreathed in the violet and pink remnants of long mid-summer daylight, the famed white roses in full bloom, their scent wafting on the air of the garden.

'The roses are legendary. They date back to the Plantagenets,' he told her as they walked.

'The white rose of York?' She smiled.

'Yes, exactly so. Meltham sided with the House of York. It was in the early days of our title, so I am told. The white roses also symbolise purity and innocence.'

He stopped and plucked a rose from its stem to ensure there were no thorns. 'May I?' He tucked the bloom behind her ear, securing it in the depths of her auburn tresses. She'd changed into a pink gown for supper and the colour looked extraordinary with her hair. 'I didn't think redheads wore pink.' He gave the bloom a last adjustment.

'We can if we're brave enough and our dressmakers are smart enough,' she replied with a laugh. 'I have a gown in a blush pink, too. It's one of my favourite colours to wear. This is the first time I've actually worn this one. I'd bought it before...' Her voice trailed off. They both knew what before signified. 'And then it wasn't exactly something I could wear last year.'

No, he didn't imagine this bright, pure pink would have been appropriate during mourning. He was touched that she'd worn it for him. He was the only man to see her in it. This dress was his alone, something that didn't belong to Dead Adam. 'You match the sunset,' he complimented.

The comment obviously discomfited her a bit, this usually confident woman who always had something to say. Perhaps she was rusty at receiving them, another sign that she'd been alone too long. She quickly recovered, a teasing flare in her green eyes. 'By matching the sunset, surely you mean stunning, fiery, blazing.'

He shook his head and covered her hand where it lay on his arm. She was trying to downplay the compliment and by doing so the sentiment that went with it. 'Those adjectives describe the sun. I am talking about the *sunset*: calm, quiet, serene. You can be those things, too, Fleur. You needn't be fiery all the time.'

'Needn't I? I beg to differ. I think I would be eaten alive.'

'So *you* must be the fire? The consumer?' He gave her a thoughtful look. 'I feel that way, too, when I'm in London. I must protect the family, even myself. There is always business to take care of. I must always be on guard. Everybody wants something from me: money, time, patronage, an introduction, an acknowledgment. But not here. When I'm at Rosefields I am entirely myself. Certainly, there is work. Managing land and people always requires work, but there is also time to be me, to be quiet and still, to lay down my guard and rest.' He gave her a long look. 'I want Rosefields to be that for you as well while you're here.' There was a shadow in her eyes that confused him. Had he not been sincere? Had he not just laid the best gift he could conjure at her feet in a token of his goodwill?

'It is an impossibility, Jasper. Here is the place where I can lay down my guard the least. This is your ground. Not an inch of it is mine. In London there was at least some parity, some neutrality.' Restaurants and ballrooms were neutral territory. Theatre boxes and ballrooms were public. Homes were not.

'Do we need that neutrality?' he asked quietly in the gathering darkness. She did not trust his overture and it stung because it meant that she'd agreed to their alliance last night even though she hadn't fully believed him, trusted him. 'You are safe with me.'

She gave him a long, searching stare. 'But I shouldn't be. You have much to lose and yet you've brought me to your sanctuary.'

Jasper sensed she meant the words to put him off, to remind him of their circumstances. Fleur loved to fight. It was her protection. But the words did not rouse argument within him, only sorrow. This past year had done more damage to this woman than she knew. It was not only grief she carried with her, but suspicion and mistrust of everything and everyone in her world. Was there truly no one she could turn to?

He knew that feeling. A marquess must, by the nature of his position, be somewhat alone. *He* was alone except for his brother, a few close friends and his mother.

Despite her ceaseless matchmaking, his mother was a bellwether for him, a compass. And he had Orion. He relied on them both. Who did Fleur have? Her husband was dead. Her best friends had remarried and left England. Her board of directors seemed more like sharks than supports and her aunt and uncle had deserted her.

'You say I have much to lose and you marvel that I've invited you here. But I say the reverse is true. You also have much to lose and still you have come,' he ran a thumb gently over the back of her hand in a soothing gesture. 'Contrary to your conclusion, I think my invitation and your acceptance of it indicate that there is indeed trust between us, *not* suspicion.' The shadow did not diminish from her gaze. She was wary even now. Good lord, how deep did her hurt go? How did he reach someone that far adrift, that heavily protected by the walls they'd built to hide the damage of loss?

'Are you not afraid of what we might find here?' she asked. It was the first time she'd ever used that word 'afraid'. In the beginning he'd never have associated such a word with her. She was bold, daring, but not afraid. Now, he saw those things as decoys.

'Yes,' he confessed. 'I am concerned about what we might find. However, I am not afraid of how we will respond. I have every confidence that you will handle the information with discretion and professionalism, that you will understand the gravity of how that information might affect people. Likewise, I have every confidence in myself to respond fairly. Our intentions come from a place of goodness. You believe it, too, or you would not have come.'

At least not with him. She might have come alone

eventually, an avenging angel with a flaming sword looking to prove herself. A position of anger was not the way he wanted her to approach this fact-finding mission.

The spring moon had risen above the garden and the night birds had begun to sing. He led her to a low stone bench set amid a bower of white roses. 'You can see the stars from here as they come out. Look, there's the beginning of the Plough.'

He heard her sigh, felt her gaze follow the arc of his hand as he traced the sky, his finger connecting one star to the next. She shifted on the bench as she spoke, her voice soft in the dark, the weight of her head leaning against his shoulder as it had in the carriage this afternoon. 'The country *is* beautiful. It is so quiet out here. A person can hear themselves think. It's not like that in London. London is all busyness and schedules and moving from one activity to the next. It's a good day if I can go to sleep with my list completed. I'm not sure a completed list *should* be the mark of a good day.'

He could feel the rise and fall of her breathing, deep and slow, relaxed. He took comfort from that. She did trust him a little even if she'd not admit to it. He said nothing, waiting and wanting her to speak again. He'd been telling stories all day in the hopes of putting her at ease and in the hopes that she'd share stories of her own. Eventually, she did.

'I haven't spent much time in the country since I made my debut. It's hard to believe that was over ten years ago.' Her hand was idly picking at his sleeve. He liked her touch on him, casual and soft.

'Do you not have a country property?' A man with her husband's wealth could have afforded to buy an estate and many did, thinking it another notch in their belts to show the world they were someone.

Fleur rolled her head on his shoulder. 'No, we lived in London year round. Adam didn't like being too far from the *Tribune* offices. Whenever we left London it was to go to the other papers: Bristol, Leeds, York, Sheffield. We did stay a few times at Antonia and Keir's or Garrett and Emma's places. They had estates not far from each other in Surrey and not far from London. Adam felt he could get back quickly enough if there was trouble.'

Dead Adam was starting to sound like a selfish bastard, Jasper thought, but he knew he *was* biased. The man had had this incredible woman as his wife and his first thoughts had been whether or not he lived close enough to his work. Admittedly, Jasper recognised he knew little about the lives of businessmen. The concept of going to work, of keeping hours, and meeting deadlines was entirely foreign to him in some ways.

'And you worked at the paper as well?' he asked idly, careful not to scare her off with too much prying. This was the most she'd ever spoken of her previous life. His arm had tired of tracing the stars and had gone around her. Lord, this was nice, holding her, talking in the darkness, watching the moon. No London evening could be finer.

'Yes, I did. I wrote feature stories for the *Tribune*. I went in every day.' She gave a little laugh. 'Otherwise, I wouldn't have seen Adam at all.' Aha! Jasper thought. Dead Adam was indeed a selfish bastard. But then her next words deflated his sense of private victory.

'We were very lucky. We enjoyed our work together. We spent our days together. Some couples become strangers with no shared interests, the wife going one way with her charities and ladies' teas and the husband going another with his work and clubs. Soon, they're two different people living in two different worlds.' She gave a light sigh and snuggled closer. 'It's not necessarily their faults. I think the world sets people up to fail when it divides responsibilities, women to the private sector of the home and men to the public. There's not much opportunity for sharing or for paths to cross.'

Jasper ran a hand up and down her bare arm in a languid pattern. 'I suppose that's one way to look at it. Being at work all day doesn't leave a lot of time for family, though.' It was a dangerous question. He knew it the moment he asked it. He felt her tense where his hand ran down her arm.

'Adam did not wish for a family. He felt he was too old. He turned fifty the year we wed and he felt we should have some time to ourselves before we contemplated adding children in the mix. He believed it was important that we get to know each other.' She gave a little laugh against his chest. 'Ours was a whirlwind courtship.'

'Yes, you've mentioned that,' Jasper said wryly. He couldn't forget it. One kiss from Dead Adam and she'd fallen for the much older man. 'But once those years of settling in passed, surely children would be a natural progression to a marriage.' It would be for him. He wanted to be a father, not just for the duty of the marquessate, but for himself. He wanted to give to another what his father had given to him. He yearned for it, but he wanted children with the right woman, not simply any woman.

'By then Adam felt he was too old. He said he didn't want to die and leave behind a half-raised child.' She'd talked a lot about what Dead Adam had wanted. What did she want?

'But you felt differently? Did you want children?' Did she still want children?

'Yes,' she breathed the answer quietly into the night. 'It was a point of contention between us, the one thing we never agreed on.' Ah, so she and Dead Adam had fought. Argued. Had unresolved issues. Children. Time in the country. She'd given up a lot for that marriage. Did she see that? With Griffiths's fortune, she could have spent her days any way she chose: shopping and charity work, decorating and redecorating the town house. Instead, she'd chosen to spend it working at the *Tribune* in order to be close to her husband. Perhaps she'd understood the risk of not doing so—the risk of losing him, the risk of watching her marriage disintegrate.

Something potent, part admiration and part envy, stirred in Jasper. Fleur Griffiths was loyal to the bone. To be the recipient of that loyalty, that devotion, would be the honour of a lifetime. Such dedication should not be given idly to just any man or woman. A person would need to be worthy of it, would need to earn it. Sitting here in the moonlight with her, he realised *he* would like to be worthy of it, even if only for a short time.

'What of you? Have you ever been in love?' she asked. She was deflecting and exacting a little *quid pro quo*. But wasn't this also a sign of trust, proof that she'd meant it last night when she'd said she cared for him?

'I thought I was once. I was young and foolish, though.

It didn't work out, obviously. Hence, my mother's need for a list. I am more cautious these days.' He'd not truly understood how attractive a title could be for ambitious young ladies in those days.

She elbowed him in the ribs playfully. 'And yet you're here with me. That doesn't sound like the cautious choice.' There was nothing cautious about Fleur Griffiths, it was what he liked about her. She was bold but vulnerable, brave but scared. But despite the vulnerability and the fear, she did not hold back, did not let those things stop her.

He felt her draw away from him and some of the magic went out of the evening. He was losing her. 'I should not have said that. It was very leading.' She rose and shook out her skirts.

He rose with her, a hand at her arm. 'It was very *bold*. You know I like that about you. You admit your feelings. You speak your mind. Don't ever change that. Not for me, not for anyone.' Perhaps that had been the appeal of Dead Adam besides his kisses. He'd allowed her to speak her mind. Few men would. Fleur was a lot of woman to handle. No, not to handle. No one handled Fleur Griffiths. He'd do best to remember that. 'You may be as you please here, Fleur. *We* may be as we please.' He let his eyes linger on hers, his gaze conveying the unspoken message of his words. Rosefields could be their sanctuary. Here, they could be Jasper and Fleur until it was time to return to London. Did she understand?

Chapter Fifteen

Her breath caught. He was asking her to trust him,
to be his lover in this place where they could keep the
world out, where others wouldn't dictate whether or
not they could be seen together. It was a chance to answer the question she'd posed for herself at the station in London just this morning: what could they be if
they had a chance to just be Jasper and Fleur, removed
from the circumstances of their association? Her body
thrummed with the innate recognition that she wanted
to know. She wanted to know that answer very much.

'If you dare, I dare,' she breathed, the realisation settling on her that she dared more than trusting him, she
dared her heart, she dared a testing of the feelings she'd
not yet been willing to name. She was falling for Jasper Bexley, the man. She could not keep shoving that
knowledge to the side.

He moved into her, hands at her waist, his mouth
hovering inches from hers as he whispered, 'I dare.'
He sealed it with a kiss, claiming her mouth with his.
This was not like the ravenous kisses they'd shared before in her office or at the Harefields'. This was unhur-
ried, but no less heated for it. The slow burn that spread

through her body carried its own brand of intoxication, its warmth searing away opposition in its wake until it was impossible to not want this, to not want him.

All the reasons why this would be a poor idea were obliterated with the stroke of his tongue against her lips, the press of his body against hers, reminding her of the possibilities between them, not the problems. He made her hope—perhaps she did deserve a second chance— it was a wild, reckless hope, full of moonlight's magic and none of daylight's realities.

Her hands reached for his neckcloth, moving to untie it. He chuckled against her mouth, his own hands disengaging to reach for hers. 'Tonight, I want to be with you in a proper bed, without worry of discovery hastening our lovemaking. We have all night; I want to make the most of it.' It was a promise of pleasure, a pledge of protection. He would not take her here, out of doors.

All night.

The prospect sent a delightful tremor through her even as the thought came to her that he'd also want things in exchange—not merely physical passion.

I want to be with you in a proper bed.

She was ready to give that, ready to feel the comfort of being with another. He'd want the things that went with it. He'd not said he wanted to *have her* in a proper bed, bedding her like some archaic medieval lord, but that he wanted *to be with her.* He was asking for her trust, for her presence in a way she'd not given it to him before. This was going to be a deliberate act of lovemaking, not the outcome of spontaneous, riotous emotions, which could be excused in the morning.

And I want it. With him, came the warm thought.

Upstairs, his bedroom was lit with a single lamp that bathed the space in a soft light, a welcoming light. Covers on the tall, carved oak four-posted bed had been pulled back and Jasper's robe had been laid out. The small intimacies sent a shiver of anticipation through her, a reminder that lovemaking was a domestic act, a large intimacy full of smaller ones.

'Shall I play the maid tonight?' Jasper whispered at her ear, his hands already working the laces of her gown, making it a rhetorical question. He pressed a kiss to her neck and she let the warmth of him seep into her skin as he continued his slow seduction. He undressed her with his hands, his mouth dropping kisses to welcome the newly bared skin.

She gave an appreciative sigh as he pressed a kiss to her back. 'You are remarkably good at undressing.'

'Not undressing,' he murmured, his hands unfastening petticoat tapes. 'Unveiling.' The word was punctuated by the soft landing of her petticoat and the silent fall of her crinoline cage shortly after. The last of her undergarments gave way. She was entirely nude, entirely free to feel him against her skin—his chest to her back, his hips to her buttocks, the hard length of him making itself known through the fabric of his trousers as it butted up against her.

His hands cupped her breasts, kneading them gently, thumbs brushing over her nipples in languid strokes, his mouth at her ear. 'Have you ever seen Michelangelo's sculptures *The Slaves*?' he whispered. 'They are statues cut from marble, but they are not entirely finished, on purpose so that it seems as if the marble is a chrysalis the figures are emerging from.'

He nipped at her ear. 'What makes them magical is the sense of effort, of energy one senses when viewing them. It's as though the statues are actively struggling to be free of the marble, the way a baby chick struggles to pierce the membrane of an egg, or a foal struggles to be born.' He blew gently into her ear. 'Unveiling you is like that, Fleur. Each piece of clothing discarded releases you.'

Yes, yes, to all of that, her heart sang. To be free. The clothes were just a metaphor. It was the world she was being freed from. Here in this chamber, naked with this man, she need not worry about the newspaper, about the pressures of being a woman alone in a man's world. She needed only to be herself. She turned in his arms, catching his mouth in a kiss of her own. 'Let me give you that freedom, too. Let me release you from your marble chrysalis,' she whispered, her hands working loose the snowy folds of his cravat, carefully setting aside the gold stickpin.

She undid the buttons of his waistcoat, unfastened the links at his cuffs, liking the domestic feel of helping a man—her man. 'Have you ever considered why it is that a woman must be undressed from the back but a man is always undressed from the front?' She slid him a coy glance as she pulled his shirt tails from the waistband of his trousers.

'Are you going to tell me?' He nuzzled her neck, his mouth teasing her as she worked.

'I have my opinions.' She slid her hands beneath his shirt along the warm planes of his chest, wanting to feel him before she saw him. He *felt* good, warm and solid to the touch. What exquisite musculature he had. She undid his shirt, button by button, outlining her premise. 'I think it's about power, about self-sufficiency. A woman cannot help herself, even in a pinch. In an emergency a gentleman can dress himself. But the wealthier a woman is, the less likely she is able to perform that simple daily function for herself.'

Fleur finished her unbuttoning and pushed the shirt from his shoulders. She'd not been wrong. He was spectacular. 'You look even better than you felt,' she breathed. It was a bold comment, but it pleased him. She watched his eyes darken, his desire growing. He reached for her, but she staved him off with a shake of her head. 'I am not done. You are not free yet. Almost.' She promised, 'Soon.'

'Hurry,' he said in a husky whisper.

Her hands dropped to his waistband. 'Do you think that is how your sculptures felt? Hurry. Free us.' She pushed his trousers over lean hips, her sense of anticipation growing, heightening at the sight of his arousal. He kicked his trousers away and she stared in awe at what she'd unveiled. Such masculine beauty had lain beneath those clothes, a beauty that was at once both rough-hewn and smooth-carved, a body that fulfilled the contradictions she'd perceived in him that first day. She could not help herself. Fleur reached a hand to trace the musculature at his hip where the sinews tapered down towards his groin. She'd not seen such definition before.

'That's the iliac girdle.' He gave a juddering breath as her fingers feathered over his abdomen.

'And this?' She closed her hand over the length of him, feeling the hot pulse of him, his member hard and solid within her touch even as his breath came in shaky gasps. 'I believe we've not been formally introduced.' She loved that this was driving him wild, testing his restraint.

'Phallus.' He murmured the word against her mouth. She could feel him smile as he kissed her.

'You're free now.' She let him dance her back towards the big bed with its inviting turned-down covers. They were both free. The newspaperwoman and the Marquess had been left on the floor, discarded shells from which Jasper and Fleur emerged. She laid back on the bed and pulled him to her, cradling him between her legs. Her body was wet and hot and wanting and his answered. There would be time later for exploration, for lounging in one another's arms. This was not Harefield's garden. There'd been no time then, no unveiling. There'd been only sensation, combustible and bright like a firework and just as fleeting.

He came into her and she let the feel of him fill her, let it purl through her as she gave a slow arch of her back in response, savouring him, welcoming him. The old urge came to close her eyes, to fall into the sensation, but he would not have it. 'Stay with me, watch me as I watch you,' he murmured the instruction, his hips moving against her, setting an easy rhythm. 'Don't leave me. Tonight we are together.' Yes, and for now that was enough. For now that was everything.

She fastened her gaze on his topaz eyes, locked her legs about his hips and took up the rhythm with him. There was wildfire in his gaze, encouragement in his words, adoration in them as his body worshipped hers until restraint broke and they were lost together, gasping and crying, desperately seeking the culmination that waited just beyond them. Then she was there, *they* were there, on the shores of ecstasy, and she was coming apart, eyes wide open as a climax rippled through her body, gaze transfixed on him in his most vulnerable, most complete moments.

Watching him was a mesmerising experience. It left her breathless to see this powerful man wild and undone *with* her, *because* of her, his pleasure a mirror of her own, as was his satisfaction and completion. Yes, despite the undone, deconstructed, bone-shattering quality of their lovemaking, there was also a sense of wholeness, rightness. She wanted to drift in that rightness for ever. Rightness was rare. Nothing had been right or whole for her for a very long time.

She curled into him, fitting her body against the curve of his, her head at his shoulder, her hand at his abdomen. She could feel peace come to him as his breathing settled and slowed. There was a sheen to his skin, testament to their efforts. Their bodies told the truth better than words in those moments and she was content to be quiet, content to let her hands wander idly over his body.

'Clavicle,' he murmured, half asleep.

'And this?'

'Trapezoid.' His body became a litany of words. Pectoralis major, the ticklish spot beneath his arm. Serratus anterior. Rectus abdominus.

'That's amazing.' Her hand came to rest low on his hip on the so-named inguinal ligament. 'How do you know so much anatomy?'

He chuckled, lacing his fingers through hers. 'If I could have been anything I'd have been a scientist.'

'Hmm.' She gave a drowsy, considering sigh. 'That makes sense, I suppose. It explains why you knew about the stars tonight and the anatomy. Why? What do you love about science?'

'Science is precise, dependable. The same efforts get the same results. There are guarantees. Hypotheses are testable. Results can be confirmed. There are sureties not found elsewhere. What about you? If you weren't a journalist, what would you be?'

'I've never given it much thought,' Fleur confessed. 'Perhaps because being a journalist isn't too far from what I might have been. I've always liked writing. I may have fancied being a novelist like Mrs Radcliffe at one time, but writing for the newspaper is close enough and it gave me a chance to…' She didn't finish her sentence, didn't let the words *be with Adam* slip out. She didn't want Adam here tonight in this bed with them, between them. Tonight they were free. Just the two of them.

'To use my writing for good,' she amended hastily. 'News promotes literacy both through reading and information. It also promotes social access, a gateway to participating in the world instead of letting the world happen to you. Wherever there is a newspaper, people have access to information, to reading.'

She gave a little laugh. 'I don't mean to pontificate. The news is off limits tonight.'

Sweet heavens, there were so many things they shouldn't talk about here in bed and she'd nearly broken all those rules. Perhaps it would be best if she stopped talking and turned the conversation back to him.

'How interesting that you are a mar—err…uhm…
man who likes science. What else do you like? I want to
know everything about you.' She snuggled back down
beside him, aware that she'd almost made another conversational mistake. He did not want to be the Marquess
tonight any more than she wanted to be Adam's widow
or a newspaperwoman. Yet for those rules to hold, there
were limits to their conversation. It was a sobering reminder amid the pleasure that tonight was a fantasy.
They weren't as free as they thought.

He'd been free with her last night, at liberty to be
himself and she with him. But now that night was ending. The first tentative fingers of morning were stretch-
ing across the floor while Fleur slept in his arms,
exhausted at last. Such nights didn't happen often for
him. Even with the occasional mistress, he must always be the Marquess, sex was more of a performance
than a pleasure. But not last night. Last night with her,
he'd been himself. He did not want to waste a moment
drowsing even if it was only to stay awake to watch her
sleep and to remember, to savour.

It had been exquisite to hold her in his arms, to know
that she was with him when they'd found completion.
He'd lost himself in the emerald depths of her eyes as
assuredly as he'd lost himself in the pleasure of a jointly
achieved climax. Even so, lost as he was, he'd been conscious enough to protect her from any repercussions—
both times—because talk had led to more lovemaking
and then more stories.

He'd told her stories of his boyhood growing up here
at Rosefields, stories of his father and the adventures

they'd had, fishing in Rosefields's streams, hunting grouse—which he far preferred to hunting elk—in the dales, hiking the hills amid the brilliance of autumn foliage and in the spring amid the purple heather. 'I wish you could see Rosefields in the autumn,' he whispered, knowing she would not hear.

'And at Christmas,' he added, thinking of the evergreen boughs that would drape the mantels and lintels and the Yule log that would crackle in the hearth, the house crowded with villagers and tables groaning beneath Christmas delicacies. She would like that, all the children running around. Fleur was a caretaker. It was what she did with her news stories. She used news as a means of caring for people, of connecting them to their world, of broadening their horizons, and she used it as a tool by which she could advocate for them. He'd rather loved her impassioned impromptu speech earlier about what a newspaper could do. Weren't those the very reasons he championed a free press? It was something they had in common in the real world.

He stretched with a groan, aware that the morning was full upon them. It would be a difficult day for her. They were going into Holmfirth to speak with some people about the dam. It would take her back to the scene of the crime, so to speak, to a place that held only sadness for her. He'd rather stay here at Meltham where there was happiness, where there was this bed and where obligations and memories did not intrude.

She stirred in his arms, her hair a tumbled auburn cloud against the pillow. He thought she was the loveliest woman he'd ever seen. 'Is it morning already?'

She groaned and opened one eye. 'How long have you been awake?'

'A while, sleepyhead.' He gave a lazy smile.

'You should have woken me.'

'You needed the sleep. We have time.' Their eyes met, a bit of the night leaping between them.

'Time for what?' she teased.

'For this.' He rolled her beneath him, his manhood morning ready for her. He might not be able to guarantee how the day played out, but he could make sure it began with a good morning and it could end with a good night.

It did not take long for morning desire to run its course and, though he would have liked to have stayed abed with her all day, duty called for them both. They helped each other dress, taking turns playing valet and maid. He brushed out her hair and sat on the bed watching her braid it into a twist. This was what it would be like with a wife, he thought. He would be privy to these little intimacies, things one could only learn about another by observing them, absorbing them, over time. Osmosis, a scientist might call it. It was another kind of unveiling, the revealing of layer upon layer until all was peeled back.

When she was done, Jasper went to her, putting his hands on her shoulders and pressing a kiss to her neck. He loved kissing that neck, loved breathing in the scent of her where she dabbed her perfume. 'Are you ready?' he asked, meeting her eyes in the mirror over the dressing table.

She reached a hand up to grip his. 'Yes.' She paused and sighed. 'But I hate to leave this. Last night was beyond words. Not just the pleasure, Jasper,' she tried to explain. He nodded. He knew what she meant. He did not think there were words *for* it.

'We will come back. Our room will be here for us, waiting.' He squeezed her hand in assurance. 'We *can* have more.' *If* they were careful. It would be too easy to let the practicalities of the day ruin the magic they'd created last night. With luck, the spell would hold. Magic. Luck. Spell. He laughed at himself. These were not the words of a scientist. But neither was love. He'd best tread carefully here or he'd forget himself entirely.

Chapter Sixteen

She'd forgotten the intensity and extent of the devastation. She'd not thought she would. But somehow, over the course of the year, it had become muted. Not erased, just mitigated perhaps against the grief of her personal loss. Fleur stood in front of Quarmby's Butcher Shop on Victoria Street, staring at the stone that marked the depth of the floodwaters. The water must have been six feet deep at least here.

'Extraordinary,' Jasper murmured beside her. Perhaps it was the very extraordinary quality of it that had indeed caused it to become muted. One could not live with such horror in full force day in and day out. But today, she felt she must. The reminder kept the need for justice fresh. Distance and time dulled the exigence and the pain.

Jasper was her rock as they walked the town. He listened to her recount the night and the days that followed. 'In the dark, we could only hear it and in the morning we could see the wreckage it had left,' she said as they turned towards the river where the damage had been greatest.

The weather was fair, an early summer day with blue sky overhead, but the weather could not disguise the lack of progress that had been made. After a year, the damaged bridge had not been rebuilt and several mills lining the river were still not operational. She understood the recovery effort would take time, that it was no easy task to dredge a river or to haul away machinery that weighed tons, or to bring in new building materials, draw up new plans and all that went with rebuilding. But that didn't change the practical reality that every day a mill didn't operate, people didn't work, didn't eat, didn't provide for their family. Delays cost people money and jobs. Quietly, her heart went out to the families that continued to suffer residual effects of the disaster.

'Whole mills collapsed that night,' she explained as they walked. 'Cottages gave way under the weight of the water flooding them. Mill equipment littered the streets along with livestock and furniture. All the pieces of people's lives gone in a matter of minutes. If I hadn't seen it with my own eyes, I would have thought such destruction impossible.'

She told him about the dish cabinet with the blue set. 'It was indiscriminatory, what was saved, what was lost, who lived, who died. The waters were no respecters of status or money. We learned later that there was a wealthy man, Jonathan Sandford. He had stock in the London Northwestern Railway. He was in the process of buying an estate and there was a rumour he had nearly four thousand pounds in his house the night of the flood, a small fortune. But he lost all of it and his life. His money was never recovered.'

She shook her head. 'There are sadder stories than his, but his stays with me. He was successful, a good steward of his funds, he'd built a comfortable life for himself and his family. He was on the brink of attaining all he'd aspired for and there was no reason he should not have it. It took only thirty minutes for it all to be wiped away. A lifetime destroyed.'

She shot Jasper a strong look. 'Logically, he should have had more. Science might offer sureties, but real life does not.' Perhaps the story of Jonathan Sandford stayed with her because it was so much like Adam's. Adam should have had more, too.

She traced the route of the river that night for him as their walk continued. She stopped every so often to write in a little book, making notes for an anniversary story. To keep interest in Holmfirth alive, it would be good to do a 'where are they now a year later' style story about how the villagers and townspeople had recovered and how they had not. Mills weren't the only things that had been lost. Farmland had been lost, too. When they met people along the river road, she took a moment to interview them about their lives in the past year, their stories affirming the broader conclusions she'd drawn about the effects of the flood.

'This is where Holmfirth gives way to Hinchliffe Mill.' She paused at an unseen border. Water Street lay ahead. The one place she was most loath to go. She'd not even gone there in the days following the disaster. It hadn't been possible. But now there was nothing holding her back except her own choice.

'You don't have to do this,' Jasper said quietly at her side. All day he'd been her strength. He'd walked beside her, reliving the disaster with her and through her. He'd waited patiently as she'd interviewed people, showing empathy and making enquiries of his own. He'd been impressive. People had responded to him.

She had responded, too. Seeing his sincerity in action, directed at people he didn't know, affirmed that Jasper Bexley was a good man. He would go with her to Water Street if she asked it. He'd probably go even if she didn't ask because that's who he was. And he was right. She didn't *need* to go there. She could choose to turn around and go back to the Rose and Crown Inn, have her meetings, and return to Rosefields. Seeing Water Street would not impact her ability to investigate Lord Orion Bexley's involvement.

'I have to go,' she said solemnly. It would bring a different type of closure than the closure she sought with her legislation and her call for justice. This would be a personal closure, maybe a chance to shut the book on her life with Adam, here at the place where they'd last been together.

'Then we'll go together.' Jasper gripped her hand and they made the rest of the walk, slowly and with the dignity of a funeral dirge as if to endow the importance of the event with the respect it deserved.

Fleur did not know what she expected to see on Water Street. Something. Remnants of the place they'd rented, perhaps. It was an unexpected shock to see that there was nothing. Just a gap where the row of houses had been. A woman hurried past with a child. Fleur stopped her. 'Madam, do you know if there's any plan to rebuild these houses?'

Leery of a stranger, the woman shook her head and scurried on. But the impact of that headshake sent Fleur reeling. She'd come to Water Street, treating it as a pilgrimage, a chance to memorialise Adam and the others. But there was nothing she could make into a personal, mental shrine. Adam's part in the tragedy had been entirely washed away, as if he'd never been, as if their stay on Water Street had never happened. There was no stone like the one at Mr Quarmby's Butcher Shop to mark what had happened. A man had died here, a marriage had died here. The life she'd known had died here and there was no marker for it. Rage began to boil. That wasn't right, that couldn't be right. There had to be more.

'Fleur, are you well?' Jasper had a steadying hand at her back. 'You've gone pale, perhaps you should sit down.' Only there was no place to sit. 'Or lean. Lean against me,' he instructed. 'I am worried you might faint.'

She took a shuddering breath. 'I'm f-f-fine', and felt his arm go about her. It took all her willpower not to sag into that embrace, to not simply give up.

'I have seen fine, Fleur, and you most definitely are not,' he scolded. 'You're also a poor liar.'

'I am fine,' she insisted, the need to argue bringing her some resilience. 'It's just the shock of seeing it. Or rather, *not* seeing it.' Then, with his arm about her, concern for her clearly expressed in his eyes, the words began to come, how she'd stayed to play whist at Mrs Parnaby's and the men had gone back early. Then came the words she'd not shared with anyone, not even Antonia and Emma. They'd had their own grief to bear. They hadn't needed her grief and her guilt as well. There'd been no one else to tell. Besides, these were not things anyone wanted to hear.

'I didn't kiss him goodbye. I was angry with him. We'd argued earlier that evening. We argued a lot.'

Guilt jabbed hard. She should not have pushed Adam that night on the issue. Her anger rose. Guilt and anger pushed at her, the pressure of those emotions building. Why hadn't she done better? Chosen better? If she'd only known. The strength of Jasper's chest bore the brunt of her guilt, of her anger, her fists pummelling at an unseen enemy as the dam of her grief broke. 'I should have been a better wife. If I had only known. I squandered our last hours. I should have apologised. I was too stubborn, too selfish.' She sobbed.

'What did you fight over?' Jasper's voice was soft at her ear, calming as his hands ran over her back in a smoothing motion.

'A baby.' She drew a harsh, ragged breath. 'I thought I was pregnant. Adam didn't want the child and I said horrible things to him.' She rocked against him, the horror of those memories sweeping her. 'He told me I was asking the impossible, that it was selfish for me to want a child, to put that burden on him when he didn't want it. I told him he loved himself more than me, that he was cruel and self-centred. That I was sorry I'd ever married him.'

A wail escaped her. What an awful thing to say to someone. She'd never said anything of that magnitude to him before. 'I didn't mean it.' She gulped for air. 'I swear I didn't mean it, but I didn't get to apologise.' Now he was gone, the house where they'd fought was gone. She would never get to make reparations to him directly. The best she could do was to seek justice.

'Breathe, Fleur. Just breathe. It will be all right.' Jasper repeated the mantra over and over, until he felt her body quiet and still against him. He would be calm for her sake. For his, though, he was boiling with rage. He wanted to do harm to Dead Adam. Too bad the man was already beyond his efforts. How dare a man make his wife doubt her place with him?

She lifted a tear-stained face. 'I wonder if he hated me in the end? I can't bear the idea that he died hating me, resenting our life together. It wasn't all bad. We were in love. Most of the time.'

He could give her obliteration, but he could not give her what she really wanted: absolution. He had not known Adam Griffiths, had no guess as to what Adam had thought or felt. He had no insight to offer that wouldn't sound like naive platitudes, that of course Adam loved her. Hell, he had no idea. But his heart broke just a little further. Damn Adam Griffiths and his work-obsessed heart. If he had such a woman as Fleur Griffiths, Jasper would be damned sure he made time for her, that he gave her children, as many as she wanted. 'You've done enough for today. Let me take you home, Fleur.' Home to Rosefields where they could walk in the peace of the garden, talk on the terrace in the still of the evening and make love in the bedroom until the hurt was eased.

'I am sorry I went to pieces,' Fleur said quietly as they took in the garden by starlight, sitting on the stone bench where they'd sat the night before. 'I had not expected to see it all gone. The finality of that was overwhelming. I thought I had come to grips with it, with all of it. I was wrong. Sometimes the grief just comes out of nowhere.' Even now her voice trembled a bit.

'You needn't apologise. When my father died I felt

much the same way. Everyone was looking to me as the new Marquess. They expected me to be strong, to make decisions, to immediately step into my father's shoes. It was, as you say, overwhelming. There was no time for me to grieve privately. I imagine it was much the same for you with the newspapers to run.'

And she would not have given herself a break to adjust. It wasn't her way. In the time he'd known her she was always at work. She'd been 'at work' at the Harefield's ball, garnering Parliamentary support. The only time she'd not been at work had been the night he'd met her at the theatre. She worked because it was what she knew, because it was what she and Adam had done together. Maybe it was part of her grieving, a tribute to him. Jasper wasn't sure Adam deserved such a tribute.

'How did your father die?' She leaned her head against him and he took a quiet pleasure from their closeness and the ease of it.

'He got pneumonia one winter and never recovered. One would not think a cough would bring down such a man as he was, always out riding, exercising. He seemed invincible to me.' Jasper smiled at the remembrance.

'Adam seemed invincible to me, as well.' She sighed. 'I thought there was nothing he couldn't do. But I learned otherwise. He was not so perfect. His newspapers were in debt before I took them over and he didn't tell me. He left me with a struggling newspaper empire, he left me alone and without a family, and there are days when I am furious with him for it. You see, I am truly terrible. I am angry at a dead man who left me behind to sort out his mess. Then I get mad at myself for being mad at Adam.'

He pressed a kiss to the top of her head. 'You are not terrible. You are human, you are honest and something bad happened to you, something unpredictable and unanticipated.' And it had changed the trajectory of her life. He would not have met her if it hadn't happened. But other things wouldn't have happened either. His brother would not be in jeopardy. It was a reminder that while today had been tense with its remembrances, tomorrow would be more so.

'What would you like to do tomorrow?' he asked quietly. They had yet to meet with the regional bank where Orion kept his accounts. The accounts would tell a critical truth about Orion's culpability. In his heart he hoped that they might delay that visit because of what the revelations might do to them. He wanted more time with her before that happened, more time to think about how to survive this because every day he was with her, the more he wanted that: to survive this latest crisis with this relationship intact.

She thought for a moment, perhaps weighing the choices and consequences as he had done, perhaps, he dared hope, she wanted the same thing. After a while she said, 'I want to stay here and write, if that's acceptable? I thought we might also draft that bill for better dam oversight.'

He allowed himself the luxury of relief. He would have her, them, for a while longer. Of course, she would seek refuge in work. After seeing the wreckage, still so visible after a year, it was clear that the region needed help and that something had to be done to prevent other disasters. But there was something else in her eyes that he understood and it warmed him even as he recognised it as a delaying tactic. She, too, wanted more time. With him. Not the Marquess. Just him.

Fair enough. He wanted more time with her, enough time to sort through what happened next, after the accounts revealed a truth that would support one of them and dash the hopes of the other. How could he navigate the outcome without losing her—her sharp wit, her intelligence, her forthright nature, temper and all, without losing her *presence* in his life. There were so many ways to lose her…and, he suspected, his heart. He'd not meant for that to happen.

Jasper lost no time in planning the days they did have together. After all, she wouldn't write the whole day every day. He took her riding in the mornings, something she hadn't done since she'd left her aunt and uncle's, and watched her delight at being on horseback, cantering across Rosefields's meadows. Morning rides turned into afternoon picnics beneath a June sky. There were strawberries to pick and stories to tell, of his childhood and hers. In the evenings there were al fresco dinners for two on the terrace and strolls in the garden, punctuated by stolen kisses and the final stroll upstairs to their bed accompanied by two realisations: the longer he was here with her the more obvious it was to him that he was falling in love and that each day moved them closer to the end. This could not last for ever.

'I wish we could stay here for ever.' Fleur stretched beside him on the picnic blanket one lazy afternoon when the blue sky was greyer than it had been lately.

There were more clouds and they'd been playing the child's game of seeking shapes.

'Well, why not? We have food,' he teased, reaching for the strawberries in a bowl. He popped one into her mouth. 'We have a large blanket between us. We have each other.' He grinned wickedly. There was no chance of being bored with Fleur. 'What more could we want?' He fed her another strawberry from their freshly picked horde. 'I am glad you like it here. I'll say it again, Rose-fields suits you.' And it suited him to have her here, to share this important place with her.

She turned on her side to face him, her auburn braid falling over one shoulder, her expression content. 'It reminds me of my aunt and uncle's home, only Rose-fields is a much grander scale. My uncle had an endless amount of bridle trails. He was the master of the hunt for our bucolic corner of the world and I had a pony from the first day I came to live with them.'

Fleur gave a soft laugh. 'My uncle took me to show me the stables before my aunt had a chance to even show me my room. He had a beautiful white pony waiting for me. I named her Sweetie and I thought she looked like a unicorn minus the horn.' She was silent for a moment. 'Sweetie became my best friend. She was exactly what a lonely little girl needed to start life in a new place.'

Jasper threaded his fingers through hers, taking advantage of the moment. Fleur had never talked before so specifically of her childhood, of life before Adam. 'How old were you?' It was the first of many questions he wanted to ask.

'Eight. Old enough to know that something bad had happened, old enough to remember my life before and old enough to know everything was going to change.' She shook her head. 'I didn't want it to change. I wanted my parents to come home. I wanted to stay at my house. Uncle's house was larger, but I liked our manse with its ivy-covered brick walls, and Papa's messy study and Mama's tiny parlour.'

Jasper could imagine how uncertain the world must have felt for an eight-year-old. His own world had felt unstable when his father died and he'd had the benefit of being twenty-two. Perhaps we're never old enough to lose our parents, he thought. 'How did they die?' he ventured softly.

'It's quite dashing, really. They were in the Mediterranean on one of Papa's explorations—he was a cartographer—and their ship was boarded by pirates. Papa was also quite good with a sword and he stood to fight. It didn't go his way. So, I became a permanent resident at my uncle's.'

'I'm sorry.' Jasper meant it. He gave her a considering look, a new understanding of Fleur Griffiths emerging: a woman who'd first been a girl betrayed by love. She'd lost her parents, then she'd lost her aunt and uncle, then she'd lost her husband.

'I was, too, but I also know I was lucky. It was an entrée into a whole new lifestyle. I went from being raised as a country gentleman's daughter to being raised as a baron's daughter. Life changed, opportunities changed and so did expectations.' She'd mentioned those expectations before. Perhaps it was no wonder she'd been protective of herself in this relationship, less willing to give of herself emotional than physically. Until the day in Holmfirth, she'd kept her emotions—all except anger—on a tight leash.

In that regard, she was not any different than himself. He, too, felt betrayed by love. He, too, tiptoed around embracing sentimental emotions. And yet, here they were on a picnic blanket beneath a summer sky, falling for one another, their worlds turned upside down by the one thing they'd sought to avoid. It made no sense. It lacked all logic. Until one looked beyond social trappings of position and circumstance. In their hearts, they were alike: their hopes, their fears, the things they valued at their core like integrity, honesty and truth. The realisation shook him. It made him reckless.

'I want to be your Sweetie. I want to be like that pony at your uncle's. I want to be the person that makes it possible for you to step into your new life, the safe place you can run to when the world is too much.' In this moment, he wanted that with all his being—to be *hers*, to make up for the disappointments with Adam, for the loss of her aunt and uncle who had stood by her until she chose a different path.

There was a flare of alarm in her eyes; she was rearing back even as he was reaching forward. 'You should not want that,' she warned. 'I lose everyone I love.'

Did she love him?

He knew she meant it as a caution, but his heart sang at the implication. He would not press her on it. She would only retreat, only throw up her guard. He would instead quietly treasure the near-admission and the knowing that he was not in this struggle alone. But her next words tore at his heart. 'I sometimes wonder if I deserve the right to love again. I bungled it so badly with Adam, with my aunt and uncle.'

Anger sparked in him on her behalf. 'Why ever would you think that?'

She sat up and he sat up, too, ready to reach for her, to comfort her. 'My aunt and uncle gave me everything, every advantage, treated me as their own, and I disappointed them by marrying down, by not advancing the family.'

He took her hand. 'Love doesn't work that way. If there is any fault it is theirs. Love is not conditional. If it were, I would have stopped loving Orion a long time ago. He was a difficult brother and I failed him, too. I wasn't ready to be a father and brother to a teenage boy. But we've forgiven each other for our shortcomings.' He paused. Adam was a different matter. 'It is all right your marriage wasn't perfect. How could it have been when people aren't perfect?'

'I was selfish. I wanted more than he could give, and I was not content with that.'

He would not let her get up from this blanket believing that. Jasper pushed a strand of loose hair behind her ear and tipped her face towards his. He wanted her to look at him when he told her the truth he saw. 'He could give less and so you gave more.' Jasper called on everything she'd told him about her years with Adam Griffiths. 'He wanted to work and so you worked alongside him. He went to the paper daily and so did you. You wanted to be a collector of stories, but you made yourself into a reporter to fit his world. You gave up your lifestyle, your ambitions, your family, your dreams for him. That is not selfish.'

If anyone had been selfish it had been Adam Griffiths. The man had either been selfish and arrogant or he'd been entirely oblivious to his wife's sacrifices. 'Worst of all, Fleur, you're *still* doing it. You're running a newspaper syndicate, wearing yourself to a nub trying to overcome his debt. Where is your life in that? What, my darling, do you want? When do you reach out your hands and take it?'

For the second time since they'd arrived at Rosefields, Fleur Griffiths was crying. He had her in his arms, consoling her, but he did not regret sharing the hard truths in an attempt to reshape the narrative she carried in her head. When she told her story he wanted her to tell it right—with herself as the strong, resilient, selfless woman at its core. And he wanted to be there in that story beside her.

'You mustn't say such things, Jasper. I hurt the people I love and I will hurt you, too—you know it's true.' There it was again, that implication that she loved him.

'No, I don't know that,' he argued fiercely. 'You haven't hurt me yet, nothing unrecoverable at least. I have a new set of tumblers on order,' he tried to joke. But he knew what they faced. The trials to date were nothing compared to the last trial that loomed before them. Still, they had a good record of overcoming differences. Just maybe, they'd overcome this one, too. And they were stronger now—surely that worked in their favour as well.

'I don't want this to be over,' she whispered against his shirt.

'Then it won't be.' He hugged her close. He would find a way to prove to her that she deserved a second chance at love, that they deserved each other even as their personal Armageddon loomed.

She drew a shaky breath. 'We can't get over it if we don't go through it.' By 'it' she meant the bank, Orion's records. So the time had come. Their Rubicon called.

He nodded, his grip about her tightening. 'We'll go tomorrow.' Then they'd be on the other side of it. They'd know what their future looked like. He'd not come out on this picnic imagining it to be their last before…the bank. Perhaps it was better this way, to have the decision made without planning and posturing, without argument and formal consideration but instead here in the quiet of the afternoon, after picking strawberries and talking of childhood. The biggest moments of one's life didn't always come with a blare of trumpets but on the whisper of suggestion.

'It will be all right, Fleur. We will find a way to survive it.' He breathed the words into her hair as thunder rumbled in the distance, presaging a summer storm as if the weather understood just how momentous tomorrow would be.

Chapter Seventeen

How would she survive the coming days without losing everything? Without losing herself, without compromising her sense of justice, her task, the newspaper, but most of all, without losing Jasper? And always the answer kept creating the same equation. To save Jasper, she would lose herself, sacrifice justice and perhaps the papers along with it. To keep all she held dear, Jasper would have to be surrendered. There was simply no way to have it all. The realisation of that created a most impossible dilemma, one that had not existed a month ago.

Fleur looked up from her writing at the library table to sneak a glance at him at his desk, wire-rimmed glasses and all, his own gaze intent on his own letter writing. He'd rolled his sleeves up a while ago to spare them from errant ink blots and his forearms with their sprinkling of dark hair were on masculine display. She'd never found rolled-up shirtsleeves and exposed forearms particularly sexy before, but on Jasper they were proving to be quite the aphrodisiac and quite the impediment to the last of her evening work.

She could not give in and set aside her work for another day. She must finish this article tonight. There was no guarantee that tomorrow she'd be back here at Rose-fields enjoying its hospitality. In fact, chances of return-ing here seemed slim regardless of tomorrow's outcome. Tomorrow morning they would go to the bank and call for Lord Orion's accounts. Tomorrow they would know what they'd come to find out. Tomorrow, their affair would end.

Jasper glanced up, catching her staring. 'Is there something you want?' he drawled. Indeed there was. She wanted him. She wanted this damned quest to be over. She wanted for there to be a way between them that wouldn't cost her everything and he the same. She wanted more of this, of days spent side by side, of eve-nings in the garden talking of everything from politics to the personal, of nights spent in bed making love. Did he want that, too? Wasn't he worried at all about tomorrow?

Fleur set aside her pen and walked towards the desk. 'There is something I want.' She gave a wicked smile and came around to his side. This might be her last chance. She'd spent the afternoon since they'd returned from the picnic thinking of every 'last': last luncheon in the countryside, last supper, last walk in the garden. Had he spent the time that way, too? She hiked her skirts up to her thighs and straddled his lap.

'What are you doing, Minx?' He was startled, but pleasantly so. She could see the flames of intrigue light-ing in his eyes. She'd come to know those eyes so well in the past weeks: how they glowed in interest, dark-ened with desire, narrowed with disapproval, how they became coals when he was angry, a deep amber when aroused. It would be easy for someone to mistake one for the other.

She wriggled closer. 'It would be cliché to say I've wanted to do this since I first saw you…' she reached for his glasses, removing them gently '…so we'll say I've wanted to do this for a while.'

He slid down slightly in the chair to better accommodate her. 'What is that, exactly?'

'To take off your incredibly sexy glasses and run my fingers through your hair while sitting on your lap.' She moved against him, feeling him rouse beneath her hips.

'Since the first day we met? Really?' Teasing lights glimmered in his eyes. He rested his hands at her hips. 'I thought you didn't like me.'

'I thought you were over-confident. It didn't mean I wasn't interested.' She pressed a kiss to his lips. How was it possible to fall so fast and not realise it? She'd fallen fast before, with Adam. She thought she would have recognised the signs. Or perhaps she *had* recognised the signs—the heat between them, the mental and physical chemistry of being together on her part as well as his—and explained them away as something else— an antidote for loneliness, nothing more, because for them *to* be more was a frightening prospect that brought risk and uncertainty at an already uncertain time.

Was this what it had been like for Emma and Antonia? Only they had happy endings to their stories. She wouldn't be so lucky. There was no happy ending for her. She knew. She'd run the numbers on this. One of them would be right and the other would be very wrong. That would be a chasm too wide for a relationship to overcome even if they managed to survive it on a professional level.

And what do you care? What do you want from Jasper Bexley beyond an affair anyway?

Those were questions she refused to answer.

'You are sad all of a sudden. What is it, Fleur?' His eyes were soft with concern and she felt her heart crack just a tiny bit. She didn't want to hurt him. Why did she always hurt the men she loved? She'd hurt Adam, and she was going to hurt Jasper. Her research was good. There was little chance Lord Orion Bexley was not guilty of negligence on the Bilberry Dam. Jasper loved his brother. Tomorrow would devastate him.

'Aren't you worried about tomorrow?' She smoothed his waves away from his face. It felt domestic and wifely to make such a small, intimate gesture, to have the right to do it, to sit here on his lap, to talk so openly. These were just a handful of the intimate privileges she would lose tomorrow.

'I can't change what we'll find. The reality is already out there. The answer we're looking for already exists.' He reached for her hands and took them in his own. 'And I trust us, Fleur. We have pledged to handle whatever we find with discretion and good faith.' His calmness and logic were soothing. He might be the only man she knew who would draw on the concepts of Plato in the midst of a crisis. She wanted to believe them, but they were incomplete and only addressed half of her worry.

'What does Plato have to say about us? Have *you* thought about what happens to us tomorrow? Do we go back to being business partners?' Or perhaps they went back to being nothing at all. This was her greater worry and that realisation carried its own shock. A month ago, her first worry would have been support for legislation. But tonight, she wondered if she could go back to business-only with him? Every time he was in a room, she'd think about Rosefields, about his big bed, about every consideration he'd shown her, how, for a short while, she'd been cherished for herself. And yet what other choice was there? How did she think this would end?

She pressed a finger to Jasper's lips. 'You don't have to answer my question. Forget that I asked.' She'd known the ending from the start and nothing had happened that would change that. Even if Lord Orion Bexley was miraculously expunged of his guilt, the ending for her and Jasper would not change. He would still be a marquess with expectations to marry a well-titled young gentlewoman.

His fingers curled warmly over hers, gently moving them away from his lips. 'What do *you* want to happen with us? Don't we get to decide? You talk as though the world will happen to us instead of the other way around.'

'It doesn't matter what I want. The facts are indisputable. I'm not on your mother's list.'

'You are on *my* list. Maybe that's more important.' He nipped at her ear, but she had fallen out of a mood for teasing. She moved her head away.

'I will not be a married man's mistress,' she said quietly. 'Nor are you a man who would keep a mistress once he had a wife and family. Don't you see? It's no use. If we do not end now, we will end later. It is inevitable. Marquesses and newspaperwomen have no future together.'

His hands framed her face, warm and confident.

'That is not the sum of who we are. We are people who share the surviving of loss, who know the true value of trust and deep commitment. We are not just our titles.' He kissed her softly. There was more than one Rubicon to cross and this one was definitely more personal, more than the sum of what they found with Orion. 'If we want our relationship to happen, we'll find a way. Not even the findings at the bank will stop us. *That's* the kind of people we are.' He smiled. 'For instance, I want to find a way to get you upstairs.'

'You might start with asking,' she said coyly, sensing that the time had come to accept the inevitable even if Jasper wouldn't. This was likely their last night together. They might as well enjoy it. She could hold tonight as a shield against all the lonely nights to come.

'Asking? Is it as simple as all that? Who would have thought?' Jasper laughed, rising from the chair with her in his arms. It was not a heavily disguised allegory.

'For being a man of science, you're not being very logical, Jasper.' She laughed to cover the severity of her comment.

'Perhaps you've changed me, just a little, or perhaps I don't think my claim illogical to start with.' He juggled her in his arms, passing the library table and her half-finished article.

'Wait, I can't leave it. Put me down. I just need five more minutes,' she protested.

'You can finish it tomorrow. We've done enough work tonight,' Jasper said sternly, never breaking his stride. 'In fact, we've done more in a week than Parliament does in a month. I am very proud of us and you should be, too.'

He turned sideways, manoeuvring them through the door into the hall and began the trek upstairs to their bedroom. 'You're smiling. Are you marvelling at my strength or the amount of work we've accomplished?' They had achieved a lot. One day had turned into a week in which they'd stayed at Rosefields, isolated from the world, drafting a bill, writing letters to potential supporters, and she had written her articles. It had been a productive excuse to forestall their visit to the bank.

'Can I marvel at both?' She *was* marvelling at his muscles. 'I don't think I've ever been carried upstairs before.' She laughed up at him. 'You've done well, you can set me down.'

'No.' He grunted. 'We're not at the top yet and I am no quitter.' There was allegory in that, too, and Fleur duly noted it. He was making this hard on her, on them. Perhaps she should have let him answer her impossible question. Perhaps if he could hear his thoughts out loud he'd realise that their time together had come to an end.

Fleur was afraid. Jasper felt it in her touch and tasted it in her kiss. Jasper held her close, watching her sleep. That fear was a base-note which had underscored their lovemaking. There'd been desperation in that lovemaking, too. Her fingers had traced him as if they wanted to memorise every line and plane and she'd wrapped her legs about him so tightly he'd worried she'd not let him go in time. As delicious as the prospect of spending within her was, Jasper did not want to take the risk. Although that would certainly resolve things. A child would push past the barriers she was so good at erecting, it would strip away all discussion of choice.

A child with Fleur. Perhaps a curly, auburn-haired daughter with her mother's boldness and her father's love of science? He'd build a university just for her. Or maybe a dark-haired son with his mother's green eyes. Or a tall, broad-shouldered son with hair the colour of Rosefields's autumn leaves. He laughed at himself spinning endless possibilities in the dark. Fleur would say they were *impossibilities*.

To be sure, he knew it was a notion born of midnight and madness. Marriage had never come up between them other than that he had to wed. They could not even agree on what happened after tomorrow. It seemed unlikely they could agree on something as big as marriage. And yet, hadn't they implicitly tried it on this week with their prolonged retreat?

They'd made a good team. He'd liked working with her even as he understood the pattern that was enacting itself after her breakdown at Water Street. Work was her answer to grieving. Water Street had hit her hard and she was compensating for that with work, just as she'd once compensated for the loss of Adam. She'd tried to do it again tonight, too, by wanting to work on her last article instead of coming upstairs and facing what she thought would be their last night together. He'd not allowed it. Fear had to be faced if it was to be overcome.

'I'm afraid, too,' he whispered to Fleur's sleeping form. He was afraid of what the bank accounts would show, afraid he would not be equal to the tasks required of him, equal to being the man Fleur would need him to be. If he could not rise to the task, he would lose her.

Tomorrow would just be the beginning of the battle and he wasn't sure his record in battle was all that good.

Look at Orion. For all of his best efforts to be a brother and father to him, Orion was struggling to make the transition to responsible adulthood. He was thirty. It was time, even well past time. Perhaps he shouldn't be so eager to be a father. If he couldn't raise his brother, what made him think he could raise a child? He pushed the thought away. Orion had been spoiled early on. He could not shoulder that blame. Midnight was a cruel mistress, prompting madness on one hand and maudlin reflection on the other. Such introspection was best left to the light of day.

His day started with an empty bed. Jasper rolled over with a groan, his hand meeting a cold pillow. She'd been up for a while and he hadn't even heard her. He must have been deeply asleep. A little smile curved on his face as he thought of the reason for that. They'd worn each other out thoroughly last night. If she was up, she would be in the library finishing her article. His smile broadened. He liked imagining her at Rosefields. Then the smile faded when he looked about the room.

She was gone from his bed and her things were gone from this room. Last night, she'd left a chemise hanging over the chair. The chair was empty now. Jasper got out of bed and padded over to the bureau, pulling open the two drawers she'd claimed as hers. They were empty, too. Gone. No, not gone, he reasoned with himself. She was just downstairs. But she'd packed. Even her gowns were gone from the wardrobe.

A sense of betrayal stabbed at him. She planned to return to London tonight and yet all this time she'd said nothing about it. She was leaving him. After everything that had been said and shared last night, she was *still* leaving him. His immediate reaction was to run downstairs in his banyan and confront her, half-naked and raging. He'd not lied last night. She *had* changed him. Her emotion had rubbed off. It took all the logic within him to realise confronting her *while* he was angry was his worst option. It was, perhaps, even what she preferred. Fleur *wanted* a fight. A fight would make leaving easier. He would not give her one. A fight would allow her to run away...from Rosefields and from them. She would not thank herself for it in the long run.

Jasper shaved and dressed slowly, methodically: grey summer trousers, crisp white shirt, a white waistcoat embroidered with blue forget-me-nots, a grey jacket and neatly tied cravat. The morning rituals helped to restore his equilibrium. Today had to be taken one step at a time even as he kept the larger circumstance in mind.

He took the stairs, recalling how he'd carried her up them just hours before. He found her in the library, breakfast and coffee beside her writing implements, her auburn head bent as she worked, the morning sun catching the highlights of her hair, picking out the rare gold hidden within the red flame. She was ready for the day in a sage-green skirt and a thin, plain white linen blouse trimmed in tiny loops of cotton lace. A matching green bolero-cut jacket lay on the chair beside her with gloves and a straw hat. She was ready to leave on a moment's notice.

'Good morning, Fleur. You're up early.' He entered the room as if he hadn't noticed her jacket and gloves or that she'd left his bed in a manner highly uncustomary of the morning routine they'd established. He dropped a kiss on her cheek as he passed her chair on the way to the coffee urn. 'Did you finish your article?'

'I did. Would you like to read it before I send it in?' She smiled. 'I hope you don't mind that I asked for breakfast to be served up here?'

'You may have breakfast anywhere you like, my dear. Rosefields is at your disposal.' He sat down with his coffee and a roll. 'I'll read your article this afternoon when we get back from the bank.' He arched his brow. 'You let me oversleep. I should have been up long before now.'

'You were tired.' She looked up briefly from organising her papers.

'For good reason,' he teased, but she didn't flirt back.

'I don't want to rush you, but I'd like to be at the bank when it opens.' She fixed him with a straightforward stare. He understood that boldness better now. The bolder she was, the more worried she was. That was how Fleur Griffiths operated. The boldness was real, but it was also a shield.

He set down his coffee cup to meet her eyes without distraction. 'I'll have the coach ready. We'll go as soon as I'm done eating.' The battle was about to be joined.

Chapter Eighteen

The Huddersfield Banking Company was an inauspicious building on Cloth Hall Street, austere and plain fronted with the exception of the tooled double door and its two large discs for knobs. To Fleur, the unexceptional mood of the building seemed at odds with the import of what would happen within its walls this morning. Justice would be satisfied. Her quest fulfilled. By evening she'd be home in London. All of this would be behind her.

She should be pleased. Her tenacity had paid off. Amid struggle and grief, she'd continued to fight. She ought to be proud of herself. But all she could feel as Jasper held the door for her was trepidation. Somehow her quest had become less just, less right.

'My lord, it is good to see you again. How may we be of service?' A neatly groomed man Jasper's age, dressed in a banker's plain dark suit hurried forward, recognising the Marquess of Meltham on sight.

'Mr Sikes, I need to go over the family accounts, particularly my brother's, from 1846,' Jasper said smoothly, recognising the man in turn.

Fleur's sense of trepidation tightened in a knot in her

stomach, her coffee and roll churning. She did not like relying on Jasper for access to information that would betray him. But she could not have hoped to have access to these accounts without him. On her own, she would have had to go through legal channels, made petitions and a fuss to look at anyone's financial records, let alone the relative of a peer. But Jasper had made it easy for her. And private. She shouldn't forget that. This was not a decision entirely without benefit for him.

'Mrs Griffiths.' Jasper turned to her with a formal tone. 'May I introduce Mr Sikes? He's a valued assistant manager at the bank. He's handled the Meltham account since I inherited. One might say we've come up the ranks together. I have no doubt one day he'll make managing director.' He smiled warmly at Sikes. 'Mr Sikes, this is Mrs Griffiths, the head of the Griffiths News Syndicate. She is my guest today.'

Mr Sikes shook her hand. 'It is a pleasure to assist you and to meet you in person. I am sorry about your husband. Allow me to offer belated condolences. One of your papers published an editorial of mine a couple years back about the importance of extending access to banks to the working classes for the purpose of creating savings accounts.'

He cleared his throat. 'I think of all the money people lost in Holmfirth when the dam burst, actual coin that was never recovered, all because money was kept in their homes instead of in a bank. I think, too, how much comfort it would have offered families to know that even in the wake of destruction they had the security of a modest savings to help them start again.'

Fleur managed a smile, knowing the man meant well

and that he couldn't possibly know what was at stake today: truth, justice and a lonely heart that had only just now come back to life. 'Thank you for your kind words and thoughts. I am glad our paper was able to be an outlet for your cause.' Inside, she was sinking, her resolve wavering. She didn't want Lord Orion Bexley's perfidy revealed in front of this man who clearly held Jasper in great esteem. She'd not started this quest to shame the Marquess of Meltham or to ruin a family that was respected in the local eye.

Sikes led them to a small room off the lobby of the bank, which was as austere as the exterior, and left them to fetch the account books. Jasper laughed when she commented on the excess of plainness. 'The board felt the bank would inspire more confidence with local clients if it was less ostentatious. The bank was formed after the panic in 1828. My father was one of the first to invest in it. He admired its mission to focus on local business and to focus on local growth. I was happy to continue banking here when I inherited. I should tell you that the Holmes River Reservoir Commission did much of its banking here.'

'Yes,' Fleur said quietly. She'd noted the bank in Captain Moody's report and in her own documents. There'd been a two-thousand-pound loan the bank had made to the commission for repairs. She drew a deep breath, guilt eating into her. She had to say something before Mr Sikes came back. Her conscience demanded it. 'Jasper, I am sorry.' It was hard to say what she was sorry for. There was so much that required her penitence. She wasn't sorry for the whole situation, certainly. For instance, she was not sorry to have been in his bed, to have had him as a lover. But she was sorry to repay those moments with trouble and scandal. 'I didn't mean it to be like this.'

Jasper held her gaze, his topaz eyes steady. She was feeling penitent. He knew what she wanted to hear, but he wouldn't give her absolution. 'You knew it could be like this, Fleur. You knew this was a risk.' Then he added, 'As did I. Still, I think it is better we face what is in those accounts as friends rather than foes.' He hoped that was the case. This morning had been difficult on them both. They were in the belly of the beast now, forced to face the truth, forced to face their feelings and somehow reconcile them both in a way that didn't leave them broken.

Mr Sikes came back with the records. 'These are the accounts. Let me know if you need anything else,' he offered before leaving them.

Jasper immediately set aside the family accounts, which he'd only requested to divert the bank's attention from his brother. 'This one is Orion's account book,' Jasper said solemnly, opening the ledger. He was aware of Fleur coming to stand beside him, positioning herself to read over his shoulder. He appreciated that she was letting him take the lead on combing through the ledger. He bounced his knee surreptitiously under the table, hoping they found nothing.

There were the usual deposits, the quarterly allowance from the estate, the payments made to tailors, club memberships and other young man's pursuits. He winced at one large payment made to a club off St. James's. There was another further down, and another.

'Is that excessive?' Fleur asked, pointing to the recurring entries.

'Yes. Gaming hells are the vice of many young men.' Jasper grimaced. 'This was seven years ago. Orion had some trouble at a gaming hell.' In customary Orion fashion, his brother had played over his head in an attempt to recoup his losses. When that had failed, Orion had tried to handle the debt on his own, but his allowance was not large enough.

'Who are these people? Brown and Whitaker?' Fleur leaned closer, the scent of her perfume intensifying with its nearness. Jasper swallowed, not against desire, but embarrassment on his brother's behalf. He did not want another to see Orion like this. Orion was his brother, a fun-loving, caring, often short-sighted young man who was still looking for his place in the world. He was not what these numbers suggested. Jasper hadn't even told his mother about it.

'Those are some gentlemen who will make short-term loans at high interest rates to other gentlemen who find themselves short on cash.' Instead of turning to him and asking him for help, Orion had taken a loan from Brown and Whitaker in Cheapside. 'It was the beginning of a snowball of debt that got larger each month until I found out the hard way.' He paused, remembering that horrible night. 'Orion was found in an alley, badly beaten.' Brown and Whitaker had taken their pound in flesh when coin had not been produced in a timely manner.

Fleur's hand squeezed his shoulder. 'How awful.'

'I paid the debt the next morning and put Orion up at a hotel until he was fit for Mother to see him.' Jasper pushed a hand through his hair. 'I cut off all credit for him at the gaming hells. When his own funds ran out, he was not to be allowed to play.' Jasper sighed. 'He was not happy with me. We had many fights that spring.'

'Well, it appears to have worked,' Fleur said as they reached the end of the spring quarter account book. 'There doesn't seem to be any more payments to Brown and Whitaker or other such folks.'

Jasper reached for the summer and then the autumn books. 'You take autumn, I'll do summer. Then we can trade to double check each other.' He hated this. Going through someone's finances was like going through their underwear drawer. Yet it was the only way if Orion was to be vindicated. He'd just finished with summer, having spied nothing, when Fleur looked up. Her expression grim.

'There's a deposit in October of 1846 for seven thousand, eight hundred pounds,' she said in a near whisper. Jasper froze. That was the exact sum request for dam repairs in the August work order.

'Who is it from?' Jasper asked, although it didn't matter. What else could it be? It wasn't Orion's quarterly allowance. The timing was wrong and so was the amount. It was too much.

Fleur shook her head. 'It doesn't say.'

'I'll get Mr Sikes and have him check the bank records.' It was the next logical step. Leaving the room also gave him a chance to get his emotions under control. Good God, Orion had really done it. He'd filed a work order and pocketed the money. And a few years later eighty-one people had died.

Jasper calmly made the request for Sikes to find the

deposit record, but all the while his mind raced. What was he going to do? This would devastate his mother. What had Orion been thinking? Why had he done this? Had he got in trouble again and tried to find his own way out?

He waited until Sikes returned with the bank's record of transactions. 'Here's the cheque.' Sikes showed him the grey and mauve note used by the Huddersfield Banking Company. Jasper studied it, his eyes landing on the signature at the bottom, his gut tightening. It had been issued from Parliament for the express purpose of reservoir repairs. The only saving grace was that it had not been issued directly to Orion. It had been issued to the Holmes River Reservoir Commission.

Jasper furrowed his brow. 'If this cheque was not issued to Orion, how was it possible he was able to deposit it into his account?'

Sikes set down the big book that kept track of deposits. He turned to the date the cheque had been deposited. 'It didn't go to his account. It went to the Commission's account. You can see the amount right here. Then, a day later, one of the commission members transferred the funds to Orion's personal account. I imagine whoever was the drawer at the time did the transfer.' At which point, Jasper surmised, the funds fell out of the public eye. They were mixed with Orion's personal monies and no longer traceable. Or maybe they were. 'Sikes, I'd like the family ledgers for forty-seven.'

Fleur looked up when he returned, new ledgers in hand. 'The cheque was a match, sort of.' He explained how it had been deposited to the commission's account first and the whole sum was later transferred to Orion. 'I want to see if we can find where the money went. Was it frittered away on new purchases?' Jasper tried to remember back that far. Had Orion gone through a spending phase that was over and above his usual? 'Or...' he offered another suggestion fearfully '...did it go to pay more debt?' He handed Fleur a ledger. 'If it went to pay debt, there would be a large outlay all at once.'

After an hour of combing ledgers, they'd come up with little. 'There is nothing except for these four payments, made quarterly,' Fleur remarked. 'They caught my eye because they were regular occurrences, and because when you total up the amount, it comes out to seven thousand, eight hundred.' She shook her head. 'I didn't want it to.'

'It's not your fault.' Jasper slouched in his chair. Perhaps it was his fault. Why had Orion done this and thought he could get away with it? That no one would find out? It didn't make sense. 'Who did the payments go to?' He did not think for a moment the payments had gone for reservoir repairs. At some level, it didn't matter where the money went. The bottom line was that Orion had taken it.

'It doesn't say. Your brother doesn't seem to be a prolific record keeper. He just writes down the basics.'

Perhaps because he didn't want anyone to know. If only he knew where Orion was now. He could get some answers, talk some sense into him. Jasper forced his mind to work. He had to think of next steps. 'You were right. My brother embezzled money from the reservoir commission.' When he looked at Fleur, she was pale, her expression tight.

'I would prefer not to be right about this,' Fleur said apologetically.

'That's not how you felt when this all began,' he corrected. 'You don't need to feel that way now simply because things changed between us.' No, this couldn't be about them. This had to be about Orion. 'What will you do with the information?' It was the last piece she'd been looking for, the piece that proved a single man had been responsible for the collapse of the dam. If the money had gone to repair the waste pit, none of this would have happened.

'The *Tribune* will break the story.' They were speaking in whispers now. If they didn't speak these horrible things too loudly, perhaps they wouldn't become real.

'The board of directors will be pleased. You will sell a lot of newspapers. It isn't every day a peer's brother is caught stealing money from the government.' Just saying the words made him sick to his stomach. How could he tell her not to print the story when she had her evidence? That had been the only condition he'd asked her for, that if she did want to connect the deaths to Lord Orion that she have proof for it. Would it be enough? All that was left was the press of causal arguments. Could it be proven that this money had been given to the commission for the express and singular purpose of the repairing the waste pit? Or had it been meant for other repairs? If so, it was still embezzlement, but at least it wasn't manslaughter.

'How long until the story breaks?'

'A week at most. With something this big, I do need the board of directors to approve it and they will need time.' To her credit, Fleur did not break. He admired that. Perhaps another woman would have given in to the relationship between them and decided not to publish. But Fleur was made of sterner stuff, and he loved her all the more for it—for her conviction, for her strength, for her dedication in doing what was right even when it hurt. This was not easy for her. Nor for him.

He'd chosen the right words in his head a moment ago. He *loved* her, that very thing that brought pain with the joy, that very thing he'd sworn to avoid because he knew that pain first-hand from losing his father and watching his mother fall apart. Fleur had turned his well-protected logical world upside down and he *loved* her for it despite the cost. He would do it all again to have had this time with her, to have *her* in his world no matter how briefly. How ironic he should realise that now, here at the end.

'I do not want to cause you pain, Jasper. I am sorry it didn't turn out another way.' What other way was there? With her losing her papers? Her position? That would not have helped them any more than this did. Perhaps she'd been right last night. A future for them was impossible.

She rose from the table. 'I want to commend you for your integrity. I understand I'd never have been able to access these records without your co-operation. You could have obstructed all this. You could have lied to get what you wanted and you didn't. And I am repaying you poorly.'

'Say nothing more, Fleur. We are past words now. I'll take you back to Rosefields.'

She shook her head. 'No. There's an afternoon train to London. I think it's best that I take it. Good bye, Jasper.'

She made a clean break of it, then, walking out of the room and towards the front doors, the sound of the click of her heels diminishing on the tiles until the door shut behind her and she was gone.

She would go to London and he would go to Rose-fields to plot his next move. He had a week to find Orion, to find a barrister with an impeccable reputation or to send Orion out of the country, which seemed fairly appealing at the moment. The legal system couldn't prosecute a man they couldn't find. Orion would never be able to come home, but perhaps that was better than the alternative. Then, when that was settled, he would try to put his heart back together, perhaps settle for one of the girls on his mother's list, assuming anyone would have him with the taint of scandal on the family name.

Jasper pounded a fist on the table. Damn it. He'd been right all along. Love hurt. Why the hell had he decided to test that hypothesis once more? The results had been the same.

Chapter Nineteen

Rosefields was not the same without her. Jasper wandered the garden at sunset, his footsteps aimless, his thoughts picking over each scene, each moment of the week they'd shared here. How was it possible that a person could make such an impact on a place in such a short time? Perhaps because it wasn't the place they impacted, but the people in it. Wasn't that why he loved Rosefields? Here was where the reminders of his childhood lived, of days spent with his father, of happy summers and snowy Christmases.

Jasper kicked a pebble, watching it roll away. Rosefields was the home of his childhood. By necessity, London was the home of his adulthood at present. But he'd always imagined Rosefields would be the home of his own family when the time came. He'd marry here in the little chapel on the property in the off season, not at St George's in town. His children would be baptised here as he and Orion had been. A family would give him reason to spend less time in London, to run his politics from a distance.

Now, he wondered if that time would ever come. He stopped to watch a bee burrowing deep in a rose. Had that time, perhaps, already come and he'd missed it? Had Fleur been his chance? For a moment he stilled, thinking there'd been a sound in the garden, the crunching of gravel beneath a foot. He looked up, wild, illogical hope beating in his chest. Had she come back? But the garden was empty. There was just him and his thoughts.

Jasper pulled out his pocket watch. She would be in London now. Had she gone home, or had she gone straight to the office? Would she stay up all night crafting her article? He snapped the watch shut. Would she think of him and Rosefields at all? She belonged here with her love of the countryside, with her desire for family and children.

He could give all of that to her here: a country home, children, time away from the paper. These were all things Adam Griffiths had chosen not to give his wife. By doing so, he'd chosen her life for her. Which begged the question: would she give up the syndicate for Rosefields? He supposed the question bore asking in the little hypothesis he was testing. If he ever were to offer her Rosefields and a family, would she take it? Or was she wedded to the ghost of the life she'd had with Adam? Did she stay at the paper for Dead Adam, or did she stay for herself?

He gave a harsh chuckle. What did any of these questions matter? She was gone and Orion was in trouble. Her newspaper was going to expose what he'd done and how that act had led to the Holmfirth flood deaths. He needed to think about Orion now. He couldn't save his relationship with Fleur, but perhaps he could find a way to save his brother.

* * *

Two days later, Jasper had something of a plan. He'd consulted the family solicitor on retainer in Huddersfield, who'd recommended an excellent barrister with ties to the region. Both Jasper and the solicitor felt that a home-grown connection might help if the time came. Or rather *when* that time came. Short of Fleur not publishing the article, that time *would* come and it was coming quickly. The article would not print before tomorrow at the earliest and he hoped that it was more reasonable to assume it would print the day after.

Jasper poured himself a drink and settled in to pass the long evening reading. All that was left now was to go back to London and brace his mother. His trunk was packed, ready to go to the station tomorrow for the morning train.

'My lord,' the butler interrupted shortly after nine o'clock. 'Your brother is here to see you. Shall I show him in?'

'Orion is here?' Jasper leaped up. Despite the trials of the week, his first reaction was one of relief. 'Yes, show him up. No, I'll go down.' He was in too much of a hurry to wait. His brother was home, safe, a bright spot in difficult times.

'Orion!' he called from the top of the stairs, his brother turning to face him. Jasper raced down the stairs and pulled his brother into a tight embrace. 'I was so worried. I didn't know where you'd gone or how long you'd be.' He hugged his brother and then stepped back to look at him, relief giving way to concern. Orion was well dressed as usual, sporting an elegant silk waistcoat of lavender paisley, but he was tired. There were dark circles beneath his eyes and his typically lively gaze was dull concern.

'Jasper, your welcome makes me feel quite the prodigal.' He gave a half-laugh.

'Where have you been?' Jasper asked.

'Everywhere, nowhere. Thinking, or at least trying to think. I keep reaching the same conclusion. I am in trouble, Jasper, and I need your help.' Orion pressed a hand to his mouth in a visible effort to hold on to his control. It took a moment for him to recover himself. 'I am sorry. I am so sorry.'

'Come, sit. You don't look as if you've eaten. I'll have a tray sent to the library and we can talk.' Rather, Orion would talk and he would listen. Jasper led his brother upstairs. He could guess what this was about, but he wanted to hear it from Orion. He poured his brother a drink and settled him in a chair. 'Now, tell me what this is all about.'

'It's about those articles regarding the Bilberry Dam accident, the ones that name me as being primarily responsible.' Orion looked down at his drink. 'I am afraid of what the newspaper will find if they keep digging.'

'Why would you be afraid of that?' Jasper asked carefully.

'Because there was a deposit made to my account for a sum meant to be used for repairs to the waste pit. It will look as though I took the money and the waste pit repair never happened. It's why the dam burst. We need to make sure the paper can't get a hold of my accounts. You can block that, right?' Orion's blue eyes held his in earnest desperation.

'I suppóse I could. But it wouldn't be moral, Orion. It would be deliberately hiding evidence.'

Orion's eyes sparked. 'I would think philosophical ethics would be the least of your concerns. Do you know what it would mean? The case could be reopened. I could go to trial and be convicted for embezzlement, for manslaughter.' His voice rose in panic.

'Calm down, Orion. That hasn't happened yet,' Jasper said in careful, evenly measured tones. He wanted to tell his brother it would be all right, that they would fix it. In part because he couldn't—it was too late for that—but also in part because he shouldn't. Perhaps that had been his Achilles heel with Orion all along. He'd been so intent on helping him, on cleaning up Orion's messes instead of making Orion clean them up. He'd made the messes go away without asking for atonement. And Orion had learned a very different lesson than the one he'd intended to impart.

'Since you've been gone, some things have happened. I need to tell you, so please listen without losing your head,' Jasper said sternly. 'The paper has indeed dug deeper and they have found the deposit.'

Orion blanched. 'How did they get my accounts? Surely that is an inadmissible sort of evidence. They can't go get a man's private accounts without a warrant or something.'

'I gave permission. I went to the bank with Fleur Griffiths. I was the one that went through the account book and had the bank cross-reference the cheque with their deposit records.'

Orion exploded out of his chair and began pacing. 'You! Do you understand what this means? You've all but delivered me for trial and admitted my guilt *for* me.' Orion flashed a hurt look. 'All for a woman? She really got to you. But she'll sell you short, too. Do you think you'll emerge unscathed? That you will look like a hero? This will touch all of us. Think what it will do to Mother. She won't be able to hold her head up. Think of what this will do to your marital prospects. Who will want a scandal-tainted marquess for a son-in-law?' Orion shoved a hand through his hair. 'Was she worth it? I never thought you'd throw me over for a woman. I thought you were better than that.'

Orion made him sound like a traitor and Fleur a harlot. 'I will not obscure the truth for you, Orion.' It took willpower to keep his temper on a firm leash. 'Yes, what you have done will have ugly consequences for innocent people like myself and Mother, and that is not fair to us, but that doesn't mean you should be excused of the responsibility. Perhaps I've excused you from too much responsibility in the past.'

'You would see me face a trial? Be sentenced for crimes?' Orion was aghast. 'All to teach me a lesson?'

The leash of his control slipped a little. He'd been desperate to see his brother and relieved to have him here. But now he wanted Orion to accept responsibility for what he'd done and Orion would not. Orion only wanted a way out. Yet, to not give him a way out would be to condemn him. 'Eighty-one people died, Orion. Whole families were killed. Babies drowned in their sleep. Children washed away while parents looked on helpless. Homes were destroyed, mills were destroyed. I saw Holmfirth last week, over a year since the flood. The place still bears scars. Bridges have not been replaced, mills have not been rebuilt, some wreckage has still not been removed. People lost homes, lives and live-lihoods. They can't work if the mills don't run. No work means no wages, no way to support families.'

There was a long silence between the brothers, the tray of food untouched. Jasper hoped the import of what had happened was weighing at last on Orion's conscience. 'I have engaged a barrister with an excellent reputation,' he said after a while.

Orion glared. 'You've engaged a barrister? That is your idea of help? Let the newspaper print the opportunity and drag me to trial? And then what? Just throw up your hands and hope for the best? How am I supposed to be vindicated when they've got the cheque and the financial records?'

'We can make arguments of causation. If we can show that the money was for repairs in general, that it wasn't specifically for funding only the waste pit, we can argue you weren't directly culpable. If we can show that there were other problems with the dam that con-tributed to the accident, we can mitigate the role of the waste pit. We can show it to be one of many flaws in the dam's engineering. Those arguments stand a good chance of being successful since they've already been made and the original findings conclude there were a variety of factors. I do think the burden of proof is on paper.'

Orion shot him a sardonic look. 'And if you're wrong? This is my life you're playing with. It's bad enough you are willing to trot me out into the public eye and let the Griffiths news syndicate attempt to pin this on me.'

Jasper answered with a solemn stare. 'All right then,

let's back up. Did you do it? Did you take the money? Did you place the work order and not see it carried out?'

'Yes. No.' Orion shook his head. 'It's complicated.'

'That's not an answer. Try again. First, have a sandwich. There is no rush. We have all night.' He couldn't save Orion if Orion was not willing to save himself.

Orion sat and Jasper waited patiently while his brother ate. At last Orion was ready to talk and the eating had done its job in settling his emotions.

'I sent in the work order requesting repairs on the waste pit,' Orion began. 'It was a request that came from all three of us assigned to oversee the Bilberry reservoir. My name is on the order only because I drew the short straw and had to fill out the paperwork. It just happened to be my turn. When the money was awarded, it went into the commission's account first. Then, William Hendricks, who was the current drawer and who was also on my subcommittee for Bilberry, asked if the money could be transferred to my account so that the money could be easily accessed by us to oversee our repairs. He said he was concerned that the money would get used by other reservoirs or eaten up by other expenses. He wanted it separate, given the commission's history of insolvency.' Orion gave a tell-tale fidget and Jasper interrupted.

'The ledger shows evenly quarterly distributions over the course of the year that total up to the deposit amount. Did those go to repairs?' Even if that money hadn't gone to the waste pit repair, it would definitely eradicate charges of embezzlement. It would be a start.

Orion shook his head. 'The money went to Hendricks. He volunteered to be in charge of hiring engineers for the repairs.'

'Did he ever hire anyone?' This would also be helpful. If someone had been hired, they could find a contract. It would show that Orion had not wilfully ignored the need for repairs.

'I don't know. Hendricks rotated off the subcommittee at the end of his term. By then, the money had all been transferred to his account.' Orion was nervous. He was bouncing his leg. There was something amiss here.

'Let me understand. You transferred the repair funds to Hendricks once a quarter and yet no repairs were made and no one was hired. Did you question him about that? Make him accountable?'

Orion fiddled with a sandwich. 'No. But neither did our third member.' He let out a sigh. 'What do you want me to say? That I didn't follow up? That I didn't hold another committee member accountable for his actions? That I was lazy? That I didn't take my position on the commission as seriously as you would have? A position, by the way, that I didn't want and you foisted it on me not for just one term, but two.'

'I was trying to give you purpose,' Jasper explained. 'I thought after the engineering corps, that dam work would put some of those skills to use. I thought it was a good fit.'

Orion took a savage bite of his sandwich. 'Except that I *hated* the engineering corps. I was a horrid engineer.'

'It was better than *your* option, which was do nothing,' Jasper shot back, remembering how difficult Orion had been after university—which he hadn't quite finished. The don had felt academics weren't Orion's calling.

Orion gave him a baleful stare. 'I'm not you, Jasper. I don't have answers for everything. I don't have a sense of purpose. I just move from disaster to disaster, or perhaps I am the disaster. I suppose every family has to have one.'

'None of that is true, not even the part about me.' Jasper blew out a breath. If it was, he might not have lost Fleur. They were getting sidetracked now.

'Being incompetent is unfortunate, but it is not a crime,' Orion drawled.

Jasper nodded. 'Where is William Hendricks these days?' He could hunt down Hendricks, make him accountable. Orion had not acted alone.

Orion took a swallow of brandy. 'He's dead. Died last year in April in a hunting accident on the moors, although some say it was suicide because April isn't exactly hunting season, is it?' There'd certainly be no hunting down Hendricks, but Jasper could still get his hands on Hendricks's accounts. Hendricks's accounts could clear Orion while still giving Fleur a story. Jasper made a note of the date of Hendricks's death. Just two months after the flood.

Jasper swirled the remainder of the brandy in his snifter. 'Why did you do it, Orion? Surely, something must have seemed off to you after that first disbursement and no one had been hired to start repairs?'

Orion was silent for a long time and Jasper felt that he'd at last come to the crux of the matter. Orion met his gaze, regret etched in his face. 'Because I owed him money and he offered to wipe the debt clean if I'd just let him park the reservoir funds in my account.' Orion sighed. 'I couldn't really say no. I didn't have the funds to pay him back. It seemed like a good option at the time. It was true that there was concern the funds would be used for other expenses. His argument wasn't illogical. It did make sense to have access to the funds.' Orion shook his head. 'But when he didn't actually disburse those funds for repairs, I couldn't call him out on it.'

'That was a better option than coming to me?' Jasper put in, hurt.

'Yes, given that I had just so recently disappointed you with my little run-in with the moneylenders.' Orion closed his eyes, struggling for control. 'That was eight years ago. I haven't gambled over my means since. You know that.' He opened his eyes and Jasper saw real regret there. 'I told myself it wouldn't matter. The reservoir waste pit was fine as long as the water didn't exceed a certain level. Chances were the waste pit would never reach excess. I took a gamble on that. Who would have thought the whole dam would go?'

'Hendricks was using extortion in order to launder money through your account.' Jasper drummed his fingers on the arm of his chair. 'It would be harder to trace that way. It would have been too obvious if the whole sum had just shown up in his account all at once and then no work materialised.' A hypothesis was forming. Perhaps Hendricks's death had been a suicide after all. Riddled with guilt over the dam deaths, fear of being found out for extortion or connected to the dam accident, and whatever other problems the man had—it would be interesting to find out—Hendricks had taken his own life before he could be discovered.

As the clock chimed one, Jasper came to certain conclusions. Yes, Orion had put himself in trouble's way, yet again. Yes, he'd need to bear responsibility for his part in it. But his part was no longer the role of the perpetrator. He was guilty of negligent oversight, for not calling for accountability, but he was also the victim of extortion. Orion was guilty of many things, but not the failure of the dam, at least not any more so than of the other commission members.

'What are we going to do?' Orion asked.

'We are going to get some sleep. Tomorrow, we are going to London to stop the presses. There's an afternoon train and with luck we'll make it.'

Fleur Griffiths had the wrong man. For his sake and for hers, Jasper hoped they got to London in time.

Chapter Twenty

It was nearly time. Fleur glanced at the clock on her office desk. She would leave herself twenty minutes to take the stairs down to the basement of the *Tribune* building where the presses were housed, far enough away from the daily business of running the paper that their noise didn't interrupt. The feature story on the Bilberry reservoir would go to print and be out in the morning edition. She'd taken the story down this morning for lay out and she wanted to be on hand this evening when the first copy of the paper came off the presses.

She'd stayed late tonight especially for that reason. Last night she'd stayed late for a board of directors' meeting. The night before that she'd stayed late to write. The night before that... She stopped right there. She didn't want to think about that night or the one before it. Suffice it to say, there'd been a lot of reasons this week to stay late. Here, she was busy. She didn't have time to think about anything outside of work.

And why would she? Work had been good this week for the first time in a long time. There had been successes. The board of directors was thrilled with being able to break the Bilberry Dam story. It was going to be the biggest story of the summer and into the autumn once a trial was called for. Circulation would go up and that meant revenues would go up. The board had actually applauded her and complimented her work.

Two weeks ago they'd wanted her head on a pike, blaming her for losing money even though the losses had pre-dated her tenure. And now, they were so pleased. Her position was safe. Adam's newspaper syndicate was safe. She sat back in her desk chair and raised a teacup to the empty room. 'I did it, Adam. I found the culprit and he is going to pay for your death.' She was going to have justice for Adam, Keir, Garrett, Antonia, Emma and herself, just as she'd vowed after the tragedy last year. So why didn't she feel better about it? Why wasn't the thrill of victory thrumming through her? She'd triumphed. Breaking this story would also give momentum to her call for better oversight legislation. By rights, she should be on top of the world.

The higher the pedestal, the further the fall. What a long way down it would be with no one to catch her. It was an incredibly morbid thought and a lonely one, too. But she wasn't going to fall. She'd done her research, she had her proof. Her story was airtight. Adam's syndicate was rallying. Why did none of this fill her with satisfaction? With pride? Why did it all of this good news leave a sour taste?

Was it a sour taste or just no taste at all? Where was the joy? There was no one to celebrate it with. She'd achieved the improbable, she'd discovered what Captain Moody's inquest could not. For her efforts there'd been a round of applause in the boardroom and a perfunctory champagne toast. Then the board had shook her hand and headed home to their families to celebrate their own good fortunes with those they loved. It was what she would have done. In the past, Emma and Antonia would have celebrated with her. But they were long gone, off to new lives. Adam wasn't here. There was no one.

'Damn it, Adam. You should be here,' she scolded out loud. 'I became a reporter for you. I learned about the newspaper business for you and now you aren't here to do your part.' This was for him. It had always all been for him. They'd dedicated their lives to his news syndicate because it had been his dream. She'd kept that dream alive for him. But this was not her dream, it did not feed her happiness. She saw that more clearly now.

For so long whatever Adam had wanted, she'd wanted, too. She'd not stopped to consider her own dreams. Not until Jasper. He had been just for her because he couldn't be more. He was a dream she couldn't have. They could never go out into society. She didn't belong in his circles and now she was bringing scandal to his family.

Whatever he felt for her would not withstand the firestorm her article would stir up. He would hate her, knowing that she'd done this to his brother. He couldn't possibly love a woman who would strike such a blow against those he loved. It didn't mean she was doing anything wrong. This story must be told. It was right to tell it. But it did mean she couldn't have him.

'What can your story change? It can't bring anyone back.'

His words had haunted her this week amid the champagne and congratulations. She had her success but at what cost? At the cost of hurting him, of ruining his brother's life, even though his brother ought to have shown better judgement to begin with. There was cost to her as well. She'd lost Jasper, a man who cared for her. She'd never thought to feel again the way she felt with Jasper: on fire, alive and it was better than anything she'd ever known.

Even with Adam.

Such a thought bordered on heresy. Adam had been the sum of her world for so long it seemed wrong to let anything or anyone challenge his place. Life with Adam had been fiery, passionate, an adventure. There'd been wealth at her fingertips and unique opportunities that appealed to her bolder nature. But there'd also been a limit. She'd never truly been Adam's partner, had she? Their life was Adam's life. She was just invited along for the ride.

With Jasper, she was a partner in truth. He'd invited her into partnership that night at Meltham House and never looked back, knowing the risk he took in doing so. He'd never flagged in that partnership, not even when the account books squarely implicated his brother.

She'd not easily forget the pain on his face when she left him at the bank. Even in his own private agony over his brother, he'd offered to take her back to Rosefields. She'd left because she couldn't bear to see him suffer, knowing that she was the cause of it. She'd not trusted herself to hold on to her principles. One halfway decent argument from him and she would have let the findings go. Now, it didn't matter. She had put herself beyond him with this article.

The last of the clerks were locking up the offices as she walked through on the way to the stairs. Only the print crew would remain throughout the night to have the morning edition ready when London awoke. She stopped and looked about the space. It was quiet with everyone gone. Jasper would like that. He appreciated the value of quiet. Did she really want to give all this up? Could she? She rather thought she could. It would not be easy. The adult years of her life had been spent in these offices. But what and who was she keeping this for? Not for herself, she saw that now. This did not bring her joy, not without Adam.

She thought of the conversation she'd had with Antonia earlier in the spring. She'd urged Antonia to think about why she was holding on to Keir's company. Perhaps she ought to ask herself that question, too. Why was she holding on to the papers? Out of habit? Because she felt she owed it to Adam? Because running the syndicate brought her joy and fulfilment? Two of those answers were not reasons to stay involved. The third one was, though. Could she answer yes to it? The last few weeks with Jasper had caused her to question her choices and reasons. Perhaps it was time to start exploring those answers, and perhaps for the first time since Adam's death she was actually in a mental and emotional place from which to do that exploration.

She was about to turn the knob on the door leading to the basement when the night security guard called out, running towards her, 'Mrs Griffiths, wait. There's a gentleman here to see you. I told him we were closed for the night, but he insisted it was important.'

He panted his message as two men came up behind him, one, an immaculately groomed dirty blond, the other dark-haired and tousled. *Jasper.* Her reaction was physical and real, after almost a week without him. Her pulse raced, the sight of him enough to fluster her. She'd missed him so much.

'Fleur.' Urgency underscored that single word. 'Have you printed the article yet?' There was desperation and hope mixed in his eyes as if everything hung by the thread of her answer.

'Um, no. It runs tomorrow morning. I was just going down to see the first editions come off the press in a few minutes.'

Jasper's hand gripped her arm with a gentle pressure, his eyes intent on her. 'You have to halt the presses, Fleur. That story cannot run.'

She had to be strong here at the eleventh hour even when faced by the temptation of seeing him again, all those feelings of want and need that only he could satisfy surging to the fore. 'Jasper,' she said in low, private tones, 'we've discussed it. You know I cannot ignore the evidence.'

'I know, Fleur. That's not why I'm asking.' She'd never seen him like this, so stern, so intense. 'You've got the right idea, but you've got the wrong man. The story is bigger than you think. Trust me,' Jasper ground out. 'I'm asking for your sake. That story will be the ruin of you. I cannot let you run a piece that I know is false.'

That was when she knew just how much he loved her. This was not a gambit to save his brother or even himself. He'd come to save her. After all she'd put him through, he'd still come for her. Halting the presses was no small consideration. The board of directors would be furious to discover the piece was pulled. They'd have to lay out the front page differently. The paper might even be late. There'd be a price to pay for her decision. But Jasper had come for her. The least she could do was listen to him.

'We'll have to hurry,' she said gravely, making the decision on the fly, hoping they weren't too late as it was and racking her brain for what she was going to use to replace it.

They made it with a minute to spare, Fleur bellowing at the top of her lungs, to stop the presses before tying on an apron and taking charge of the needed alterations. Jasper stepped back, keeping himself and Orion out of the way. As far as he was concerned, he had the best seat in the house. It was impressive to watch her work as she moved from group to group, helping with the typesetting to rearrange the layout and to find a new article to substitute.

'It's not going to run, right?' Orion asked nervously at his side.

'Not that version of events,' Jasper said sternly. He and Orion had engaged in serious discussion on the train trip to London. 'She will run your complete version of events when the time is right. She will want to interview you tonight. You must tell her about Hendricks and the extortion, just like you told me. Then she will want to go out and get proof. When that is done, the story will run.' And Orion would be named. He would have to own up to his part in the debacle, but at least it would be honestly and fairly presented and the backlash for the family would be mitigated. For the Marquessate of Meltham it would be a survivable scandal thanks to her.

* * *

After two hours of work, the presses began to hum and Fleur made the rounds, congratulating the press crew on their effort. At last, she came to join him and Orion. 'We've got it all under control.' She smiled as she wiped her hands and took off her apron. 'Now, you need to live up to your end of the bargain.' She gave him a sly smile that was part coyness, part seriousness. 'I stopped the presses for you, you'd better have a great story for me. Come upstairs to my office and we'll talk.'

After a day of not having enough time, of wanting time to slow so that the train delays would not prevent them from arriving in time to beat the presses, it seemed to Jasper that there was suddenly too much time—too much time between Orion having a chance to tell his story and his being able to have Fleur to himself, to ask her the questions that mattered most to him. It took all of his willpower to sit patiently and quietly—two things he was usually very good at—while she listened and Orion got the lion's share of her attention.

She finished questioning Orion and set her pencil down, turning her gaze in his direction, an apprecia-tive smile on her face. 'You were right. The story is big-ger than we thought. I can start tracking down leads on Hendricks right away. We'll need proof before we can print.' A palpable tension crackled between them, nei-ther of them sure what to say next.

Jasper cleared his throat. 'Orion, take the coach back to the town house. I'll find my own way home. Mother will be pleased to see you and you can see to getting our trunks unloaded.' To Fleur he added, 'We came straight from the station. I didn't want to risk waiting too long.'

When Orion departed, he asked, 'Will you be all right? You made an enormous sacrifice for me tonight.'

'You also made one for me. You could have hung me out to dry, let me run the story and then sued the paper for slander. You could have ruined me, could have had a nice piece of revenge,' Fleur said. 'But in truth, I don't know how the board of directors will respond. They will be disappointed. I will have to answer to them. Still, I will have a better story, later, so I am hopeful that they can be pacified with an exclusive interview from Lord Orion Bexley himself.' She gave a tired smile and for the first time, Jasper noted the faint circles about her eyes.

'You've been working late.'

'I didn't want to be home alone. I don't think I've even unpacked yet.' Her gaze flickered over his face, doing its own assessment. 'How are you, Jasper? Are you holding up?'

'I am doing much better now that I've seen you.' He reached for her hand, the first contact they'd had in days, his gaze steady. 'I missed you, Fleur. Rosefields didn't feel right with you gone. I spent a lot of time thinking about you, about what a great team we made—and still make. Not just in politics or in bed, or in problem solving, but in life.' His grip on her hand tightened. 'I want to pursue the possibility of that life with you, Fleur.' He watched a flurry of emotions scuttle across her face, none of them the emotion he hoped for. It would be so much easier if she simply responded by throwing herself in his arms. Instead, her answer was in the form of a question.

'What exactly are you asking me, Jasper?' Her green eyes were sharp and wary.

'I am asking you to marry me.'

Chapter Twenty-One

What did one say when a fantasy came to life? This was madness, something that was both possible and impossible and she didn't know how to respond. 'After only six weeks? Jasper, are you sure?' She could feel herself trembling with shock and delight, and surprise and, yes, with uncertainty.

'I am sure, but perhaps you are not?' Jasper seemed disappointed with her response. Dear heavens, she was hurting him all over again in a different sort of way. She seemed doomed to hurt him. He made to disengage his hand, but she held on, refusing to let him go.

'It's not that. I am overwhelmed by the asking,' Fleur said hurriedly. 'Perhaps too overwhelmed to think straight.'

'I love you, Fleur.'

Her voice shook a little at hearing the words for the first time from him. 'I know you do. I saw it in your eyes tonight. You came to save me, not yourself. That was an act of true love, an act that was entirely selfless.'

'I want you to be my partner in all things and I want to be yours. I want a life with you in the country at Rosefields, children with you, the family we both want.'

Fleur nodded, unable to speak against the emotion

conjured by his words and the images that went with them. He offered her everything she craved and true partnership to go with it. She understood implicitly that partnership had made tonight's outcome possible. If he'd not compelled her into partnership with him, if they'd remained opposing enemies, tonight could have hurt them both—exposing his brother in an unfair, incomplete light in a way that cast aspersions on him and the family, as well as hurting the paper's reputation. But the honesty of their partnership, their trust in each other, had prevented that two-way disaster.

'It would be easy to say yes, Jasper. But I am not sure it would be right or fair to either of us to jump headlong into this.' She paused. 'I've been doing a lot of thinking since I've been back. This week, I had everything I thought I'd been searching for. I had justice for Adam, validation of my hold on his news empire, recognition. And it wasn't enough. Those things didn't fill me. They were things that were important to Adam and, without him, they were no longer important to me. I still think the values that Adam championed are important—literacy and access to information as cornerstones to a society that practises real equality.

'I still want to fight for those things, promote those things. But I don't know if I need to do it at the helm of a news syndicate. I certainly couldn't run the syndicate from Rosefields. It is too remote. But maybe I am ready to give all of that over to someone else and start fresh with those efforts on a more local level. Perhaps I should take a leaf out of the Huddersfield Banking Company's book and focus on regional literacy efforts close to home at Rosefields.' She leaned close. 'Do you hear what I am saying, Jasper? I just don't know what the right direction is for me. I have to work some things out about what I want and how I want them before I can invite someone into my life on a more permanent level.'

Jasper smiled. 'That doesn't sound like no.'

Something warm blossomed in the vicinity of her heart. Perhaps that was what hope felt like. 'It's not "no". It's "I need a long engagement". I think you do, too. Between the newspapers and Parliamentary legislation, we have a big year ahead of us, Jasper, plenty of time and ways in which to test our partnership.' She could feel relief sweeping him and she let herself be drawn into his arms until she was on his lap. She reached for his glasses. 'I'm looking forward to most of it.'

'What part are you not looking forward to?' Jasper teased, stealing a kiss.

'Meeting your mother. I'm not on her list.' That would be one more item they'd need the year to sort out.

'You're not on the list…yet. But you will be.' Jasper grinned. 'So, this time next year, you'll marry me?'

She twined her arms about his neck, letting her fingers play with his hair. 'Yes, but I have conditions. I want a small ceremony at Rosefields, family only. No big celebration. Just something intimate. Quiet.'

'Perfect.' He laughed against her lips. 'Just as I imagined it. Until then, we'll have one whirlwind of a year.'

One year later

'We made the front page,' Fleur whispered, startling Jasper in the tiny antechamber of the Rosefields family chapel.

'What are you doing here?' Jasper scolded in surprised tones that conveyed more pleasure at the surprise than displeasure. 'It's bad luck to see the bride before the wedding.' But from the look in his eyes, he didn't seem to mind. She gave a twirl in her wedding gown, showing off the delicate raised white roses embroidered at the hem. The gown was made from a pretty white cotton, fresh and simple with its three-tiered skirt and tight-fitted bodice. She'd chosen to wear white even though she wasn't a new bride: white for new beginnings, new chances.

'You've been seeing me all year. I can't think today makes much of a difference.' She laughed, twining her arms about his neck.

'What's this about the front page?'

'We're the headline on the front page of the *London Tribune*. *"Newspaper Mogul Makes Marriage Deal with Marquess"*,' she recited happily. 'They ran a whole article about us: how we met, what we've done together this year and our plans for the future.'

'They need a whole special edition for that!' Jasper chuckled.

'It was a pretty spectacular year.'

They'd spent the year lobbying for legislation that would prevent lax accountability on dam commissions. Just last week, they'd celebrated their bill passing the House of the Commons. They'd also spent the year making decisions about life going forward. Fleur decided it was indeed the right choice for her to scale back her active role in the news syndicate.

She still held stock in the company, but her role was now focused on overseeing the regional paper out of

Huddersfield so that she had time working with a local committee dedicated to establishing a public library open to everyone without fees. She even had time now to devote to her own personal writing and had a novel in the works.

Socially, the year had been spent navigating new social circles for Fleur. The Duchess of Cowden and Jasper's mother combined efforts to ease that transition. When she was in town, Fleur enjoyed re-joining the Duchess's charity circles and in November, she and Jasper had attended both the Duchess's Christmas fundraising ball and Lady Brixton's literacy ball. There would always be those who looked down their noses at her and who would think Jasper had married beneath himself, but she'd found many people quite welcoming and even a bit awed by her.

'Thank you,' she whispered to Jasper.

'For what?'

'For this year, for giving me the time I needed to sort through my life so that I could come to you whole and ready to commit to *our* life together.' She kissed him just as Orion poked his head into the little antechamber.

'Ahem. Ten minutes, Brother. Really, you two, could you wait just a little longer?'

Fleur flashed him a look over her shoulder. 'Absolutely not. We were just practising.' The door shut and they could hear Orion laughing. 'Now, where were we?'

'Right about here,' Jasper murmured, picking up their kiss where they'd left off.

'You can tell a lot about a man by how he kisses,' Fleur whispered.

'And what can you tell about me?'

'That you're the one.' She'd come through grief and guilt, anger and resentment to arrive here, to be here with this man. 'What does my kiss tell you about me?'

'That you are worth waiting for.' He hoisted her up on the flat surface of a cabinet built into the wall.

'We're going to be late.' She laughed.

'Not to worry. They can't start without with us.'

Epilogue

1864

The summer of champagne and roses had started. June was well underway, the gardens were in full bloom at Rosefields, and the estate was alive with the sounds of laughter and children. Fleur would not have it any other way. This summer, Emma and Antonia had come to England with their husbands and children for business and for pleasure and Fleur was intent on making the most of the opportunity.

A footman approached with a tray of ice-cold champagne and lemonade, the champagne courtesy of Emma's husband, Julien Archambeau, the Comte du Rocroi. Fleur took a glass of lemonade while Emma and Antonia opted for the champagne as the three women lounged in the shade, stealing a moment of quiet to be together while their husbands taught the children battledore on the court they'd put up for the summer.

'Cheers, dear friends.' Fleur touched her glass to the others. 'Here's to having come thousands of miles for a reunion.'

'And here's to safe travels for all of us,' Emma said

solemnly. 'The distances we've come can't all be measured in miles, especially when it's a journey in love.'

Fleur couldn't agree more. If someone had told her eleven years ago that they would all three find love again, have the families and lives they wanted after such incredible, devastating loss, she would have thought it impossible. And yet, here they were. Out on the battledore court, she caught fragments of instruction as Jasper showed their son, five-year-old Michael, named after Jasper's father, how to hold his racket as they set up for a match against Julien and nine-year-old Matthieu-Phillippe. On the side-lines, Antonia's husband, Cullen, tanned a deep bronze with long tawny locks bleached by the Tahitian sun, stood with Emma's youngest—Etienne—and their own boy, Manahau, ready to play the judges should a shuttlecock go out of bounds.

'There's not a daughter among them.' Emma sighed wistfully. 'I love my sons, but how is it that we didn't conspire to have at least one girl among us?'

Fleur slid her a coy glance, her hand dropping to her stomach. 'Well, maybe this one will be a girl. Jasper and I started after all of you. We're not finished yet.'

'I thought so!' Emma cried joyfully. 'I didn't want to say anything, but then when you didn't take any champagne…'

Fleur smiled, beaming. 'We're halfway there. Just four and a half months to go.' She'd have preferred there be fewer years between Michael and this new child, but that was not to be. There'd been a miscarriage three years ago early in her term and she and Jasper had been careful after that not to conceive too soon. Then she'd not got pregnant as easily as she had with Michael.

Antonia squeezed her hand. 'It's wonderful news. A real blessing.' One Fleur knew, boy or girl, she'd not take for granted.

'This one will be our last, I think. I'll treasure every moment of it.' Fleur smiled at her friends, seeing the echo of her words in their eyes. They all knew the import of savouring each moment. They'd experienced the fragility of life and how quickly that life, the things one thought they could count on, could be swept away. They'd all made the journey to Holmfirth a couple of days past to see the flood marker at the butcher shop and to walk the streets. The homes on Water Street in Hinchliffe Village remained unbuilt, their absence a gaping hole and strong reminder of the power of nature and human vulnerability.

'I am excited for this child, but a little sad, too,' Fleur confessed. 'I wonder if either of you will see him or her? I am happy for us, but I am unhappy that we live so far apart. It's been what? Eleven years since we've been together other than through letters.' Letters that came only twice yearly from Antonia. Tahiti was still a long way off.

Emma smiled, eyes sparkling. 'Perhaps you will be seeing more of us. We've established an office in London as British importation of champagne has grown astonishingly. My brother will handle most of the day-to-day operations, but we'll need to check in regularly. Julien's been talking about a champagne Christmas here in London this year. He wants to give the children the same experience of growing up in both England and France that he had. You and the new baby will be up for visitors by then, I assume?'

Fleur laughed with gratitude. 'If you're angling for a Christmas invitation to Rosefields, you've got it.' Jasper's mother would be in her element with so many children to love, and Orion was perfect uncle material even if he wasn't quite husband material...yet. She could imagine nothing better, unless it was Antonia being here, too, but that was too much to hope for. They would have barely reached Tahiti by December.

'Would there be room for one more family?' Antonia put in with a broad smile. Tahiti agreed with her. 'Cullen told me today that he's decided to stay through winter to work with the Duke of Cowden on expanding the South Seas arm of the company. The good news is that we can be together for Christmas. The bad news is that if Cullen is successful, and I know he will be, we won't be back for another ten years.' She gave a wistful sigh. 'Matthieu-Phillippe will be nineteen by then, practically all grown up.'

'Tahiti is good for you, Antonia. You belong there,' Fleur consoled.

Antonia smiled. 'I love it. I wish you could see our house with its thatched roof and bamboo poles and barely any walls. It's big and airy and unlike anything I ever dreamed I'd live in, and I love it. The water is warm, you can swim all year. It's a little boy's perfect playground. I couldn't imagine Manahau growing up anywhere better. I have everything I want.'

'I'll drink to that.' Fleur raised her lemonade. 'We are the luckiest of women. We have everything we want.' Although there'd been a time, long, long ago, when she'd not thought she was lucky at all, that she hadn't deserved the love of a good man. She was happy to be wrong. Today, she had a man who loved her, who had made her a true partner in that love and in the life they were building together one day after another, through good times and bad. Jasper had been right that night so many years ago when he'd argued for them. They were indeed better together.

* * * * *

*If you enjoyed this story,
you can catch up with the previous
books in the Enterprising Widows series*

Liaison with the Champagne Count
Alliance with the Notorious Lord

*And pick up Bronwyn Scott's
Daring Rogues miniseries*

Miss Claiborne's Illicit Attraction
His Inherited Duchess

*Or one of her other captivating
Historical romances*

The Captain Who Saved Christmas
The Art of Catching a Duke